# THE
# TEMPLAR
# INHERITANCE

**Mario Reading** is a multi-talented writer of
both fiction and non-fiction. His varied life has
included selling rare books, teaching riding in
Africa, studying dressage in Vienna, running a
polo stable in Gloucestershire and maintaining a
coffee plantation in Mexico. An acknowledged
expert on the prophecies of Nostradamus,
Reading is the author of eight non-fiction
titles and five novels published in the UK
and around the world.

*Also by Mario Reading*

**THE ANTICHRIST TRILOGY**
The Nostradamus Prophecies
The Mayan Codex
The Third Antichrist

**THE JOHN HART SERIES**
The Templar Prophecy
The Templar Inheritance

# THE
# TEMPLAR
## INHERITANCE

## MARIO READING

CORVUS

Published in paperback in Great Britain in 2015 by Corvus, an imprint of
Atlantic Books Ltd.

Copyright © Mario Reading 2015

The moral right of Mario Reading to be identified as the author of this work
has been asserted by him in accordance with the Copyright, Designs and
Patents Act of 1988.

10 9 8 7 6 5 4 3 2 1

A CIP catalogue record for this book is available from the British Library.

Paperback ISBN: 978 1 78239 533 1
E-book ISBN: 978 1 78239 534 8

Printed in Great Britain.

Corvus
An imprint of Atlantic Books Ltd
Ormond House
26–27 Boswell Street
London
WC1N 3JZ

www.corvus-books.co.uk

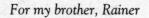

*For my brother, Rainer*

I have loved in life, and I have been loved
I have drunk the bowl of poison from the hands
of love as nectar.

Hazrat Inayat Khan (1882–1927),
from *Nirtan, or The Dance Of The Soul*

Listen, O drop. Give yourself up without regret
And in exchange gain the Ocean.

Rumi (1207–73)

# ONE

# As Sulaymaniyah, Iraq

Later, John Hart came to feel that he had anticipated the explosion by a split second. That there had been a momentary vacuum before the blast during which he had reached towards Nalan Abuna, his guide and translator in Kurdistan, and taken her hand in his.

Either way, the makeshift metal screen that separated their private seating area from the main expanse of the teashop had undoubtedly saved their lives. Hart had awoken on the shard-bedecked tiles with Nalan curled tightly against him, hip to hip, as if they had dozed off on the floor together in flagrant disregard for public decency.

Hart let Nalan's fingers reluctantly slip from his. He pressed both hands to his ears and swallowed. Ten times. Twenty. He knew enough about the percussive effects of bombs not to risk getting to his feet before he could hear again. It would be like succumbing to an attack of acute labyrinthitis.

For Hart was no stranger to sudden outbreaks of violence. He had undergone his first major bombardment in Sarajevo, twenty years before, when he was cutting his milk teeth in photo-journalism. The memory of that bombing could still jolt him awake at night, his sheets drenched, his body aching with a form of muscle memory that led his limbs to flex and contract with no discernible input from his conscious mind. It was at that time, too, in Sarajevo, that he had seen what they call the 'dervish effect' at work. People flailing around in the immediate aftermath of a bomb strike, their faces blank, their eyelids ticcing, their arms, if they still had any, feeling out for non-existent support.

No, Hart decided. He would have none of it. He would lie there on the ground until his hearing and his senses returned. Only then would he act.

When next he awoke, Nalan was crouching over him. She was cradling his head in her lap and encircling his face with her arms. He could see her lips moving, but he could not hear what she was saying.

A man lurched past them and then turned back, in slow motion, as if he had forgotten something. A single red star appeared in the centre of his forehead.

Hart began to make out Nalan's voice through the fog that was inhabiting his head.

'They are firing at us. They are massacring people. We must leave here. I know where to go. It is very near. There are high walls. They will not get in.'

Hart tried to get up. He pitched forward onto his knees, as if that single wild movement was what he had always intended to do. Nalan took him by the hands and helped him to his feet. Her touch felt familiar to him now, despite the fact that their physical knowledge of each other had barely progressed beyond the most fleeting of handshakes.

He had known Nalan Abuna for a total of three days. To all intents and purposes they were strangers. Until this moment – this freak occurrence – their relationship had been an entirely formal one. Businesslike. Mutually convenient. He was a forty-year-old freelance photojournalist, with all the collateral damage that such a profession entailed, and she was thirteen years younger than him and his paid employee. A Chaldean Christian and a Kurd. Engaged to be married, as she had swiftly informed him, no doubt in a bid to anticipate, and thereby disarm, any likely passes. Strictly out of bounds.

Hart began to run. He lurched from side to side, with Nalan keeping pace beside him. He saw more people fall. Out in the street, bodies and body parts were scattered across the asphalt like the tossed pieces in a jackstraws game. Hart saw the remains of the burnt-out car in which the bomb had been hidden upended on the pavement three doors down from the teashop. As he ran, he inadvertently kicked a woman's unattached hand. He knew it belonged to a woman because it was freshly painted with henna in honour of the public holiday which had been due to begin that day at sunset.

Ahead of him another man spun round and fell to the ground. The firing intensified. Hart pulled Nalan down beside him. They flattened themselves on the asphalt, fully expecting to be killed.

As he lay beside her, with his cheek pressed tightly against the warm tarmac, Hart could feel his wits slowly returning. This wasn't the first time that he had been pinned down by gunfire. As a photojournalist, guerrilla warfare and street-fighting were his stock-in-trade. He knew he needed to get a grip on himself, or they'd never get out of this. But he was still shaking from the seismic effects of the bomb.

Hart drew in three lungfuls of air through his nose and expelled them loudly through his opened mouth in a bid to alter the direction of his consciousness. Then he steadied his breathing back to normal and tried to filter out the clatter and clamour of the automatic weapons and focus on the intent behind them. It took him less than ten seconds to realize that the gunmen were not concentrating their fire on him and Nalan, but on a group of people huddled a hundred and fifty metres away, near the entrance to a mosque.

'We need to move now. It's our only chance.'

Nalan rose with him, as if they were twin parts of the same person. They ran. Each eternal second they were out in the open Hart expected the deadening thump of a bullet in the small of his back, or to see Nalan pitch to the ground beside him in a welter of blood and tangled limbs. He urged her ahead of him so that he might protect her, at least to some extent, with his body. She glanced back at him in surprise. It was a look only a woman can give a man. To Hart, the look she gave him offered a sort of completion. If he had died at that precise moment he would have died happy. But he did not die.

Nalan led him to a steel-grilled gate set into a high concrete wall. A teenage soldier in a khaki uniform and an antiquated Kevlar vest was standing behind the grille, holding a sub-machine gun. He was so scared that his shoulders rocked like an old man's in the throes of a coughing fit. When Hart tried to force open the grille, the soldier raised his weapon.

Nalan shouted at the soldier in Kurdish.

The soldier drew back a little at the sight of the woman. He flushed. Then his shoulders steadied, as though at the orders of an unseen officer. He indicated with his head that Nalan should retry the gate.

Nalan pushed it open and she and Hart stepped inside. Hart glanced back down the street to see if anyone was following them. Bullets pinged off the concrete wall twenty feet above his head.

'We need to lock this gate,' he said. 'Right now. They've seen us come in. They are killing everybody. This boy won't be able to protect us. Look at him. He's still in fucking nappies.'

Nalan talked to the soldier again. Intently. Quietly. Pointing first at the grille and then at them.

An older man ran up. He pushed the soldier to one side and began shouting at Nalan.

She shouted back.

After a moment the older man withdrew a large key from his jacket pocket and locked the grille. As he did so, an armed figure came into view thirty yards away across the street and started firing.

The older man took two steps backwards and fell heavily onto his buttocks. For a split second the movement seemed almost comical – like a toddler who has lost his footing in the fleeting instant before tears begin. He pitched onto the ground, blood welling from a sequence of bullet holes stitched like poppies down the line of his suit.

Hart hustled Nalan away from the gate. The young soldier followed them.

Nalan pointed to a narrow passageway, thatched with barbed wire, that snaked between two high walls. 'This is the way.'

They zigzagged down the passageway and out into a large courtyard filled with rusted tanks, superannuated field guns, and the exoskeletons of trucks and armoured personnel carriers. To one side of the courtyard stood the ruins of a building. It was pitted and scarred with the ancient marks of shell holes and bullet gouges. Near to the building was a life-sized plaster memorial depicting six facially bandaged human beings bound so tightly together that they resembled a tree. A tree of death.

'What is the name of this place? Tell me quickly, Nalan. I need to pass this information on to someone I know.'

'This is the Amna Suraka Museum. They call it the Red Interrogation House. It was the Ba'ath Party's intelligence headquarters until 1991. It is here that the Mukhabarat tortured, raped and killed hundreds of Kurdish freedom fighters on the orders of Saddam Hussein.'

'Jesus Christ.'

'It is the only place we will possibly be safe, John. It is built like a fortress.'

Hart sprawled against the courtyard wall and took out his mobile phone. His battery was at half power because he hadn't bothered to recharge it the night before. Hell. Why would he? He wasn't on active assignment. He was on a reconnaissance tour for photographable locations for a piece his ex-girlfriend Amira Eisenberger had been commissioned to write on Kurdistan's economic resurgence. No one was meant to be shooting at him. No one was meant to be bombing him. Kurdistan was notoriously safe. Not like Mosul. Or Fallujah. Or Baghdad.

'Amira? It's John. Don't talk. Just listen and record.' He waited for a moment while she set the recorder. 'There's been a car bombing. A hundred yards down from the Amna Suraka Museum in As Sulaymaniyah. My interpreter and I were having tea three doors away from the blast. We're okay. Shaken, but okay. But we're pinned down here in the museum. The people behind the bombing are killing everybody. It's bedlam out there. It's like the Taj attack in Mumbai. You'd better check what's coming in on the wires. I suspect they've made me as a journalist thanks to the cameras I'm carrying. I'll be prize meat for them. I've got only Nalan Abuna with me and a boy soldier, who looks about ready to piss his pants. And I'm halfway through my battery.'

'Is the museum secure?'

'Tight as a drum as far as I can make out. It used to be Saddam's torture house. But they'll blow the gates before too long. Then we'll be for it. I'm switching off now. We're going to make for one of the upper floors.'

Hart saw Nalan shaking her head.

'No. Hold that. Where are we heading for, Nalan?'

'The basement. We are going down into the basement.'

'We'll be in the basement, Amira. Nalan knows this place. I'm taking her word she knows the best spot to hide up in. I'll call you again when we're safe.'

'No, you won't.'

'What do you mean?'

'You'll get no signal down in the basement.'

Hart glanced again at Nalan. She shook her head a second time.

'That's a risk we'll have to take, Amira. The bastards are at the gates. We need to go.'

# TWO

They ran past a sequence of small cells, some little larger than a man. Each cell had a metal door with a peephole let into it.

'They can get to us down here, Nalan. We'll be sitting ducks.'

'Wait.'

The young soldier, too, seemed content to follow Nalan's lead. She's a guide, thought Hart. It's not surprising she knows this place. I understand nothing of her language. Perhaps she knows this soldier? Knew the man in the suit who was lying dead just beyond the grille. That would explain things.

Nalan pointed behind him. 'Now. We shut this connecting door and barricade it. Here. There are wedges. And a bar. The door is made of sheet metal. It was built to keep prisoners in. They will not blow it without dynamite. Grenades will not work against it. Our soldiers will be here soon. If they come quickly, we shall be safe.'

Hart and the young soldier began barricading the door. How certain this young woman was of herself, Hart found himself thinking. How secure in her knowledge. Looking at her, it was hard to believe that she'd been the near victim of a car bombing ten minutes before. Had seen people killed before her eyes. Had run down a street awash with blood and body parts while the bombers had used her as a moving target. From where had she derived her courage? From what source?

'What is this, Nalan? What is this figure of a man?' Hart was looking at a life-sized plaster model of a prisoner in one of the cells flanking the doorway. The man was chained to the wall by one hand in a purposefully uncomfortable position, so that he could neither stand fully upright nor lie stretched out on the floor to sleep.

'He is a Kurd. Like me. It is what they did. They made this model to remind the Kurdish people of all that happened to them during Saddam's time.'

In a further room, another full-sized model of a man hung from a pipe in the strappado position: his arms stretched out behind him, the full weight of his body bearing down onto his shoulders. An electrical cord, attached to a magnetic field telephone, hung from around his neck.

'I can tell you who this man is.'

Hart inclined his head. Nalan's face had taken on a haunted aspect, as of someone who senses a malevolent presence just beyond them, but still marginally out of sight.

'This is my father, John. And many others like him. Men and women both. This is what Hassif did to them. His favourite places to electrocute you were the tongue, the fingers, the little toe, and the sexual organs. He spread the places he electrocuted you as far apart as possible so as to cause the most extreme spasms. The muscles themselves conducted the electricity. So you were electrocuting yourself, so to speak. When this happens you cannot think. You cannot breathe. Your heart goes into spasms. They wet your body with salt water so as to better distribute the current. They even use luxury gels and creams so that the skin is not burnt at the point of contact, giving the torturers away if the prisoner is ever released. This is what they did to my father over many weeks so that he could no longer use his arms.'

'How do you know about this? Did they release your father? Did he tell you?'

'He told me this before he died. Yes. He wished me to remember. To carry the memory of it in me.'

She ushered Hart ahead of her. The young Kurdish soldier hung back, as though he suspected what Nalan was telling this English stranger who had intruded on his life, and did not wish to interfere.

'I want you to look in here, John.'

Nalan stood back and pointed to the entrance to a cell. The steel door was open, but this cell was darker than the others – the only light that entered came from out in the corridor. It illuminated the life-sized model of a woman leaning against a concrete pillar. Her head was thrown back and her eyes were shut. A young girl, less than half her size, was clinging to her legs and looking down at the ground.

11

'This is my mother. The young girl is me. I was five years old in March 1991 when they came to liberate Amna Suraka. I had been here since I was three.'

Hart couldn't take his eyes from the two female figures. 'This is you? This little girl?'

Nalan nodded. 'This is my mother, yes. And this is me.'

'So this is how you know this place? This is how you knew to bring us here?'

'This is how I know this place. There were forty women and children imprisoned in this room. You see those blankets on the floor? The dog bowl over there to drink from? That is how they saw us. As dogs. The women left those behind when they were released by the Peshmerga following a two-day gun battle. You saw the bullet marks outside in the courtyard where we came in? The shell holes? Our soldiers found the rape rooms and the torture chambers and the isolation cells when they broke in. It sent them crazy. They killed 700 Ba'athists in this place. It was far too few. Guards. Torturers. Rapists. Spies. But not Hassif. No. That man managed to get away. Later, when the Allies eased off their air attack, Saddam came back. For a while it looked like he would get his revenge. That Hassif would return to torment us. But the no-fly zone was implemented. For the first time in a hundred years, the Kurds were free.'

'And your mother?'

'They raped her too many times. Humiliated her too many times. It was too much for her to bear. She and my father committed joint suicide in 1993. I was brought up by my uncle and aunt. They were very kind to me. I am very lucky.'

# THREE

Hart glanced down at his watch. It had been two hours since they had heard the last of the hand grenades exploding against the outside door of the museum. For a while after that there had been silence in the streets. Now the gunfire was starting up again.

The young soldier stood up and walked across to where Hart was sitting. Wordlessly, he handed Hart his abbreviated AK47. He returned to his corner, sat down, and turned his head to the wall.

Hart hesitated, unsure what to do.

But Nalan knew.

She got to her feet and approached Hart. She opened her hands. He understood immediately. He handed her the AK47.

She walked across to where the young soldier was sitting and touched him on the shoulder. He turned to look at her. She held out the gun. He refused to take it. Nalan stood in front of him with the gun held out.

Finally he took it.

She cupped his face in her hands and looked into his eyes. She said something and he acknowledged it. She repeated it, and he acknowledged it a second time.

She went back to sit beside Hart.

'What did you say to him?'

Nalan shrugged. 'I asked him if he was a Kurd. I asked him if the men outside were his enemies.'

'And what did he tell you?'

'He said yes. He was a Kurd. And they were his enemies. Then I asked him again. But more forcefully this time. When he answered me the second time he was a man again.'

Hart shook his head. He was utterly bewildered by Nalan. Bewildered by his feelings for her. Bewildered by the fact that she could come back to this place after twenty-two years and confront her demons without cracking up. If he had gone through a fraction of what she and her parents had gone through, he would have wished the place blasted off the face of the planet. Razed. Its fields planted with salt like those of Carthage.

'Who are they? The gunmen outside?'

'They are Shiite. Paid by Iran. Or they are Sunni. Paid by Saudi Arabia. Take your pick. It amuses them to try and turn Kurdistan into a war zone. They are jealous of us. Jealous that we have security. Oil. The beginnings of an autonomous nation. They hate us. They want a civil war. But we shall not give it to them.'

'Do such things happen often?'

'No. Not nowadays. Not here. This is a bad thing. Very bad. They will try to do much damage. They know you are in the museum. They know by your cameras that you are a journalist. They will try to kidnap you. Or kill you. Either way you will be news to them. A triumph if they can get to you. A way to make the West listen to what they are saying.'

'But you think we're safe here? For the time being?'

Nalan looked at her watch. 'For another hour. Maybe two. When night falls they will try again.'

'Then we must escape.'

'There is no way out of here but that door. They will be watching it. We must hope that it holds.'

'And your soldiers?'

'The entire area will be sealed off and surrounded. But the bombers will be well prepared. They have come here ready to die. They will have weapons. Food. Water. Suicide vests. They will have done their surveillance many times in the past months. They will know the area and its weak points. They have done this before. It is second nature to them. Our soldiers need to act quickly. If they do not, we are lost.'

'I still think we must try to break out before the bombers come. There must be another way.'

Nalan looked at Hart, although her attention seemed elsewhere. 'There is one way. Perhaps. But we must wait. We must use the darkness too.'

"How long before darkness starts falling?"

She glanced at her watch again.

'Another hour.'

# FOUR

Hart tried his phone again. Still no signal. He glanced up. Nalan was staring at him with a peculiar intensity.

'You? Are you married?' she said.

He was tempted to laugh at the abruptness of her question, but something in her expression stopped him. 'No.'

'Why not? You are an old man?'

Hart made a face. 'No. I'm not an old man. I'm forty.'

Nalan burst out laughing. 'Don't look so serious. I was teasing you. In Kurdistan you are barely old enough to be a leader at forty. To be respected. We look at age differently here.'

'That's a relief.'

Nalan arched her head to one side and peered at him again. 'Why are you not married? Why do you not have children? A man your age should have a family. A wife. Responsibilities. All you have are those cameras.' She pointed to Hart's chest. 'Is that all you have? Those cameras?'

Hart looked at her in amazement. Nalan's hair was the red gold of weathered bamboo. Her complexion was pale, her nose straight, her mouth a perfect crescent. Her eyes, which almost matched the colour of her hair, were set far apart in a broad, unlined face. She was a smallish woman, maybe five foot five inches tall, with delicate features and emphatic eyebrows. She wore six or seven bangles and bracelets on each arm, and on her nose, high up, just above her right nostril, a diamond chip glittered.

Nalan's crowning glory was her hair, Hart decided, at the end of his unexpected re-evaluation. It framed a sharp-jawed, intelligent face, whose owner looked you unwaveringly in the eye. The red-gold ringlets reached all the way down to the small of Nalan's back, and were swept away from her forehead to leave a small widow's peak, akin to but less pronounced than his own. Around her neck she wore a simple green bead necklace. Her hands bore no rings, nor any sign of them. Hart found her presence mesmerizing, and he was finding it increasingly hard to hide his interest in her. 'Yes, I suppose these cameras are all I have.'

'But you like women? Not just your cameras?'

'You already know I like women. That much must be obvious to you.'

Nalan gave him a secret smile. She crossed her arms. 'So? Tell me. Tell me about all these women of yours.'

Hart sighed. Why were women – and especially beautiful women – always so damned inquisitive? There were moments when he roundly cursed his susceptibility to their charms. 'So. I had a long-standing girlfriend. The woman I spoke to on the phone before we entered here. But something happened and we aren't together any more.'

'What happened?'

Hart squirmed internally. All his life he had been wedded to truth as to a jealous lover. He could no more avoid answering Nalan's question than he could abandon a wounded, car-struck animal on the side of the road. 'She aborted our baby without telling me. That's what happened.'

Nalan stared at him, her face livid with shock. 'She aborted it?'

'Yes. It's what women do in the West when they don't want children.'

'Then she did not love you?'

Hart shook his head. 'She did love me. I know that now. But she did not want our baby. She is a journalist. She had seen too much bloodshed. She refused to bring a baby into a world she did not care for.'

'This I can understand. But you? You wanted this baby?'

'Yes.'

'So you left her?'

'Eventually. Yes.'

'Does it make you sad?'

'No. Not any more.'

'Does it make her sad?'

'I believe it does. And I am sorry for that. But it's not something I can help.'

They sat in silence for a while. Then Nalan cocked her head to one side in the particular way Hart had noted in her when she wanted to ask an indelicate question. 'No one else?'

Hart rolled his eyes. 'Yes. Last year in Germany. I was involved with a woman. An extremist politician. Not a good person.'

'What happened to her?'

'She was killed. She, too, was carrying my child.'

Nalan stared at Hart in horror. 'I'm sorry.'

Hart tried to laugh, but it came out all wrong. It sounded more like a sob. 'This is the moment you're meant to say, "Maybe you're just not cut out to be a father? Maybe you should lay off women and take up flying model aeroplanes instead?"'

'That would be in poor taste.'

Hart bowed his head. 'Yes, it would. I'm sorry I said it. My bitterness must be showing.' He glanced down at his watch. Another twenty minutes to go before they must move. He needed to change the subject. 'And you? Your fiancé? What about him?' He did not want to know the answer. But it was the only remotely associated question he could think of on the spur of the moment. And it would be expected of him.

'I'm a Chaldean Christian. We do not marry outside our faith. My uncle and aunt have chosen a husband for me, since I have shown no sign of choosing one for myself. They think it is time for me to stop work and have children. They are right.'

'Do you like him at least?'

'How can I like him? I do not know him. I am meeting him for the first time next week. Then we are getting married.'

19

Hart swallowed. 'Do you mean to tell me that Chaldeans would honour-kill a woman who married outside her faith?'

Nalan looked shocked. 'No. We are Christians. Only Muslims do that sort of thing.'

'What would Christians do?'

'My family would cast me out. I would be exiled from my community.'

'That's a lot more civilized.'

'Yes. Yes, it is.'

Hart realized that Nalan had missed the heavy irony in his tone. He felt ashamed of himself for injecting it into his comment. As if he had betrayed her in some way. Abused her trust. 'Are you at least allowed affairs?'

'Affairs? You mean sex with strangers? Strangers like you?'

'Well. No. Not me in particular. I meant love affairs.'

Nalan put on a serious face. 'A Chaldean bride must go to the altar a virgin, or she will shame her family for ever.'

'Ah.' Hart sensed that Nalan was making fun of him. But he still couldn't work out how truly accurate her answers were. Or whether they applied to her particular case or not. Maybe she was just fulfilling her function as his guide and trying to explain how the country worked to him? That's what she was being paid to do, after all. From her point of view, the situation they found themselves in was a freak occurrence and had created an unwarranted intimacy. She was probably just making the best of a bad lot.

There was the crump of another hand grenade at the door to the cells.

Nalan looked pleased. 'Good. They are trying to break in again. Come with me. We will take advantage of their activities.' Nalan signalled to the young soldier and he, too, got up from the floor.

Hart nodded to him in a friendly fashion, but he felt uncomfortable at having been a witness to the boy's vulnerability. There was an extra edge to the young man's expression now – a new rigidity – which disturbed him.

They made their way down a sparsely lit corridor and up some stairs to what appeared to be a mezzanine.

'These are the rape rooms.'

'I'm sorry?'

'These are the rooms where Hassif and his warders raped the women prisoners. This one at the end here . . .' Nalan pushed open the door. 'This one I know very well.' She walked inside.

Hart hesitated on the threshold. It was as though the invisible aura the room exuded was staying him in some way. He tried to fight back the question he felt driven to ask, but couldn't. 'Did they rape you, Nalan?'

Nalan shook her head. 'I was five years old. They were not interested in me for sexual purposes. They took me in here and made me watch my mother being raped instead. My father they took in too. Hassif did this to complete my family's humiliation. It was personal with him. Something my father had done to offend him in a former life. This is why they killed themselves, my mother and father. Because of the shame of what I had been forced to witness. Of what I had been forced to undergo because of them.'

Hart glanced at the young soldier behind him. Did he understand English? Did he understand what Nalan was saying? The horrors that had occurred here? The boy provided security for the museum. He must know what this place was. It would be in his blood, even though he had not been born at the time these things were happening. These outrages had been perpetrated on his own people, after all.

The young man's face was blank, his thoughts seemingly elsewhere.

Nalan seemed to intuit what Hart had been thinking. 'No one comes here. These rooms do not form part of the museum. They are used for storage now. What these rooms were used for before has been forgotten.' She pointed upwards. 'But I remember.'

Hart followed the direction of her hand. A trapdoor was set into the ceiling.

'No. I don't believe it,' he said. 'You can't have remembered the trapdoor. You were barely five years old when you left here. Scarcely old enough to remember anything.'

Nalan looked away so that he could not see the expression on her face. 'I came back. Three years ago. I asked to see this place. There was another curator then. Not the man we saw die outside. A better man. He took me here. Left me to see for myself. I spent a day and a night in here. He was very kind. He brought me food. Blankets. Let me use the staff facilities. He did not allow anyone to disturb me.' Nalan turned towards Hart. 'When I left this room I had remembered everything.' She managed a fleeting smile. 'Even the trapdoor.'

Nalan's smile was so unexpected that Hart could not find it in himself to respond. The room weighed him down with its accumulated memories. Diminished him. Tarnished him with its associated guilt. 'Where do you think the trapdoor leads? If it's just to a loft, we are no better off.'

'I do not know where it leads. But it is our only chance to get out. It will be dark outside now. Soon they will break in through the door downstairs. They have nothing to lose. They think we will be hostages for them. That is why they are holding us for last. That is why they have not been pressing hard to get in to us.'

Hart sensed that she was right. As far as the men outside were concerned, the three of them were boxed in and waiting. Like Christmas turkeys in a holding pen.

He signalled to the young soldier and they began constructing a makeshift ladder out of the packing cases and assorted junk that littered the room.

'Okay,' said Hart. 'I'm by far the oldest person here. I get to go up first.'

# FIVE

The loft space was even more cluttered than the room below. Its height was severely restricted because of the steep angle of the roof. At first, Hart couldn't work out the architecture of the place. By rights the loft shouldn't even have been there. The main building was constructed on the accordion principle – that much he'd seen before entering it. So what was this space? And what had been its function?

He crawled along the floor until he reached the end wall. Then he got to his knees and felt carefully around the roof space above him. The light from the room below radiated only part-way to where he was kneeling, so that he was in almost total darkness.

He touched what he assumed to be tiles. No lagging. No boards. As far as Hart could make out, the tiles were laid in grid formation directly onto the beams.

He crawled back the length of the loft space. He looked down at Nalan and the soldier. He lowered his voice to a whisper.

'I'm pretty sure we can break through onto the roof. I think this whole section is an add-on to the original building. It's built like an old-fashioned barn. The tiles are laid directly onto the beams and crossbars. Nailed on probably. One interleaved over the other so that they're rainproof. The thing was built on the cheap, in other words.'

'And it leads directly to the outside?'

'There's only one way to discover that. But we must do everything in the dark. A total blackout. This attic has to be on the same side of the building as the steel door. So if they're watching that, and if they happen to look up, they'll see us. So we need to switch off the light down here before we go up. And we need to knock down the makeshift ladder behind us and shut the trapdoor in case they manage to break in and come looking for us. It might buy us a couple of extra minutes. Because it won't take them long to suss this place out once they break in. But it means committing ourselves entirely. No going back.'

The soldier came up first. He reached into his tunic jacket and retrieved a torch. He handed it to Hart. Hart put on an expression of mock surprise. He pretended to offer the torch back and the young soldier laughed for the first time since he had entered the building. Hart indicated with his fingers that the boy should mask the beam in some way. While he did that, Hart leaned down and motioned Nalan to close the outside door and switch off the light.

She climbed up the stack of boxes and took Hart's hands.

'Can you hang down, if I hold you, and kick the boxes away with your feet?'

'Yes. Swing me.'

Hart swung Nalan from side to side. She was surprisingly light to hold. Barely half my weight and worth two of me, Hart decided.

When she'd kicked the boxes away he dragged her up into the loft. At one point he was forced to hold her tightly against his chest or risk dropping her. He caught her scent again at that moment – an elusive mixture of jasmine and musk, with just the faintest edge of citrus underlying it, like the discarded peel from an orange on a warm afternoon. Was he imagining it, or did Nalan rub her cheek ever so briefly against his as he held her in the darkness?

'What is the boy's name?' he asked.

'His name is Rebwar. The name means "farmer". One who knows his place in this world. One who knows his country.'

'That's a good name. Later, you can tell me what yours means.'

'Later. Yes. Perhaps I will tell you.'

They followed Rebwar down the narrow corridor that snaked between the accumulated loft clutter. At one point Rebwar stopped and pointed to the right. He briefly unmasked the torch.

'What is that?' Nalan came up beside the men and took the torch. She shone it onto the object. 'What is this, John?'

Something closed down in Hart when he recognized the old-fashioned, fixed-bracket, Cinestar camera mount. He took the torch from Nalan and aimed the beam below the object. Then he flicked the light away and covered it again with his hand. He'd seen all he needed to. 'It's nothing. Just a bunch of old metal.'

Nalan took him by the arm. 'Tell me. You know what it is. I saw by your face in the reflected light that you know.'

'Really. It's nothing. I thought it might be a weapon of some sort. Something that we could use. But it's just some old junk.'

Hart shadowed Rebwar the last few yards to the end of the loft space.

Nalan slapped him on the foot. 'You. I see you are still carrying your cameras. You never let them go. This was a camera, wasn't it?'

'Of course it wasn't a camera. You know what a camera looks like as well as I do. And that was no camera.'

'Then tell me. What did you see there that I didn't?'

Hart sighed. He lowered his voice even further. 'I'll make a deal with you. I'll tell you what I think I saw if and when we ever get out of here. Okay? The very same time you tell me about your name. Meanwhile we have work to do. And precious little time to do it in.'

# SIX

The first tile took about ten minutes to prise off with Rebwar's military-issue knife. The succeeding tiles proved a little easier to loosen. Hart decided that Rebwar must have done some construction work in his time, because he seemed to intuit the quickest and most soundless way to open the gap onto the roof space. Hart was more than content to leave him to it.

They were working in complete darkness now, and speaking only in monosyllables. Rebwar handed each tile silently back to Hart, who passed it along to Nalan. She piled the tiles up in manageable stacks of five along the floor line of the loft so as to avoid any danger of upsetting them in the darkness and giving their location away.

About twenty minutes into the process they heard the echo of a major explosion somewhere below them, followed by a concerted volley of gunfire.

'That's it. They've broken through.' Hart ducked his head towards Nalan in the darkness. 'They were using grenades before. But that was no grenade. More like an explosive charge. C-4 maybe. Or some sort of IED they made up from the grenade charges. Either way, it will have done the job.'

Rebwar was taking advantage of the noise from below to smash through the remaining tiles with the stock of his assault rifle.

'Look. Moonlight. We're out of luck.' Hart beckoned to Nalan to slide past him.

Rebwar helped her wriggle out through the hole he had made and onto the roof.

'You next,' said Hart. He pointed to Rebwar's AK47 and made a shooting sign with his hands. 'Just in case.'

Rebwar slid through the gap in the tiles and Hart followed him. Once out in the open Hart cast around himself, trying to gauge exactly where they were in relation to the breached steel door. He decided that they were maybe twenty feet over and a little to the right of it. Way too close for comfort. If one of the gunmen emerged from the basement and looked up, they would be sitting ducks.

Hart motioned for Rebwar and Nalan to precede him once again. He didn't fully trust the remaining tiles to support his weight, and didn't want to risk bringing the others down with him if the roof caved in. He was no lightweight. He measured a little more than six foot three inches in height and weighed fourteen stone.

There was a crash from inside the loft space.

'Christ. They're in there already. One of them must have tripped over the row of tiles we left.'

Hart allowed himself to slide down the angle of the roof towards Nalan, using his hands as brakes. To hell with the danger of falling through. Worse awaited him if he stuck around.

Rebwar hung back. He cast a single look over his shoulder at Nalan and Hart. Then he laid himself flat against the angle of the roof and aimed his AK47 towards the hole he had just spent the past twenty minutes making.

'Rebwar, no. Come with us.'

Rebwar made a disparaging motion with his hand.

An arm appeared through the hole in the roof, followed by a face.

Rebwar fired and the face disappeared.

Hart was now twenty feet below Rebwar, and about five feet away from where Nalan was supporting herself on the roof edge.

'Pull back, Rebwar. They'll use grenades.' He looked at Nalan. 'Tell him. Now they know we are armed, they will kill us, and they won't care how they do it. He mustn't stay where he is.'

Nalan began to speak, but the roof above them erupted before she could complete her sentence. The men inside the loft space were firing through the tiles. The light from their head torches speared through the gaping holes left by the bullets, creating mini searchlights in the sky.

Rebwar tumbled towards Hart, his AK47 skittering over the tiles behind him. Hart tried to grab him, but at the very last moment the force of gravity caused Rebwar to double over and turn what amounted to a somersault. Hart could only watch in horror as he pitched over the roof edge and into the courtyard below.

'John. The gun.'

Hart slapped one hand onto the AK47's sling as it slithered past him. The movement upset his own precarious balance, and he began sliding downwards. Only the thick rubber soles of his desert boots prevented him overshooting the edge.

Hart lay splayed onto the roof, the AK47 gripped in one hand, the fingers of his other hand locked onto the upper edge of one of the roof tiles. He daren't move. If he broke the surface tension that saw him pinned to the tiles by the slightest of adherences – if he moved even so much as one knee – he would slide over the edge and into the courtyard.

'John. Let go. It is not a long drop. Don't be scared. I can see all the way to the bottom.'

'How far down is it?'

'Six metres. Maybe seven.'

'Shit.'

The gunmen inside the loft space were shooting at random through the tiles. More spears of light emerged about ten feet above Hart's head. Very soon they would find him by default.

Hart raised his hands, consigned himself to God, and slid over the edge, twisting his body round as he did so, so that at the very least he would be facing forwards when he landed. There was a sickening pause and then he hit the ground, feet first. He threw himself to one side, just as he had been taught to do on the parachute tower during school cadet-force training. The AK47, which he was still holding by its sling, belted him on the top of the head.

Hart lay on the ground and tried to take an accounting. Was anything broken? Irremediably twisted? A trickle of blood snaked over one eyebrow and gathered in the hollow of his eye. He brushed at it with his sleeve. His limbs felt intact – his ankles, when he flexed them, appeared to work. He realized that he was lying on something soft. He turned over and saw Rebwar staring at him out of his single remaining eye.

Hart cried out. He lurched backwards and kicked the body away with his legs like a cat. Rebwar's head was at an odd angle, and one side of his face seemed darker than the other. Once he'd got over his initial shock, Hart crawled over to check Rebwar's pulse. But in the thin light of the moon it was clear that it was not the fall that had killed Rebwar, but a bullet that had exited through the tiles below him, destroying his cheekbone and one of his eyes. There would be no pulse left to find.

'John!'

Hart looked upwards. Nalan was hanging off the edge of the roof above him.

'I'm scared to let go. You must catch me. They are coming out.'

'It's okay, Nalan. Let go. I am directly beneath you.'

'I can't.'

'It's not far. You told me so yourself. Just let yourself drop. I will break your fall. I promise.'

Hart positioned himself below and just to the right of where Nalan would land. As she dropped he angled forward and attempted to sweep her into his arms. But the force of her fall from nearly twenty feet above him caused him to lose his footing. The two of them pitched headlong onto the ground.

Hart crawled over and helped Nalan to her feet, using his body as a shield to what lay beyond him. But she had already seen Rebwar. She began to moan.

'Come, Nalan. We must go. I can hear them climbing across the roof.' Hart picked up the AK47.

'I killed him.'

'No, you didn't. The gunmen did.'

'I made him ashamed. I gave him his rifle back. I killed him.' She started across the courtyard towards Rebwar's body.

Hart took her arm. 'He is dead. We can do nothing for him. We need to save ourselves.'

Nalan allowed Hart to hurry her away. But she never took her eyes off Rebwar's body.

# SEVEN

Hart urged Nalan ahead of him up the narrow corridor leading to the courtyard. The husks of the abandoned tanks, trucks and field guns that formed part of the museum's collection glittered spectrally in the thin light of the moon. He glanced back at the shattered doorway that led to Saddam's torture rooms. The gunmen would come running out of there as soon as they had made certain that only one out of their three possible targets was dead. And that would be any minute now. There was only one thing that he and Nalan could do.

'We need to get inside one of these tanks.'

'Why? It would be madness.'

'No. The men who are after us will assume we escaped via the street. The outer gate is open. It would be the obvious thing for us to do. No one will think to look for us in an abandoned tank.' Hart wasn't as confident as he sounded. But he knew the gunmen would have cleared the museum and its precincts before he and Nalan were remotely out of range of their weapons. The two of them wouldn't stand a chance against experienced street fighters. They'd either be herded up or killed out-of-hand.

Hart led Nalan away from the open grille and the body of the dead curator. He sized up each of the tanks in turn.

'Please hurry.' Nalan looked urgently behind her. 'They are coming. I can hear them.'

'Here. We can get inside number three. They won't see us unless they climb inside too. Look. The turret is fixed open. So it will seem less suspicious to anyone checking.'

'This is madness. They will find us.'

'It's too late for anything else. Trust me. This way we'll be able to hear them before they hear us.'

Nalan climbed onto the tank and disappeared inside the turret. Hart followed her. The heft of the abbreviated AK47 might be comforting, but he knew that the weapon wasn't of any significance in the greater scheme of things. It had been allocated to a wet-behind-the-ears boy guarding a museum – which meant that it was probably a veteran of the First Gulf War and the gun sights hadn't been adjusted since. The men following them would be able to outshoot and outgun him with no difficulty at all.

Hart sat across from Nalan in the cramped cockpit. A little moonlight leached in through the open turret, illuminating their faces. 'If they look inside, keep your legs tucked in and out of their sightline. Okay?'

She nodded.

'If one of them spots us, I shall kill him. When I start firing, you must run, using the trucks and field guns as protection. I will stay inside the tank and cover your escape – the armour plating will shield me. I want you to agree to this now. Before they come. I need to be able to concentrate on them and not to have to worry about you.'

Nalan watched Hart's face intently, as if she were searching for the real truth behind his litany of words. Finally, after a long pause, she nodded, her expression that of a child listening for a distant bell. 'Yes. I will do as you ask me.'

Hart was taken aback by her sudden amenability. He cradled the AK47 against his chest and began to seesaw backwards and forwards as though he were holding a baby. As he rocked he attempted to sum up their situation in his head – but the only thing he managed to do was to mire himself in trivialities.

Physically, both of them were okay. Still mobile at least. And not desperately in need of water or food. As far as concrete resources were concerned, Hart still had his cameras slung around his neck, but by now they were probably smashed and useless. For some strange reason, though, he couldn't bring himself to get rid of them. Maybe they did define him, as Nalan had suggested? Maybe he did feel naked without them? Did he really use them as his calling card to the world? As his justification for living? It didn't say a lot for him, if that was the case. He shook his head, irritated at his capacity to stray off message.

Loud voices from out in the courtyard jerked him back to the present. He tried to judge where the speakers were standing by the way their voices echoed off the surrounding buildings. He placed them near the open grille gate, close to the body of the dead curator. He counted five distinct voices – possibly six. They appeared to be engaged in a heated debate.

Thirty seconds into the debate one man's haranguing voice rose high above the others. There was an answering shout from the men surrounding him, followed by the sound of running feet. Then silence. A few seconds later there were two concerted volleys of gunfire. Then more silence. A shorter, single volley followed. Then silence again.

'What happened?' Hart hunched forwards. 'What were they saying?'

'That you, the spy-journalist, and me, whom they called your whore, had run out into the road. That we must have been recognized by our soldiers, which is why they had not fired on us. There was something about night-vision glasses too, which I did not understand. Then the leader told them to follow him outside and they shouted "Allah is great".'

'Do you think they've been killed by the army? Was that what the firing was all about?'

'I don't know. Maybe some are still waiting out there in silence? Or maybe they have all been killed and we can climb out?'

'No. We can't risk it yet. We must stay inside the tank where we're safe. If your soldiers think they have killed the gunmen, they will rush the museum. The problem is that they may think booby traps have been left here. Or that there are snipers. If so, they will come in firing. Or even mortar the place first. In that case we will be in as much danger from them as we are from the gunmen.'

Both were silent for a while. Hart tried his phone again and then put it away in disgust. The tank might as well have been lead-lined. He glanced across at Nalan.

It was clear, by the little he could make out of her expression, that she was still struggling to come to terms with Rebwar's death. What could he say to comfort her? The boy had died trying to save them – that was a given. Maybe, too, he had made that decision partly because Nalan had offered him his manhood back, alongside his weapon. But the ultimate call had been his. Hart was far too experienced in the vagaries of warfare to allocate blame or guilt in such a situation. But Nalan might not view the matter in quite the same light. She had lived through hell as a young girl, and that fact would colour all her actions. He needed to say something – anything – to reconnect with her.

He switched on Rebwar's torch and partially shaded the light with his hand. 'Your name, Nalan. You promised to tell me the meaning of your name. Remember?'

Nalan looked up at him. Her eyes seemed preternaturally large beneath the red-gold thatch of her hair. 'The light. They will see it and come for us.'

'No. They won't. We're six feet down in here. Tucked in behind a further six inches of armour plating. And the moon is high and getting higher. It will disguise the glow of the torch.'

Nalan touched the diamond chip set into her nose. Then she began to play with her wrist bangles. Her mind was clearly elsewhere.

'Nalan. You promised.'

She sighed and turned her attention full on him. 'My name means "the one who moans".'

'What?'

'It means "the one who moans".'

'What kind of a name is that?' Hart had blurted out the words before he could stop himself.

Nalan permitted herself a fleeting smile. 'It is not what it seems. The *nal* is the reed flute we Kurds play when we are sad. The word comes from the Persian. A *nalan*, then, is the one who plays the flute. Therefore "the one who moans". Rumi spoke of such a flute in the first lines of his *Masnavi*. I will translate it into English for you. But it will not be a good translation, because I am not a poet.' She hesitated. '*Listen to the reed and the tales that it tells. How it sings of separation.*'

'Can you repeat those lines to me in Persian?'

'In Farsi. Yes. Of course.' She spoke for a little in a language that Hart neither recognized nor understood.

Hart watched her face as she recited the halting sequence of verses. From time to time she would pause to think, her eyes fixed upon him. Then she would smile and continue again as the words returned to her. She seemed at the same time 'other' to him and yet somehow familiar, as if he and she formed two separate sides of the same coin – nominally different, yet inextricably linked.

When she was finished, Hart steepled his hands and inclined his head. He smiled for the first time since the bomb attack. 'Thank you. That was beautiful.'

'Now you tell me. . .' she began.

'Wait.' Hart held up one hand. He knew exactly what she was about to ask him. It would be about the apparatus they had seen in the attic. What it was. What its purpose had been. Hart needed to deflect her from any such questions.

'Before you say anything, I have something to show you. Something very special.' He reached into the inside pocket of his jacket and took out a glassine envelope. 'I want you to look at this. It is dated the winter of 1198. More than eight hundred years ago. It was written by Johannes von Hartelius, a former Knight Templar, on the very day of his execution for treason. I carry it with me wherever I go.'

Nalan frowned at him. 'Why are you showing me this now?'

'I don't know.' Hart's neck was stiffening up after the roof fall, and he tried to ease it. He was acutely aware of the white lie he was about to promulgate. Of its bullshit quotient. But there were times in life when displacement activity was needed. 'Because it bothers me, I suppose. Because I don't understand it. Because the past matters. And because we are sitting here in this abandoned tank, in a suburb of As Sulaymaniyah, with no idea whether we are to live or die.'

Nalan bowed her head to indicate that she understood, and even sympathized with, his motives. That she was happy to accord him her time if he felt he needed it. 'Who is the man who wrote this?'

Hart let out an inaudible sigh of relief. 'My paternal grandfather – only twenty or so generations back. I had no idea that I was related to this man until events a year ago proved that he was my direct forebear. At first I understood him to be a hero – the hereditary Guardian of the Holy Lance.'

'The Holy Lance?'

'The spear that was used to puncture Jesus's side on the cross.'

'Ah yes. I know of this thing.'

'Then I found a letter hidden inside the gilt sheath that surrounds the Holy Lance, and my certainties vanished. A letter written nearly a thousand years ago. My ancestor wasn't a hero, it transpired – he was a villain.'

'You have the Holy Lance in your possession? The true Holy Lance?'

'Yes. It came into my possession through my father. A friend is now holding it for me.'

'This is incredible. People would kill to have this.'

'They have already done so. An extreme right-wing party in Germany killed my father, his lover and their driver. Others died too. The thing is jinxed. But it has enormous symbolical value. Adolf Hitler was obsessed by it.'

'I am sorry, John. I am sorry for your father and his people.'

'Thank you. But the bitter truth is that I hadn't spoken to him since I was five years old. I can't pretend that we were close.'

'How can you be sure this is the true Holy Lance?'

'The letter I found inside proves beyond a doubt that this is the real spearhead – the one carried on the Third Crusade by Frederick Barbarossa – and not one of Adolf Hitler's fakes that he got up to fool the Americans.'

'What does the letter say?'

'It's written in old German. I had it translated. I've read it so many times that I know the text by heart. It reads: "I, Johannes von Hartelius, Baron Sanct Quirinus, hereditary Guardian of the Holy Lance, lawful husband of Adelaïde von Kronach, lawful father of Grimwald, Paulina, Agathe and Ingrid von Hartelius, former Knight Templar, exonerated from his vows of chastity and obedience by Frederick VI of Swabia, youngest son of the Holy Roman Emperor, Frederick Barbarossa, acting lawfully in the name of his brother, Henry VI Staufen, do dictate this letter on the day of my execution, to be placed inside the Holy Lance as a warning to all those who may come after me. Swayed by my unlawful love for Elfriede von Hohenstaufen, former lawful sister of the king and former intended wife of Margrave Adalfuns von Drachenhertz, military governor of Carinthia, I turned against my king and misused the Holy Lance which had been placed in my care. In doing this I refused to heed Horace's warning, passed down to me with the guardianship of the Lance: *Vir bonus est quis? Qui consulta patrum, qui leges iuraque servat* – 'He is truly a good man who observes the decree of his rulers and the laws and rights of his fellow citizens.' Instead, I purposefully misunderstood the words Catullus handed down to all unvirtuous men: *Mulier cupido quod dicit amanti, in vento et rapida scribere oportet aqua.* I thus deserve my fate. May God have mercy on my soul."'

'What does the second quotation mean? The one from Catullus?'

Hart smiled. 'That a woman will tell her besotted lover whatever she thinks he wants to hear.'

Nalan was silent for a moment. 'Not all women. I would not do this.'

Hart nodded. 'I believe you. But you are not all women, Nalan. The woman I was with last year, for instance. She told me many things. I believed them all. And they were all lies.'

Nalan looked up sharply. 'And so you mistrust all women now?'

Hart shook his head. 'No. I don't. I don't mistrust you, for instance.'

'Why do you say that? You do not know me. All I have said to you about my past may be lies.'

'No,' he said. 'What you have told me is true. After what has happened to us in the past few hours, I know you. Viscerally. Just as you know me.'

Nalan turned away from him. After a moment's hesitation she reached back and took the torch from Hart's hand. But still she refused to look at him. She hunched over the manuscript, her red-gold hair drifting forwards to frame her face. She shone the torch downwards. She read for a long time. Finally, almost shyly, she met his eyes. 'There is more writing here.'

'No,' said Hart. 'That's all there is. What I have read to you. That's all there can be.'

'There is more writing.' Nalan glanced at the sheet of vellum in her hand. Her tone brooked no argument.

'What are you talking about? There is no more writing.'

'Yes. Between the lines. There is. Look.' Nalan handed the torch and the manuscript to Hart. 'Maybe he has written it in – how do you call it? Urine.' Her face went blank for a moment, as if something inside her had been switched off. 'My mother and my father and some of their companions used to do the same here in the prison to communicate with each other. Some used urine. Some used semen or other bodily fluids. All of these things work. At least to some extent. And providing they are not checked too closely by the guards. If you heat the paper or the cloth later on with a match, or hold it up to the candlelight or against a strong bulb, the words will appear as if by magic. Hold the torch beneath the letter, John. You will see that what I am saying is true.'

Hart upended the torch and shone it through the parchment. For a moment he refused to believe what his eyes were telling him. There were words, exactly as Nalan had said – dozens of words, maybe even hundreds of them – squeezed between each line of the text, and travelling up either side of the vellum sheet. They were a fraction of the size of the visible writing. But they were clearly legible in the light emanating from the torch. The only possible conclusion was that they had been written with a pin or a finely sharpened quill, using some natural substance that would not reveal itself in daylight.

Hart looked at Nalan in consternation. 'Why did I not see this before?'

'Did you translate the text yourself?'

Hart shook his head. 'No. I don't know old German. A lady, nearly ninety years of age, who grew up with this language, translated it for me.' He gave a rueful laugh. 'A lady with cataracts that are so bad that she had to translate the manuscript through a magnifying glass. Even then she could hardly see it.'

'But you looked at the letter yourself afterwards? You inspected it closely?'

Hart cast Nalan a look of terminal embarrassment. 'No. Not that closely. Once I had the translation safely in my hand I put the letter back in this envelope and left it there. I don't know why I still carry it around with me.' He paused for a moment. 'Actually, I do know. It's because I feel connected to the man who wrote it. That my relationship with him, despite the nine centuries that separate us, is still unresolved. That he let me down in some way. Let his family down.'

'Then you must take this letter back to your old lady and you must get her to translate these hidden words for you. Then, maybe, you can achieve a resolution.'

'You are forgetting one thing,' said Hart.

'No. I'm not.' Nalan glanced towards the open hatch above her. 'No. I am forgetting nothing.'

# EIGHT

Hart climbed out of the tank ninety minutes later. There had been no further gunfire in the streets during that time, and no sounds from inside the compound. No sign, either, of the expected assault on the museum by the Kurdish army. It was as though everyone involved in the incursion had negotiated a truce and fallen asleep.

It was Hart's intention to find a spot where there was a good telephone signal and phone his ex-girlfriend, Amira, in England. She would then contact the Kurdish authorities, via the newspaper she worked for and the Foreign Office, to explain his and Nalan's whereabouts and ensure that they weren't shot at if they ventured out into the street. It was a good plan, and Nalan had gone along with it to the extent of agreeing to stay inside the tank until he called her and told her it was safe.

Hart stood for a moment by the side of the tank, listening. He held the AK47 flat against his flank, barrel downwards.

One part of him felt frighteningly vulnerable, as if he was already being measured for a coffin by a distant sniper using a night sight. Or being targeted by an invisibly hovering drone which would see him only as an unidentifiable orange heat spot emerging, gun in hand, from the dubious protection of the tank. The other, more rational part of his mind, sensed that the gunmen were dead – had to be. That the last suicide charge, followed by gunfire, had been their Armageddon. But then why no Kurdish army? What was everyone waiting for?

Hart moved towards the statue of the six blindfolded figures. He checked his phone. Yes. A good signal finally. He had one bar left on his battery indicator.

He put the rifle down and flicked to his last call. It was then that he saw the movement out of the corner of his eye.

He froze, the phone halfway to his ear, the number already on automatic dial.

A man stood with his back to Hart, about ten yards from the grille, partially protected by Rebwar's rickety guard post. He was clearly visible in the moonlight. The man bent down to pick something up. As Hart watched, he repeated the motion.

Hart felt with frantic fingers for the Power Off button on his phone, but he was too late. Amira's number began to ring.

The man straightened up and turned towards the noise, which, though faint, echoed spectrally throughout the silent courtyard. Hart now saw that the man was wearing a suicide vest, already partially packed with explosives.

Hart looked down at the AK47 lying on the ground beside him. He felt unnaturally calm – fatalistic, even – as if a power greater than himself was controlling events, and that whatever would be, would be.

He dropped to one knee, let go of his phone, and swept the gun up and into the firing position. He was only vaguely aware of a woman's voice calling out behind him, and of the man in front of him conducting his very own series of movements, eerily paralleling his own, as though they were both part of some mirror act in a 1930s music hall.

Hart fired first. The barrel of the AK47 swung up, and Hart saw chunks of concrete shear off the wall above the gunman's head. Hart held the barrel down and fired again. He was still reeling from the unexpected recoil from the abbreviated stock. Part of his mind was idly wondering whether, if he hit the man, he wouldn't simply explode. And was the belt packed with plastic explosive or with 'Mother of Satan' TATP? If the latter was the case, they would be dead in less than a millisecond. With plastic explosive they might have an outside chance of survival. And would the bomber have a dead man's switch?

Something tapped Hart on the shoulder and he lurched backwards. It was Nalan.

'Where is he?' said Hart, his face numb with shock.

'Don't worry. He is dead.'

Hart stumbled forwards. He looked down at the man in his suicide vest.

The vest was hanging open. Some of its explosive sleeves were still empty.

Hart realized that by a miracle he had somehow managed

to shoot the man through the heart. His white kurta was saturated with blood.

'I killed him.'

'Yes. He would have killed you. Me. Others maybe.'

'Yes. I understand that.'

Hart stood for a long time looking down at the body.

He hardly noticed when Nalan put the ringing telephone back into his hand.

# NINE

# Schloss Hartelius
# Lake Tegernsee, Bavaria

## 15 MAY 1198

When Johannes von Hartelius had been released from his Templar vows after saving the Holy Lance from the Saleph River, the Holy Roman Emperor's youngest son, Frederick VI of Swabia, had decided, in his capacity as commander-in-chief of the German crusaders, that Hartelius must immediately marry. How, otherwise, could a man formerly committed to poverty and chastity start a dynasty? A dynasty that would undertake to be Guardians of the Holy Lance of Longinus in perpetuity?

The bride chosen for the twenty-one-year-old Hartelius had been Adelaïde von Kronach, a fifteen-year-old fellow Bavarian from Upper Franconia, of impeccable pedigree and even more impeccable dowry, who had been destined for the court of the Queen of Jerusalem. Eight years into their *Muntehe* marriage Adelaïde had already given Hartelius four children – Grimwald, who would inherit the title Baron St Quirinus – Paulina, Agathe and Ingrid. Their fifth child was a breech birth.

As the result of a freakishly late snowstorm, the physician called upon to oversee Adelaïde's lying-in from outside the actual confines of her bedroom, as was the custom amongst aristocratic families, found himself and his retinue stranded across the lake from Schloss Hartelius, in Tegernsee Abbey. An inexperienced midwife and a wet nurse he had sent on ahead of him were the only people on hand to help with the birth. The midwife had never dealt with a breech birth before, and when the jet bowl and the birth girdle and the amber and coral amulets and the parchment lozenges all failed to alleviate the mother's agony, she panicked. The child suffocated. Adelaïde needed the body to be cut out of her, but no one present was capable of doing it.

The news of Adelaïde von Hartelius's death in childbirth travelled swiftly around Bavaria, where anyone with an aristocratic title, or who pertained to aristocratic privilege, was related to everyone else. Outside Bavaria the news travelled a little more slowly.

It was more than three months after Adelaïde's death, therefore, that a messenger arrived at Schloss Hartelius with orders that the newly bereaved Baron Sanct Quirinus must present himself at Mainz, in his capacity as Hereditary Guardian of the Holy Lance, in good time for Philip of Swabia's coronation.

Hartelius, who had been expecting neither the call to duty nor the royal messenger, said the first thing that came into his mind. 'Philip of Swabia? But he is the brother of the dead king. I thought the new king would be Frederick's son, little Frederick? Has something happened to him?'

The messenger responded more sharply than his nominal role might at first have suggested. 'A three-year-old king of the Germans would be an impossibility, sir, as you yourself must know. A fragmented kingdom needs a forceful ruler, or it will disintegrate.'

Hartelius was well aware that any man bearing a message from the court would, in addition to his courier duties, be tasked with spying on him and monitoring his first reaction to the news that the rightful young king of the Germans had just been ousted from that position by his uncle. It behoved him to tread carefully, therefore. 'Yes. Of course. What you say is perfectly true. Perfectly true. We are out of touch here. Little more than rustics, if truth be told. I spoke without thinking.'

He set off for Mainz via Bavarian Swabia the very next day, and delivered his four children to Adelaïde's parents en route. Adelaïde's father, Hugo von Kronach, was a bloody-minded despot with only one redeeming characteristic – that he placed his family before everything. Blessedly, Hartelius knew that von Kronach would have little to do with the children himself, being obsessed by hunting and hawking and skirmishing with his neighbours, the von Ebblings.

The well-being of his children would fall to Adelaïde's mother, Hilda von Kronach, and to Adelaïde's two as yet unmarried younger sisters, Else and Maria. Hartelius was satisfied that the children would, therefore, in accordance with his late wife's dying wishes, be in the best possible hands in this difficult time. For he suspected that something was being held in store for him, there being no precedent for a man of his minor aristocratic standing to be called upon to attend a coronation. His great-uncle, a former Abbot of Tegernsee, had been the last man of any note in the Hartelius family, and he was long since dead.

Three days after his arrival in Mainz, Hartelius was consequently astonished to find himself placed a mere two steps behind the new king – and, far more significantly, on his right – during the coronation at the newly renovated Romanesque Cathedral. At one point during the ceremony, just after the sacred oil had been combed into Philip's hair, Hartelius was required to recite a Latin motto and brandish the Holy Lance, which had been tricked up with a seven-foot-long wooden haft for the occasion. Hartelius, still bewildered by his abrupt rise to royal notice, performed his duties admirably.

The bishop then reeled off a long, carefully worded peroration which placed the newly crowned King Philip in direct line of descent, via Constantine, Justinian, Charles Martel, Charlemagne, Henry the Fowler and Frederick Barbarossa, to the military guardians of Christ's legacy on earth. The only possible explanation for this bellicose religious symbolism was that a new crusade was in the offing, and that the nobility were being prepared for their part in it.

It came as no surprise to Hartelius, therefore, when he was called into the office of the king's chamberlain a scant two days after the ceremony. It was a considerable shock, however, when he realized that he was once again to be in the presence of the king himself, but this time in a private capacity. Hartelius instantly assumed that now he was widowed – but with the significant advantage of already possessing the heir necessary to secure the position of Hereditary Guardian of the Holy Lance beyond his death – he would be required to retake his Templar oath and become a soldier of Christ once again, with all that entailed in terms of celibacy, constancy and penury. A new crusade needed soldiers, and he was nothing if not that. The thought that his four children were secured at Schloss Kronach with their grandmother and aunts afforded him some comfort in the circumstances, and he began to inure himself to the thought that he would have to hand over a significant proportion of their mother's dowry to the Templars when he rejoined their ranks.

In the event the twenty-two-year-old king had a very different task for him to perform – one that required no such financial sacrifice.

'Margrave Adalfuns von Drachenhertz, military governor of Carinthia. You have heard of him, of course?'

'Our war leader. Yes, sire. A mighty warrior.' And one of the kingdom's most troublesome barons, Hartelius might have added, endlessly fomenting nuisance and discord in a constant bid for more power.

'The margrave is to lead the next crusade to free Jerusalem and the Holy Land. In my stead. Do you understand me?'

'Yes, sire.'

'For I am needed here. To counter incursions from Sicily and suchlike.' The last part of the king's speech was almost mumbled.

Hartelius knew just why the king was mumbling. It was unprecedented for a monarch not to take the lead when a new crusade was in the offing. Hartelius kept his expression neutral, however, and his stance dignified but submissive. It didn't do to antagonize guilt-stricken monarchs if one wished to keep one's head. It was becoming clearer to him by the minute that the king's main intention must be for von Drachenhertz to stay on in the Holy Land – preferably below ground.

'I am giving von Drachenhertz my sister, Agnes, youngest daughter of my father, Frederick Barbarossa, as his wife. And I am sending him the Holy Lance as a further sign of my accord with the aims of the crusade. These two symbols will surely be enough to convince our English and French allies of the seriousness of our intent. I am needed here.'

'Of course, sire.'

'You will escort my sister to the Holy Land, Hartelius. You will hand her over to von Drachenhertz, together with her dowry, which is absurdly significant. But we need to keep the man sweet, don't we, Missingau?'

The king looked at his chamberlain. The chamberlain looked at Hartelius. Hartelius pretended that he was not in the room.

This king will never last, he thought to himself. This king is doomed. When I think of a giant like Frederick Barbarossa compared to this man, his son, my soul shrinks inside its capsule.

'Are you clear on what we are asking of you, Hartelius?'

'Yes, sire. Only . . .' Something was eating at the outer edges of Hartelius's consciousness. 'May I assume that the king's sister is a somewhat unwilling party to this undertaking?'

The king and Missingau looked at each other. Then both men turned towards Hartelius. The king shrugged, motioned to Missingau with his chin, and departed. Missingau waited until all the king's guards had vacated the room.

'What an absurd suggestion. The king's sister knows nothing of the king's plan, so how can she be against it? She lives in a nunnery. She intends to take the white. But she is far too valuable politically to palm off on God. Do you understand me, Hartelius?'

Hartelius gave no sign that he was shocked by Missingau's derogatory tone. In certain circles, a statement such as the one that had just issued from Missingau's mouth would be considered blasphemy, punishable by death. Hartelius suspected that Missingau felt himself safe from all attack. Certainly by a nonentity such as Hartelius.

'You wish me to abduct her then?'

'Abduct? Abduct? Such a misused word. No. Not abduct.' The chamberlain smiled. It was the smile of the crocodile in the presence of the stork. 'We simply don't expect you to take no for an answer.'

# TEN

The Rupertsberg Convent, built on the orders of Hildegard of Bingen at the exact place the Nahe flows into the Rhine, had lost a great deal of its spiritual authority following its founder's death twenty years before. It had become an alternative home for ladies of rank, with only the mildest emphasis on the Benedictine rite in its daily routine, derived as it was from Saint Scholastica, St Benedict's twin sister, rather than from the troublesome saint himself.

As the convent was directly subordinate to the Archbishop of Mainz, Hartelius found little problem entering its precincts, on the understanding that the twenty Templar knights accompanying him would house and provender themselves in the nearby town, and thus avoid disturbing the inmates. The abbess herself received him – after the mandatory delay of around an hour – flanked by two oblates.

Hartelius handed over his *laissez-passer* from the king. The abbess read it, then handed it to the younger of the two oblates, who glanced at it and threw it onto the table. Hartelius deduced from the comfortable familiarity – the haughtiness, even – with which the oblate treated the abbess, that the white-veiled young woman he saw before him was indeed the king's eighteen-year-old sister, Agnes of Hohenstaufen.

He tried to get a proper look at her – the margrave, after all, would hardly be amused if the king sent him a pig in a poke as a wife – but, beyond the immediate circle of the face, the veil and wimple she wore was specifically designed to discourage the male gaze, and the tunic and scapular that encased the remainder of her body allowed not the faintest suggestion of what delights – or horrors – might lurk beneath.

Hartelius focused his attention back on the abbess. 'I come from the king, Reverend Mother. My orders stem directly from him. I am to take his youngest sister, Agnes von Hohenstaufen—'

'Elfriede von Hohenstaufen,' said the oblate. 'I dislike the name Agnes. It makes me sound like a lamb to the slaughter. Which is what my brother wants of me, no doubt. Elfriede is my second name. It means "to be free".'

Hartelius was so taken aback by the oblate's intercession that he temporarily lost command of himself. 'Elfriede does not mean "to be free", Princess. The name stems from the Saxon word *aelf*, meaning an elf or supernatural being, with the second part deriving from *pryo*, meaning strength. So your name means "strength in otherness".'

Elfriede stared at him.

Hartelius turned back to the abbess. He would be on stronger ground with her, he suspected. She had a position to lose. 'I am to take his youngest sister, Elfriede von Hohenstaufen, to Acre, in the Holy Land, where she will marry Margrave Adalfuns von Drachenhertz.'

The oblate held up one of her hands, with the index and little fingers extended. 'An old goat, probably. With horns. And whiskers. And why should I lower myself to become a Markgräfin? I am a Hohenstaufen. There is nothing higher before God. My father was the Holy Roman Emperor.'

Hartelius saw the abbess's eyebrows rise and then fall again. Was there a suggestion in that brief movement that she might secretly be longing to rid herself of this worrisome young oblate of hers? Hartelius pressed on, this time with more confidence. 'I have brought the princess's marriage chest and depository with me. Also the details of her dowry and her papers of mark. Other articles, too, of which we can talk during our journey. The king has allocated the princess a guard of twenty Knights Templar for her security, together with fifty followers, including two personal handmaidens, for her comfort and convenience. She may choose a personal companion from within the bounds of the nunnery, also, if she so desires.'

The young oblate threw aside all remaining pretence. 'So you're what they call a Knight Templar, are you, Hartelius? Dedicated, like me, to poverty, chastity and obedience? But what am I saying? Of course you are. Those twenty knights my brother allocated to you wouldn't follow anyone who wasn't one of them. So Philip is entrusting me to a eunuch? Well, that's apposite. Let's hope my future husband does not embrace Templar-hood too before I can contrive to reach his bedside.'

Hartelius knew just enough about women after eight years of marriage to know when the pot he was sitting in was being stirred. 'I am no longer a Knight Templar, Princess. Your late brother, Frederick VI of Swabia, exonerated me from my vows a short time before his death at the Siege of Acre. He had inherited the leadership of the Third Crusade from your father, on the battlefield, and therefore spoke directly in his name.'

'So you are the one?'

'The one what, Princess?'

'The one who filched the Holy Lance from my father's saddle. The one who failed to pluck my father from the waters of the Saleph at the same time. The one who allowed his anointed king to drown like an unwanted kitten while he paddled off to safety and a blaze of glory.'

Hartelius sighed inwardly. 'Your father was in full armour, Princess, and I was not. The king sank to the bottom of the river before I could reach him. His horse, though injured, swam onto a sandbank. There it died. I spent the whole of a freezing night inside that horse's belly. The next morning I realized that the Holy Lance was still attached to your father's saddle. I took it and returned it to your brother two days later, further up the road to Acre. He made me Hereditary Guardian of the Holy Lance, publicly cancelled my Templar vows – with

60

the full agreement of our marshal, I should add – and married me, on the spot, to Adelaïde von Kronach.'

'So you are not a eunuch then?'

'No, Princess. No Knight Templar is. A vow of chastity is a separate thing entirely, as you well know, being an oblate, and subject to similar vows. And the twenty Templar knights of your escort will obey me because I was one of them once, and am perceived to have brought honour to our order. That is all.'

'And that scar on your face?'

'Caused by a crossbow quarrel. Fired from the very same weapon that injured your father's Turcoman and caused it to plunge into the river with your father still in the saddle.'

'Do you have children?'

'Four, Princess.'

'And your wife? Is she happy that you are abandoning her and your children back in Bavaria to transport the king's unwilling sister to the Holy Land?'

'My wife is dead, Princess. She died three months ago in childbirth. My children are well looked after in their grandfather's castle. I am the servant of the king. It is not for me to decide what I do and where I go.'

The princess hesitated for a moment. Her eyes, only partially shadowed by the peak of her veil, flashed violet, like the skirts of a Portuguese man-of-war. 'I am sorry, Hartelius. Sorry for your loss. I did not mean to be flippant when I asked you these questions. If I am to travel to the Holy Land under your guardianship I need to know with whom I am dealing.'

'Of course, Princess.'

Elfriede von Hohenstaufen glared at the abbess. 'And my vows here?'

The abbess bowed her head. 'Still formally unconfirmed. You are free to follow the king, your brother's, orders. Which, as your spiritual guide, is what I also should advise.'

Hartelius thought, for one pregnant moment, that he had lost the princess then. That the abbess's ill-advised recommendation would re-summon all her teenage perversity, and that she would choose to baulk at her brother's request.

Instead, she looked at him, her head cocked to one side, the folds of her wimple falling across her face and brow. 'What is your full title, Hartelius?'

'Johannes von Hartelius, Baron Sanct Quirinus, Princess.'

'Well, Johannes von Hartelius, Baron Sanct Quirinus, I, Elfriede von Hohenstaufen, sister to King Philip of the Germans, and intended bride of. . .' she made a face '. . . the Margrave Adalfuns von Drachenhertz, agree to accompany you to the Holy Land according to my brother's request. The only thing I ask is that you don't ignore me and put on that silent face I have detected more than once intruding on your countenance. I have been living amongst women for the past eight years. . .' she glared at the abbess '. . . and I am tired of it. Tired of all the pettiness and the machinations. Tired of all the silly laws we contrive on ourselves and the mingy restrictions that are contrived on us. You are a soldier. I want you to tell me of war and of hardship and of the things men do. You are to be the guide to my new life.'

Hartelius stared at the abbess, open-mouthed.

The abbess stared back at him. Then she gave a single shrug of her shoulders, as if to say, She is well and truly off my hands now. She is your problem, Baron. And the very best of luck to you.

# ELEVEN

For the first three weeks of their 550-mile journey from Rupertsberg to Venice, and despite all her protestations to the contrary in front of the abbess, the princess refused to see Hartelius. By day she travelled in her closed carriage with the shutters down, and at night she kept to her tent and to the company of her female servants. As a result, Hartelius found himself thinking more and more about her.

He had become used to female company since his formal release from his Templar vows, and he desperately missed his wife, whose death he mourned on a daily basis. He had therefore fancied that he and the princess might be able to spend time together talking and, yes, he had to admit it, mildly flirting according to the laws of *hohe Minne* or courtly love, as described by the *Minnesinger* Friedrich von Hausen, whose poems and songs every educated German nobleman or noblewoman had read. The truth was that Hartelius had been quite won over by the princess's extraordinary self-assurance in the presence of the abbess. Most young women of her age and class would have been cowed and submissive. The princess, instead, had dominated the proceedings. Hartelius admired courage in whatever form it showed itself. And the princess had been nothing if not courageous.

Still, he was by and large happy with the arrangement, for it freed him to concentrate all his attention on building a working relationship with his knights. For despite all that he had said in front of the princess about the amenability of Knights Templar to being commanded by a former brother-at-arms, Hartelius knew that he would need to gain each man's confidence and trust personally before he could expect anything but the most basic degree of loyalty from them.

By the end of the initial three-week stage, when they were still well short of the Alps, he felt that he had, at least partially, achieved his end. The knights – whom he had immediately split into two groups of ten, each with their own colours and standard – alternated convoy duty, with the non-guarding knights detailed to scout the terrain in front of, behind and to either side of the princess's cortege, to a distance of about a third of a league. Hartelius would accompany these knights on their expeditions and engage in war games with them, one party ambushing the other, with Hartelius sometimes contriving mock attacks on the main convoy to test the alertness of the guarding knights both by day and by night.

He anticipated few real problems whilst they were still on German soil, but there was always the outside chance of an attack by brigands or rogue knights intent on plundering the princess's possessions. News of such a large and well-armed party of travellers moving south would inevitably be noised abroad. Hartelius trusted that the presence of Knights Templar both in advance of the column and in its rear would obviate the likelihood of any such outrage, and act as a cementing measure between the men prior to the party's considerably more challenging early-autumn Alpine crossing.

It was on the evening of the twenty-first day after their departure from Rupertsberg that the princess finally called for him. Hartelius washed his face in cold water and put on his cleanest tunic, but he had hardly come prepared for polite society. He looked like what he was – a warrior knight fresh from the road and stinking of horses.

He was forced to duck to enter the princess's pavilion, for he was considerably over six feet in height, whereas the princess and her attendants averaged nearly a foot less. Not for the first time in his life, Hartelius felt like a grotesque. The environment inside the pavilion spoke of femininity and delicacy, whereas he felt more comfortable in a stable or on a battlefield.

Neither the princess nor her handmaidens were there to greet him. Hartelius took the opportunity to look around himself, as the place was well lit by wax candles. The pavilion was divided into three sections, each one sealed off from the other. He was standing in what was clearly the living section. Towards the rear of the pavilion was what he assumed were the princess's sleeping quarters, which were demarcated from the remainder of the living area by a large Flemish tapestry, with the main details picked out in gold thread.

Across from that was an area reserved for storage, and most likely also for the princess's toilet. A mobile triptych showing the Virgin standing in a field of lilies and holding the Christ child in her arms barred the way. The Virgin was flanked on her left by John the Baptist, and on her right by the prophet Zacharias. Hartelius approached for a closer look. He had never seen a rendition of the Virgin in any other than the seated position, and he found the image astonishing.

'It's in the new Romanesque style,' said the princess, who had appeared silently from behind the tapestry, flanked by her two maidservants. 'Do you see the X with the perpendicular P cutting through it?'

'Yes,' said Hartelius. 'It is the Greek spelling of the word Christ. It is a good-luck emblem. Also, the way John the Baptist is holding the fingers of his right hand, with the thumb and forefinger raised, and the last two fingers curled inwards. This represents a blessing.'

'So you *are* educated? I suspected as much when you redefined my name back at Rupertsberg.'

Hartelius approached the princess and kissed both her outstretched hands. 'I am sorry for that, Princess. I could not help myself. I apologize for my rudeness.'

Both the maidservants curtseyed to him and disappeared behind the tapestry. There was much rustling and giggling as they sat down, ready to rush to the princess's aid, no doubt, should he overstep the mark.

'Don't apologize, Hartelius. I liked it. A soldier should be educated. If he isn't, he is simply a thug, and worthy only to be served up as meat.' She sniffed. 'And speaking of meat, you are to break bread with me tonight. Kindly use the aquamanile over there on the table. The water has been warmed and perfumed, and may serve to disguise the scent of horse you seem to have carried in with you from the outside.'

Hartelius shrugged and walked across to the ewer. It was designed in the form of a seated lion, with the spigot emerging from the lion's mouth. There was a tipping handle and a sealed opening in the lion's head through which the liquid entered. The water was indeed scented. Hartelius thought he detected roses. And some elusive spice. Possibly myrrh. Or cinnamon. 'You don't like the smell of horses, Princess?'

'I smell them all day. I prefer not to smell them at night also.'

Hartelius dried his hands and turned back towards her. As he did so, the princess removed her veil and chin-band and draped it over an ivory oliphant. She smiled happily when she saw the effect her little piece of theatre had on him.

'This hunting horn was my father's. It was made in Metz from the finest elephant ivory. It was his favourite object.' She placed one hand over the pectoral cross that hung down the front of her *bliaut*. 'This cross was sculpted from the same piece of ivory. My father had it made for me as a sign of his favour.'

Hartelius noticed for the first time that the princess was wearing no cap, and that her short, auburn-coloured hair hung free. This, too, alongside the standing Virgin, was unprecedented. Her skin was pale and her eyes were violet, and very large in the context of her face, which was heart-shaped, with high Hohenstaufen cheekbones and a delicately rounded chin. Her nose was straight and full of character – what one might call a determined nose – and her ears were small, and set close to her head. Piercing the princess's ears were two gold and cinnabarine earrings. The background to the earrings had been removed with a fine chisel to reveal two peacocks flanking a vase. The peacock, Hartelius knew, symbolized immortality and resurrection. This made the princess, her accoutrements and the décor of her living quarters all part of a symbolical whole. Hartelius was hard put to conceal his astonishment at the effect produced.

'Princess. It disturbs me that you chose to take with you no companion of your own degree from the convent.'

'I have my books. I have you. I have no need of a companion.'

'Then why have you only just called on me? From what you said at Rupertsberg, I understood you wished me to talk to you of war and the things men do.'

The princess laughed. 'You didn't take me seriously, did you? I only said that to outrage the abbess. She made my life a misery for the eight years she had me in her power, despite the marked disparity in our stations, and despite my father's strict instructions, enshrined in his will, that I was to receive a liberal education, rich in the arts and in music, with regular outings beyond the confines of the convent. I therefore particularly enjoyed watching her face when you announced you came directly from my elder brother, the new king, with fresh instructions from him. She looked as though she had swallowed a lemon.' She chucked her chin at Hartelius. 'And I have only now called on you, Baron, because I needed my hair to grow out a little after the pruning those wretched nuns gave it when I turned eighteen. Wimples turn you bald, you know. And I did not wish to receive you looking like one of the minor pharaohs.'

Hartelius tried to smile, but his face wouldn't let him.

'The truth is that I am entirely uninterested in war. You can tell me about love instead. That will be far more important to my future. Sit you down, Hartelius. I am listening.'

# TWELVE

Try as he might, Hartelius found it impossible to ignore the two girls concealed behind the tapestry leading to the princess's bedchamber.

'I know nothing of love, Princess.'

'But you have been married. Did you not love your wife?'

Hartelius had never in his life been asked such a question by a woman. And certainly not in the presence of two of her servants. He looked pained, as if the princess was asking him for a loan of money he did not possess but which he still felt duty bound to give her. His eyes swivelled across to the tapestry again.

The princess caught his look. 'Both of you. Get out.'

'But, Princess. . .' said a disembodied voice.

'Get out, I say. You have lovers amongst the camp followers. Go and visit them.'

The two girls crept out from behind the tapestry and sidestepped towards the pavilion entrance. Each one curtseyed before backing out through the opening.

'That was ill done, Princess. There will be talk.'

'There is always talk *de bas en haut*. What are they going to do? Ride three weeks back to Mainz and report to my brother that I am entertaining the commander of my knight escort without a chaperone?'

'No. But they might send a message by courier from the next town.'

'And what will my brother do? Send men after me to take me back to the nunnery?'

'No, Princess. He will send men after me.'

Both fell silent for a while, looking at each other.

'Tell me something, Hartelius. Tell me something you did in battle.'

'But I thought you didn't want to hear about war?'

'I lied.'

Hartelius had encountered very few women during the course of his life. And certainly none like the princess. When a man told him something, he assumed it to be true. Otherwise why say it? But the princess seemed to say things purely for effect. As though she was trying them out on him for size.

It occurred to him then that she, too, had had very little to do with the opposite sex during the course of her eighteen years of life. She had been sent to the nunnery immediately following the king's death, eight years before. Now, aged eighteen, she was probably better educated than he was – better educated even than his late wife – but infinitely more sheltered. She would have been taught Latin, Greek and French. She would have studied philosophy and the humanities. She would have read the classics. And now she wanted to hear about war. Well, he would tell her about peace.

'Very well then, Princess. I will tell you a true story. Eight years ago – three weeks before the king, your father's, death – I was involved in a skirmish.'

'What is a skirmish?'

'A small battle. What you might call a minor attack. They happen all the time on campaign.'

The princess stood up and walked over to her marriage chest, which doubled as a sideboard. She poured them both a little wine from a pewter flagon. She carried the two chargers across to Hartelius. He made as if to stand up but she motioned him back down again. Once he had his wine, she sank to the floor at his feet, crossed her legs, and looked up at him expectantly.

Hartelius took a deep breath. The princess's perfume wafted up from below him. He was aware of the litheness of her body. Of her youth. Of the burnished copper sheen of her hair. All these things he forcibly tried to damp from his mind. But his mind wouldn't listen to him. He looked down at her, as she sat cross-legged below him, and he lost sight of himself. Of what he was. Of what he represented. A sort of madness overtook him.

'That day, after a long pursuit, I found myself separated from my companions. I had been pursuing one man. A wounded Saracen. He had been struck a glancing blow on the shoulders by one of our pike men. I had seen him fall forwards, clutching his horse's mane, and then ride off. He was mounted on the most beautiful destrier I had ever seen. I wanted this horse. I wanted to kill him and take this horse for my own. Such a thing is permitted under Templar Law, Princess. I was within my rights.'

'So you followed him?'

'Out of greed. Yes. I followed him.'

'Horses mean so much to you?'

'Horses mean everything to a knight. They are our eyes and ears. They are our soul.'

'Is this why you don't need women?'

Hartelius met the princess's gaze full on. 'We need women. I need women. There is no link between what occurs on the battlefield and what happens off it. A man is only a man, Princess. Although certain of our clerics would have you think otherwise.'

'And a horse is only a horse.' This time it was the princess who turned her gaze away.

'Yes. The horse.' Hartelius's mind turned inwards. Back to that time, eight years before. 'I have never spoken of this. There are aspects to this story that would not be forgiven if they were told in certain quarters. Maybe I should not continue?'

'Continue, Hartelius. You have my word that your tale will go no further.' Still the princess would not look at him.

'I rode. Far too far and far too fast. I was greedy. I had forgotten caution in my lust for my prize. I had forgotten good sense. I came to a valley. A fertile place in an area that was otherwise parched and blasted. A river ran through the valley. Trees climbed up either bank. Along the river lay a pasture. It was not far from dawn. Mist was rising still. I could make out the passage of the horse I was pursuing through the grasses as clearly as I can make out your face. The line of your neck.' Hartelius felt the madness come upon him again. He forced it away. 'My mare was exhausted. I climbed off her and led her to the riverbank. I tethered her there and left her to forage. I went to where the trail left by the Saracen and his horse began. I followed it for a short while on foot, looking for spoor. I could see the line the horse had made through the grasses snaking far away in front of me. I was safe. Every few yards, blood gouts coated the downtrodden herbage. My lust was leaving me. I had become aware of just how far I had travelled in my pursuit of the Saracen. Of the danger I had put myself in.'

'Did you turn back?'

'No, Princess. I was very young. My companions had seen me ride off after the wounded warrior. I did not wish them to laugh at me. I wanted to astonish them. To prove my manhood to them by killing the Saracen and returning to the camp with my prize.'

'So you continued?'

'No.'

'Why so?'

'My horse, standing on the riverbank, whickered. There was an answering whinny. The Saracen's horse came galloping back down the valley. Riderless. He had smelt my mare, you see, who was in season. Caught her scent on the wind. He was a stallion. He had thrown his weakened rider and was returning to court her. This was clear to me.'

'He could smell her? That far?'

'Just as I can smell you, Princess. It is a natural thing. Between animals. And also between men and women. Otherwise how would the world procreate?' Hartelius knew that he was edging ever closer to the precipice. But he no longer cared.

The princess trembled. Yet still she looked away.

Hartelius lost himself in looking at her. He could see both her and the valley he spoke of. Each was as real to him as the other. 'I took out my sword and followed the blood spoor left by the Saracen. It didn't take me long to find him. He had drawn himself up against a tree. He held his scimitar in his left hand. No Muslim fights with the left hand. I knew that his right must be injured. That the blow on the back had damaged his fighting side, and that the fall from his horse had probably weakened him further.'

'You killed him?'

'I circled him, watching. Fighting men are trained to sum up their opponents. Often it is what makes the difference between dying and living. This man was close to exhaustion. As I watched him he slid down the tree and lay pressed against its trunk, his scimitar still held towards me.'

'"Yield,"' I said, "and I will not kill you."

'"I cannot," he said.

'I watched him for some time. He had a beautiful face. Noble. Open. The face of a man I should like to call my friend. I approached a little closer to him. He no longer had the strength to raise his scimitar to fend me off. I had only to wait. It was simply a matter of time.'

'Then?'

'I dropped my sword and walked towards him. I cannot tell you why I did this. I still do not know. I brushed his scimitar aside with my hand and helped him stretch forwards, onto the ground. I removed his cape. Inspected his chainmail. Neither of us said a word. It was as if we were living in a place outside time itself. Outside the world's envelope.'

'Is such a thing possible?'

'It is possible.' Hartelius laid one hand on the princess's neck. He caressed her hair and her shoulders, lightly, as you would caress a child. 'The pike had driven through the linkage in his mail and damaged his right shoulder, here. . .' Hartelius touched the princess's back '. . . to the left of the shoulder blade. I made a pad with moss from a nearby tree and packed it into the wound. The Saracen was no longer fully conscious. I took his scimitar and drove it into the ground near to my sword. Later, when I had finished tending to his wounds, I collected our horses. His stallion had mounted my mare. Such a thing was clear from the condition of her hindquarters. Now they were both still. Grazing together. At peace. That night I chanced a fire. The valley was closed. What you would call a combe. It would have needed a man to walk his horse at the very top of the ridge to see the glow. And still the Saracen slept.'

'And your companions? Back at the camp?'

'I knew they must think me dead.'

Hartelius's hand was still resting on the princess. She was not evading it. Once, even, she raised her own hand and touched his lightly with her fingers.

'I felt as if I and the Saracen were in an enchanted place. Outside the war. Outside the madness of the faiths we both represented. I too slept, knowing that if he woke, he might kill me. But I knew that he would not. At that moment we were one. One soul. One unity. In the morning, when he awoke, he could move a little. I sat him up against the tree and gave him some of my biscuit and a little water. We broke bread together.

'"You wish for my horse," he said. "I can see it in your eyes. You must take him. As a gift from me. For you have given me life."

'I raised the Saracen and placed him high into the saddle of his destrier. He bent forwards at the waist like an old man.

'"I have your horse," I said. "Inside mine. Last night he took my mare. I can wait eleven months."

'He laughed. I handed him his scimitar. He sat for a long moment looking down at me.

'"Why?" he said. "Why did you not kill me?"

'"I would have been killing myself. Such a thing is a sin, is it not?"

'He laughed once more and sheathed his sword.

'"My men are camped all around this valley. It is a miracle you were not discovered. I am their commander. You are young. I would be worth much to you in ransom."

'"You are worth more to me than any ransom."

'The Saracen nodded. "I shall call them off. Leave by the way you came. You will be safe. I promise you."

'He took my hand. We kissed, as brothers would.

'"Your name?"

'"Johannes von Hartelius. Of Sanct Quirin."

'"My name is Amir Maan Ibn Fakhr-al-Din. Of Baakleen. In the Chouf. Remember or forget. The choice is yours."

'He rode slowly away. My mare called after his stallion, and the stallion called back. I mounted the mare and rode back towards our camp. I knew his men would not pursue me. I knew that I was safe.'

'And your mare? Did she have her foal?'

'Oh yes. I am riding him now. He is seven years old and in his prime. He looks just like his father.'

The princess took Hartelius's hand in hers. 'You smell of him. However hard you wash, you still smell of horses.'

'I am sorry, Princess.'

'Don't be. I like it.'

Hartelius no longer knew or cared what he was doing. Given his birth, he knew exactly the degree of mild flirtation the *hohe Minne* tradition allowed him. He was already way beyond it.

He dropped to his knees beside the princess. She was looking up at him – meeting his gaze now, equal to equal. Her eyes were large and all-encompassing – they seemed to drink him into their centres as if he were diving into a deep well. He kissed her and she responded. He lay her on the floor of the pavilion and lost himself in her scent and the tender touch of her arms about him.

'Why, Princess? Why?'

'I asked you to tell me of love.'

'But I told you of war.'

'No, Hartelius. You told me of love.'

# THIRTEEN

Hartelius visited the princess every evening after that. The moment she heard his step she would send her handmaidens back to their lovers so as to be able to entertain her own. They would talk. Kiss. Hold each other. After dining together, he would return to the camp to do his round of the pickets. Then, later, when night came, he would return to the princess's pavilion through the darkness of the camp to lie with her. His men would look the other way. There was no point trying to disguise what was happening. A moveable camp is a busy place. There are guards, blacksmiths, cooks and camp followers. Coopers, seamstresses and leatherworkers. Fires burn. Braziers glow.

Hartelius and the princess were indulging in a sort of madness, one with the other. Only people in their position could think to be so blatant. Hartelius was the commander of the column and the Guardian of the Holy Lance. The princess was the sister of the king. As long as the column kept moving, their affair could continue with relative impunity. But they were storing up trouble for themselves and both of them knew it. Neither cared.

Two weeks into their alpine crossing, somewhere near the Brenner Pass, the column was attacked by Italian *banditti*. Despite the explicitness of his indulgences, Hartelius had somehow managed to maintain the loyalty of his knights. Perhaps it was the otherworldliness of his infatuation? The near sanctity of his position as the Lance carrier? For whatever reason, his Templar knights fought nobly, despite the odds against them. The *banditti* were guerrilla fighters – mountain men. Used to dealing with merchants and their wagon trains. Soft targets.

The knights drove them off for the loss of seven of their number. Fifteen camp followers were also killed, and two of the women stolen, including one of the princess's handmaidens.

At one point in the skirmish, Hartelius had placed himself in front of the princess's pavilion, burning tents all around him, the dead and dying calling on God to save them, and had raised his sword high above his head, as a Viking berserker will, and had run at the approaching enemy, with no thought for his own life, but only that of the princess.

Three *banditti* had marked him out – men used to fighting as a team – but they had wilted beneath Hartelius's onslaught. They had merely been seeking booty – their souls were not involved in the fight. To Hartelius, death was a small price to pay for his annexation of another man's intended bride. He left it up to God whether he would live or die. The lengths of the odds he faced seemed somehow apposite.

He killed first one, then another of his assailants. Twice he was struck from behind, but his chainmail deflected the blows. A third time he was caught on the neck, near the trapezius muscle. He felt his arm go limp, and switched hands, as he had so often trained himself to do. The third *bandito*, sensing weakness, attacked low. Hartelius parried and dropped to one knee. He made as if to fall forwards and the *bandito* lunged. Hartelius feinted to one side and the man hesitated for one fatal second, uncertain what was happening. Hartelius scythed anti-clockwise with his sword arm and cut the *bandito*'s leg to the bone. The *bandito* fell and Hartelius lunged across the man's upper body, his sword nethermost. The dead weight of him as he dropped, confident that his chainmail would protect him from his own sword edge, was enough to almost sever the man in two. Hartelius lay on top of his assailant. He could feel the blood pulsing from his neck wound onto the ground.

He rolled away and tried to rise to one knee, but he could not. The princess ran from the safety of her pavilion, a dagger held out before her. She crouched by Hartelius and feverishly searched his body for wounds. His eyes were wild with looking for other assailants. Two of his knights, seeing their commander down and their princess out in the open and with no cover, made a shield round Hartelius, while the princess tried to staunch his wound.

Later, when the skirmish died down, they carried Hartelius into the princess's pavilion and laid him on her bed. The bleeding, by this time, had stopped, thanks to a pad the princess had made of part of her shift, which she had tightened in place by using her dagger as a tourniquet handle and her ornamental leather belt as a strap. The *bandito*'s sword cut had struck no artery, or Hartelius would have been dead. His wound was purely muscular.

The princess, as skilled a seamstress as all young ladies at the convent were, cleaned the cut with Rhenish wine and sewed it together with Persian silk from her depository. With the aid of the two Templar knights she stripped Hartelius of his chainmail, and then later, when they were alone, she took off his cambric shirt and sheepskin breeches and climbed into bed beside him, warming his fever-ridden body against hers.

The princess's party remained where they were for three days, burying their dead, tending to their wounded, and regrouping. On the final day, Hartelius, still weak as a kitten, emerged from the princess's pavilion to thank his men, and those camp followers who remained alive, for their loyalty. He handed out money to the injured, and small gifts to those who had distinguished themselves. All knew that the princess had been tending their commander personally, in her pavilion, but none dared speak openly of it. It was as if the princess's guilt in betraying the man she was destined to marry might infect anyone who publicly acknowledged it.

This silence carried over even to the remaining Knights Templar, many of whom stood in awe of Hartelius's insane feat of arms. For one knight, in only partial armour, to overcome and kill three of the enemy, who were attacking him simultaneously, was beyond thought. The only possible answer was that the Holy Lance had protected their leader and had made his victory possible. But what did this say about his conduct with the princess? Was God condoning it? If not, why had He allowed Hartelius to live, when any normal man, in similar circumstances, would have died?

This uncertainty continued on the far side of the Alps and down through Padua to Venice. Part of it stemmed from the fact that no priest had been detailed to travel with the princess. It had doubtless been assumed by the king that one would have been provided at the instigation of the Abbess of Rupertsberg. But the princess had been so adamant about leaving on the very eve of Hartelius's arrival, and the king's orders so very fluid, that no vicar of God had been allocated. This alone had facilitated Hartelius and the princess's affair. And the continued absence of such a figure now facilitated its prolongation.

A Venetian merchant ship had been ordered, by advance courier, to be laid to and provisioned in expectation of the princess's party. The ship had been ready to sail for two weeks now, its captain provided with letters of marque enabling him to engage any enemy vessel that might dare to interfere with his itinerary via Dubrovnik, Modon, Candia, and finally Famagusta, to Acre.

Hartelius's wound had healed well in the five weeks that spanned the *banditti*'s attack and their arrival in Venice. More letters now awaited him from the king. A second marriage chest, far larger than the first, awaited the princess. It was a gift from the princess's intended husband, the Margrave

Adalfuns von Drachenhertz. The marriage chest, which had arrived by sea from Outremer, was in painted leather, with various scenes etched into the front. A rider with a falcon. A rider hunting. A Crusader knight killing a Saracen enemy. A queen on horseback with a scourge in her hand.

'Is that meant to be me?' asked the princess, pointing to the queen.

'I fear so,' said Hartelius.

'You fear so?' said the princess.

'I know so,' said Hartelius.

'But why am I carrying a scourge?'

'It is meant to be symbolical,' said Hartelius. 'Your future husband is trying to tell you something. Something along the lines of "when you marry me you will enjoy unbridled power".' He forbore to say 'and maybe even become Queen of Jerusalem one day', but he knew that this was the hidden subtext of the margrave's message. The man was renowned throughout greater Germany both for his relentless ambition and for his cold-heartedness. He would not embark on a Crusade unless he had something significant to gain from it. Such as a kingdom.

Despite such reminders, both lovers found it next to impossible to acknowledge the true purpose of their journey. Whenever something untoward slipped out, or whenever events took over and imposed themselves on the pair, neither one nor the other would confront the reality of their situation. There was always more time. More travelling to be done. More facts to be ignored.

Venice itself was the most perfect distraction. La Serenissima was a maelstrom of different nationalities. It was, in addition, the source of ninety per cent of all European trade. Complete unto itself.

Hartelius took lodgings for the princess and his men, arguing that he and his party would need time to prepare for what could prove to be a lengthy and dangerous voyage. The captain cavilled – his secondary trading mission was already running late.

But one did well not to alienate the sister of the man who would soon be Holy Roman Emperor. Such seeming slights had the habit of catching up with a man and destroying him further down the line.

The captain reluctantly agreed to postpone the voyage for an extra week. He immediately returned to his mistress's arms. While the princess returned to Hartelius's.

# FOURTEEN

Venice was basking in unseasonable sunshine. It seemed to the two lovers as if the weather itself was conspiring to facilitate their affair.

The princess's hair was steadily growing out. By day, travelling along the canals by barge or through the streets by palanquin, she wore a cap and a veil, as modesty dictated, but by night, when Hartelius secretly came to visit her, she would allow him to undress her and revel in her beauty. Later, after they had made love, she would change into a flowing silk robe, over-threaded with roses, her limbs uncluttered beneath it, her hair falling lightly about her face. Then they would sneak out into the maelstrom of the city and lose themselves amongst the streets and markets, in sailors' taverns and kerbside eateries.

They would attend street theatres and alfresco concerts, watch jugglers from the Maghreb and acrobats from the Polish marches. Once, they hired a single-masted, square-rigged cog and had its master sail them out to the island of Murano, where they persuaded a farmer and his wife to rent them a room while they waited for two glass cameos to be made, each bearing the AGLA inscription, from the Hebrew notarikon *atta gibor le'olam adonai* – 'You are mighty for ever, O Lord'. These were to serve them as amulets against disease and ill health.

That night Hartelius gave the princess a finger-ring of gold, set with Roman sard intaglio and engraved with the figure of Jupiter, which his mother had given him on his fifteenth birthday, immediately following his father's decision that the young Hartelius must join the Knights Templar. Hartelius also told the princess that he loved her, and that he would rather die than let another man take her away from him – a man who did not love her.

The princess wept openly for the first time. She reminded him of her position, and that her intended marriage was not of her own volition but rather that of her brother, the king. That the entire tenor of her life involved duty and honour, and that she would not and could not betray who she was and the position God had given her. It was the first time they came near to arguing.

Later, Hartelius had taken the princess with a fervour out of all proportion to anything he had ever known. It was as if he couldn't slake himself of her. That he had to empty himself into her – subsume her, almost, into himself – so that the two of them became one. One body, one soul. When next he asked her about duty, and honour, and obedience, she told him that she cared not a jot for any of them unless they involved him, and that she would follow her knight to hell itself if he asked her to.

The farmer's wife made them a breakfast the next morning of eggs and truffles and morel mushrooms with fried crostini and borage tea. They had honey and oat biscuits and a confit made of plums, lemons and peaches. After they had eaten, and while waiting for the schooner to pick them up as arranged, Hartelius and the princess sneaked off behind a nearby straw stack where he raised her shift and took her from behind, in broad daylight, while she arched away from him, furtively watching him, from time to time, across her shoulder, to monitor the expression on his face – for to the princess her greatest passion lay in the reflection of herself through Hartelius's eyes.

For the bitter truth was that, during the entire extent of her eighteen years of life, the princess had lived subject to rules – a manner of being that her essential nature abhorred. She was by instinct a free spirit, although, by virtue of her position, still beholden to and bound by convention. Hartelius's gaze freed her. She could fly in his sight like the most elusive of birds. She could soar in his eyes like one of her father's falcons on the stoop.

On their trip back into Venice she watched him with a serene joy twinned with the most profound apprehension. She recognized this emotion as something that only a woman can feel. A total giving of oneself mirrored by a fear of just what that giving will ultimately entail. Hartelius stood near the gunwale of the cog staring at the multitude of islands surrounding them, his broad shoulders encased in a flannel cloak, his golden hair dancing in the wind. That he was aware of her gaze she had no doubt. Each seemed to infer the existence of the other with every exhalation of their breath. It was an utter need – with no sense and no possible resolution.

For there was nowhere they could escape to. Nowhere they could hide. Hartelius would be hunted down like a criminal wherever he chose to take her. He would be castrated, allowed to live for a while in the knowledge of what he had done and what had been done to him, and then killed, in as grotesque a way as possible. The princess's dowry would either be added to exponentially, as a sop to her future husband for agreeing to accept damaged goods, or she would be shipped back to somewhere far worse than Rupertsberg, where she would be incarcerated for the rest of her life in conditions of the most extreme sanctity imaginable.

The future looked bleak – the present infinitely joyful and with an infinity of promise. The princess swore to herself that she would hide her sadness from Hartelius and give him everything that it was in her power to give. But that when the time came, she would drive him away from her for his own good, even though such an act would effectively break her heart.

Until then she would relish every instant they spent together – squeeze out every last drop of their love, and return it to him a thousandfold. This would be her gift to him. Her lover. Her prince.

# FIFTEEN

The single-masted, lateen-sailed nef the princess's party were to travel to Acre in was constructed plank on frame, in the European style, with a steering oar rather than a rudder, and a relatively shallow draft. It was therefore prey to drifting with the wind. The captain explained to Hartelius that a course would have to be followed which never took them very far from land. This was safer, he maintained, as there were pirates everywhere, who enjoyed preying on vulnerable merchant ships.

'So we shall be a long time at sea?'

'Oh yes. Very long. Maybe thirty days. If the wind is against us, we may sometimes have to pass the same spot three or four times before we broach it. This is normal. The princess will have ample time to recuperate from the journey during our five stopovers en route to Acre; I can assure you of that, Commander.'

'And there is no hold for my three horses and those of my thirteen knights?'

'The horses can stand on deck. In a corral. They will appreciate the fresh air.'

'And the princess?'

'She can take my cabin at the rear of the ship.'

'Where do the rest of us sleep?'

'Why, on deck too. Under cerecloth. It is most comfortable, I can assure you.'

'And the oarsmen?'

'We have none. We are not a galley. We are a nef. We sail by the wind alone. If the wind is with us we are faster than any cog or galley.'

'And if the wind is against us?'

'We are doomed.' The captain laughed. 'But as you see, I am still here. So the odds are with us. And your knights can defend us, can they not? So we have nothing to fear.'

Thirty days. He had thirty days left with the princess until their arrival at Acre. Hartelius decided that there was no point in even pretending to a virtue he did not possess. Each day was precious. Each night irreplaceable. All knew of his relationship with the princess. It was visible on both of their faces whenever they were together. In the movement of their bodies. In the inclination of their heads when they spoke to one another. There was such a thing as shutting the stable door after the horse has bolted.

Hartelius resolved to share the princess's cabin *in flagrante*. The princess's remaining handmaiden would attend them, aided by the cook's wife and a twelve-year-old boy, son of, and assistant to, the blacksmith, who now found himself temporarily deprived of a job after his father had been told that no fires, beyond those necessary for cooking, might be lit aboard the nef.

The princess was entirely in accord with her lover over the matter of their shared accommodation. The very thought of being aboard the same vessel as Hartelius, but being unable to touch or to be held by him, was anathema to her. What would happen in Acre would happen in Acre. Meanwhile each day was a fresh journey – each night a journey's end.

To entertain themselves during the crossing, and to act as a necessary lacuna between their seemingly endless bouts of lovemaking, Hartelius and the princess played chess, and also a game resembling backgammon that was played using tablemen carved from walrus ivory. Each tableman represented one of the twelve labours of Hercules, one of the nine orders of angels, or one of the nine muses. The princess, who had perfected her gaming skills at Rupertsberg alongside the other bored young noblewomen immured there, invariably beat Hartelius, much to his irritation, at whatever game they chose to play that day. By the end of their first three passages, to Dubrovnik, Modon, and Candia respectively, he owed her six deniers and twelve gold bezants, and had already passed over to her a plethora of old-fashioned Fatimid dinars that he had brought back with him as souvenirs from the Third Crusade. By the time they left Famagusta he was deeper in debt than ever.

'You will ruin me yet, woman.'

'Not so. You married an heiress. I know this for a fact. You are rich.'

Hartelius squinted at her. 'But not any more. I shall never be able to go home now. My sole remaining wealth lies in the letters of credit that I hold, and which are payable at any Templar preceptory. You do realize that?'

The princess looked at him. 'But do you not think. . .?'

Hartelius shook his head. 'No. That would be an impossible hope. The margrave will have his spies on board already. They will have accompanied us all the way from Rupertsberg. That is the way these things are played. These spies will have communicated with him from Venice. Probably using the same vessel that brought you your second marriage chest. The news of our betrayal will precede us, my love. We must prepare ourselves for that.'

'Then we must return to Famagusta and you must leave the vessel there. There are Templars in Cyprus, are there not?'

'Not any longer. We sold the island to Guy de Lusignan, and his heirs now rule it. And they are not well-disposed towards us, to say the least. Which is why I kept my men aboard during our overnight sojourn. In any case, I cannot abandon you.' He took her hand in his and kissed it. 'I will not leave you.'

'Then you will be killed.'

'Sometimes it is better to die than to live in dishonour.'

The princess watched Hartelius for a long time. Then she stood up, forcibly, as if she had made a decision. She pointed to her first marriage chest – the one sent to her by her brother. 'The Holy Lance is in there.'

'I know that.'

'I am to pass it on to my future husband as a token of my brother's confidence in him.'

'I know that too.'

'What you don't know is that my brother has vouchsafed me a further object he wishes to be handed over.'

'And what object is that?'

'The Copper Scroll.'

Hartelius's chair tipped over as he stood up. His face was pale. His eyes blazed. 'That is preposterous. The Copper Scroll is the greatest of all the Templar treasures. It holds the key to the secrets of Solomon. It would never be allowed out of Templar hands. Not even if the king himself were to command it.'

The princess, disturbed at having provoked such an unintended reaction in Hartelius, turned sharply away from him. 'But you haven't fully deciphered it yet, have you?'

Hartelius reined in his anger. It wasn't Elfriede's fault, after all, if her brother was playing her for a dupe. 'Not to my knowledge, no. But then I would be the last to hear, being no longer a full Templar, but only one of the *fratres conjugati*. My understanding is that the Copper Scroll is written partly in Mishraic Hebrew, and partly in another, unknown script, that appears neither in the Bible nor elsewhere. Templar scholars have been labouring to decipher this unknown script since the scroll was discovered by our founding knights, on the Temple Mount, seventy years ago. It is only a matter of time before the script is decoded and its secrets discovered. It is therefore impossible that the Copper Scroll could be here and in your possession. Impossible.'

The princess turned back towards him. 'But it is.'

Hartelius righted his fallen chair. He was stone-cold sober now, despite the quantities of Cretan wine he had been drinking to accompany their game. 'How can you be so sure we are talking of the same artefact? There must be a multitude of scrolls available to the king.'

'But still. I am sure. Because I broke the seals on my brother's letters to my future husband.'

'You did what?'

'I broke the Royal Seal.'

Hartelius took the princess's hands in his. 'But such a thing is punishable by death, Elfriede. Even as a royal princess you would not be immune. It is called *lèse-majesté*.'

She looked up at him. 'And what have we been doing these past few months, Hartelius? What is that called, do you think?'

Hartelius's expression softened. 'What indeed?' He gazed for a long time at the young woman in front of him, prey to a profound sadness. The thought of parting from her overwhelmed him. The thought of another man holding sway over her – a man who would not, and could not, cherish her as he did – filled him with anguish.

Hartelius enveloped the princess in his arms and pressed her to his chest. He kissed the top of her head many times, as was his habit, and then kissed her around the eyes and cheeks, eventually completing the familiar journey to her mouth. When he finally spoke, he spoke over her shoulder, his eyes taking in every corner of the cabin, as if it were the last time he would get to see it. 'I think the time has come to confront the realities of our situation. We can hold it off no longer. Might I see these letters?'

The princess disentangled herself from Hartelius's arms. She walked over to her repository. She returned carrying the two letters and handed them to her lover with a rueful smile.

Hartelius inspected the seals with a crestfallen expression. 'Was it not within your capabilities to lever off the seals in such a way that they could be replaced, Elfriede? These are beyond any possible repair. It almost looks as though you brutalized them on purpose.'

The princess shrugged. 'The seals are designed so. Any tampering is permanent. Any fool knows this. There seemed no point in holding back once I had made my decision.'

Hartelius shook his head in wonder. 'So you knew exactly what you were doing when you embarked on this madness?'

The princess nodded. But the supercilious mask she had put on for Hartelius's benefit was beginning to crack, to the extent that she now appeared trapped part-way between tears of regret and tears of outraged virtue. 'Yes. I knew what I was doing. I wanted to give you no possible choice in the matter. No possible excuse to remain at my side and let von Drachenhertz skin you alive. He is all-powerful in Outremer. Your thirteen Templar knights will not be able to help you. Nobody will. You will be killed if you go ashore at Acre.'

Hartelius took her by the shoulders. 'So you broke into your brother's letters to von Drachenhertz, knowing that I would be forced to take the blame on your behalf?'

She nodded. The tears flowed unchecked down her cheeks. 'Knowing that you would insist on taking the blame on my behalf. Yes. For that is the only way I knew of to get you to leave this ship before it docks at Acre.'

'But I will not leave you.'

'You must leave me.'

'To that monster?'

'To my future husband. Yes.'

'But he will know what has happened between us. Probably knows already. You have acknowledged that much yourself.'

The princess dashed the tears away from her eyes with the hanging sleeve of her *bliaut*. 'Von Drachenhertz is an ambitious man. You told me this. Marriage to the king's sister will be crucial to him. Fundamental to his ambitions. An extra string to his bow. If you are not there as a focus for his anger, he will soon come to terms with what has happened. He will not wish to make a public fool of himself. To seem to be a cuckold. No man does. Marriages at this level are political, and not of the heart. Von Drachenhertz is a realist, from what I have heard.'

Hartelius was appalled at the princess's naivety, despite the surface confidence with which she put forward her point of view. And yet what could one expect from a young woman hauled, if not quite kicking and squealing, then at least unwittingly, from the relative innocence of a nunnery directly into the world of men? 'Elfriede. Listen to me. Such a man as you describe will invariably suffer from an excess of pride. He is a war leader – not some effete courtier hiding behind his scented handkerchief. He commands the loyalty of thousands. When he finds that you have given your love to another man in every way it is possible to give, he will punish you. Privately, if not publicly.'

'There is only so much he can do.'

'He can do anything he wants to you. A woman, even one of high degree such as yourself, has little or no power at the best of times – not even at your brother's court back in the Frankenland. In the Holy Land your position will be even more acute. I have been there. I know this for a fact. As a direct result of the Crusades, we invading Christians have gradually taken on some of the mannerisms of our enemies in terms of the way we treat our women. Certain of our leaders have even taken to keeping harems. Privately. With few outside their inner circle knowing of their existence. But such a fact has a carry-over effect. Wives and mothers are not granted the same freedoms they have at home. The same liberty of movement. You will be suborned. Confined. Humiliated. I should never have indulged my desires with you. I am your senior by twelve years. You were placed under my guardianship. What I did was unforgivable.'

'So you regret it?'

Hartelius threw up his hands. 'Of course I don't regret it. You are everything to me. Not declaring myself to you was inconceivable. Not having you was inconceivable. Not having you in the future is inconceivable.'

Elfriede managed a halting smile in response to his words. 'Then we must both flee. It is the only way.'

'That is impossible.'

'Order the captain to turn back to Venice. You have the power.'

'No, I do not. He will laugh in our faces. He knows that von Drachenhertz would pursue him to the ends of the earth and back again. Our captain may be corrupt, but he is no fool.'

'Then go alone. Have him set you ashore at Beirut. When I arrive at Acre I will make it my business to seduce my future husband into loving me. If that is the only way to save you, it will be a small price to pay. I am not undistinguished in terms of beauty – you have told me so yourself. If you are susceptible to my charms, might not other men be?'

Hartelius watched the play of emotions across the princess's face with awed respect. This one was truly a woman among women. The princess's lower lip was trembling. Her eyes were beseeching him to hearken to what she was saying, while her heart was breaking at the possibility that he might. Hartelius understood only too well, after the months of intimacy they had shared, just what her words were costing her. She was willing to sacrifice everything for him. To barter her honour for his life. The least he could do was to offer her the same consideration. To return her sacrifice and make things right for her again.

He cupped her chin in his hand. 'There is one way, perhaps. One way that you might be protected from the evil I have done you.'

'You have done me no evil, Hartelius.'

'From the evil, then, that I have brought down upon your head.'

'And how is that? Speak. Please. Do not leave me hanging like this.'

Hartelius lowered his head. It was as if he feared being overwhelmed by the sheer weight of the words he was about to utter. 'Very well then. I do as you suggest. I order the captain to set me ashore at Beirut. But I take the Holy Lance and the Copper Scroll with me when I go. Also these private letters from the king, your brother, to von Drachenhertz. This would formally exonerate you from any possibility of *lèse-majesté*. You could say, too, that in the absence of any priest in our party to safeguard you, I forced myself upon you. That you had no choice in the matter. That you were entirely in my power. That you succumbed to me for your own protection.'

'But no one would back that up. My servants. My hand-maiden. Your Templar knights would—'

Hartelius shook his head. 'Nobody credits what servants or handmaidens say. And my Templar knights will not be staying aboard. They will be coming with me. When they discover that the Copper Scroll, the brotherhood's most precious artefact, is being bartered to von Drachenhertz simply in order to get him to embark on a fourth Crusade, they will not hesitate. This I can promise you.'

'I do not believe you. They would not turn against their king.'

'They would. Believe me. There are secret reasons why I know this to be true.'

'What secret reasons? You are saying this just to placate me.'

Hartelius sighed. The acuteness of Elfriede's mind could sometimes be a hindrance, not a help. 'There is something you must understand. Something you must swear to keep to yourself.'

The princess nodded. Her eyes held the first faint vestige of hope. 'I swear. I swear it on my love for you.'

The force behind her words almost caused Hartelius to falter. To go back on what he was about to suggest. But he knew that he must not. For her sake he needed to be firm. 'The issue of King Solomon's legacy was the driving force behind the formation of the Templars seventy years ago. And it is still the driving force behind each and every one of our actions. Each Templar feels that he and his brothers are the direct heirs of Solomon on this earth. Our formal title is *Pauperes Commilitones Christi Templique Salomonis* – 'The Poor Fellow-soldiers of Christ and the Temple of Solomon'. Only in our case the word *Christi* – Christ – does not refer specifically to Jesus.'

'But that is blasphemous.'

'To some eyes, perhaps. But it is true nonetheless. The word *Christi*, according to our usage, is taken from the Greek word *khristos*, meaning the 'anointed one', which is, in turn, taken from the Hebrew word *mashiach*, meaning Messiah. And our Messiah is not, and never was, Jesus Christ. Our Messiah is John the Baptist. The first anointed. The one who baptized Jesus. The one who Herodias, through Salome, ordered slain. And the new Messiah – the one foretold by Malachi with the words "Behold, I will send my messenger, and he shall prepare the way before me: and the Lord, whom ye seek, shall suddenly come to his temple" – will make his mark by the creation of a New Jerusalem, a new Temple, established exactly on the pattern of the old. And it is the Copper Scroll alone which contains within it the blueprint for the rekindled Temple of Solomon – and also the location of the treasure with which the building of the Temple is to be funded. That much is clearly written in the Mishraic. It is unequivocal.'

'Why are you telling me this?'

'Because I wish you to understand the seriousness of what you have discovered. The only possible answer to the Copper Scroll being in your possession can be that it has been stolen from us by agents of your brother. Neither Gilbert Horal, our Grand Master, nor any of our Seneschals or Marshals, would ever have handed such a thing over voluntarily. They would rather die. So it must have been forcibly taken from us, and is intended to be used, alongside the Holy Lance, as a gathering focus – you may call it a recruiting aid – for the fourth Crusade. I will know more when I peruse these letters. But there can be no other possible reading of the situation. And once von Drachenhertz has the scroll in his possession, who is to say that he will not get his Arab scholars to decode it and steal the hidden treasure – to enrich himself or to fund his crusading army – before it can be used for the purpose King Solomon intended? Namely, to rebuild the Temple as the basis for a New Jerusalem.'

'And you believe in this New Jerusalem?'

Hartelius shook his head. 'I used to. I do not now. But I believe that others believe it. My Templar knights for a start.

They may not remain loyal to me. But they will, without question, remain loyal to their vows. Each Templar knows of the secret contained within our name. Each has vowed to guard that secret with his life. If I tell them that I have taken back the Copper Scroll, which was unlawfully stolen from us, they will follow me to the ends of the earth if by that means they can ensure that the scroll is returned to its rightful owners.'

'So you agree that I must marry von Drachenhertz?'

Hartelius threw up his hands. 'I wish you to live as free a life as you are able. I owe you that and much more besides. When I first met you, you told me what you thought was the meaning of your name. That it meant "to be free".'

'But you told me no. That it means "strength in otherness".'

'I did. But to you the symbolical changing of your name betokened freedom. Freedom from the confines of the abbey, where you had been known as Agnes – the sacrificial lamb. And freedom from the whims of men. This, I believe, is why you gave yourself to me. Because there was no formality in my request to you. No outside pressure. It was a question of free will. And free will is precious in direct proportion to what one is prepared to lose for its sake. And you have been prepared to lose everything. I cannot sanction such a sacrifice on my account.'

'It is not your choice to make.'

'But it is my right to try and convince you of the good sense inherent in my future actions, is it not? I possess such a right, do I not? Thanks to my love for you? A love which I have demonstrated, and will continue to demonstrate, until my death. There will be no other woman for me beyond you in my lifetime. You are my one and only love. You are everything to me. To the extent that I would rather see you in the arms of another man than that any hurt should befall you. With von Drachenhertz you will become a queen. You will have the protection of that title.'

'And my child will too?'

'Yes. Any child of yours will thereby be protected.'

The princess put out her hand and touched her lover lightly on the arm. 'Any child of ours, Hartelius.'

Hartelius flinched, as if her touch had scalded him. 'I do not understand. What are you saying?'

'I am saying that despite my regular use of the douche syringe, and lily root, and extract of rue, just as my handmaidens instructed me, that nature, and the fact that you are already the father of four live children and one dead, has conspired to quicken you in me. That I am carrying your child, Hartelius, probably since our sojourn on Murano.' The princess cocked her head to one side, the ghost of a smile on her face. 'Are you quite sure you withdrew from me when you raised my shift behind that haystack, Hartelius? For I seem to have no memory of it.'

Hartelius stared at the princess. 'You are carrying my child?'

'Nobody else's. My menses were due twelve days ago. They have not come. They always come. I am as regular as the seasons. I have been so since I was eleven years old. You understand the menses, don't you, Hartelius? Their significance to women?'

'Yes. I have been married. As you well know.'

'I thought as much.'

Hartelius led the princess over to their shared bed. He sat down with her and took her hand in his. Gently he kissed it. Then he laid it firmly in his lap, still grasping it with both hands so that she could not escape him. 'Listen to me. This changes everything. A man such as von Drachenhertz may conceivably accept, through sheer ambition and venal greed, the deflowered sister of the king. But he will never accept another man's unlawful child. We have no choice in the matter now. We must somehow persuade the captain to put us ashore at Tortosa. Tortosa is a Crusader citadel that the Count of Tripoli put in the hands of the Templars in 1152. The city was besieged by Saladin in 1188 but the keep never fell. We will be safe there. We can be married at the Cathedral of Our Lady of Tortosa, which the count has now rebuilt after its plundering by Saladin's men.'

'You wish to marry me?'

'Yes. I would never have dared ask you before now. You are a princess. I am a recently ennobled baron of notably low effect. Our stations in life are absurdly different. But no child of mine will be born without a name. If you don't agree to marry me, I will kidnap you against your will, like one of the Sabine women, and forcibly wed you.'

The princess laughed out loud. A broad, infectious laugh that seemed to echo from some exalted place deep within her. 'I believe I should like to be kidnapped, Hartelius. You have your princess's express permission so to do.'

# SIXTEEN

The captain of the nef ran his hand down his beard in the way a man might caress the flanks of a horse he has acquired for well below the asking price. His eyes twinkled with the knowledge that the conversation he was about to have might prove significantly to his advantage.

He had seen the two lovebirds together – how could he not? He had heard the gossip about them from his crew and from amongst the princess's paid attendants. And he had heard that gossip confirmed by the cabin boy, who had been surprisingly easy to persuade once the mate had threatened to accidentally smash his fingers with a belaying pin.

There were ways in which he envied Hartelius, of course. What man would not like to spend a month aboard a vessel in the Mediterranean fucking someone else's eighteen-year-old intended bride? But the consequences were vertiginous. No woman on earth was worth what von Drachenhertz would do to Hartelius once he got hold of him.

Despite all this, the captain weighed his words with care. It wouldn't do to spook the golden goat. Or to alienate him utterly.

'Landing you at Tortosa is an impossibility, Commander. The harbour is restricted. And three years ago I fell foul of a merchant there – a merchant with the power to make my life a misery if I ever again ventured into his waters. No. I shall take you on to Acre as I was commissioned to do. I am sure our war leader will reward me well when I hand the princess over to him as arranged.'

'And what if we were to take over your ship, Captain? I have thirteen knights at my command. You could not resist us. You could then claim that we forced you to comply with our wishes.'

The captain threw his head back and laughed. 'That would be one answer. It might exonerate me. Possibly. But it probably wouldn't. Von Drachenhertz will imagine you bribed me, and that I wanted to disguise it by affecting to be taken prisoner. No. He would hang, draw and quarter me, along with my entire crew, when he got hold of us. As he inevitably would. So it is unlikely that you and your men would be able to prevail upon us to sail this ship for you. And such a ship is no easy vessel to sail. You would likely dash yourselves on the Margat rocks if you tried to put into Tortosa. And how, pray, would you navigate? You would probably end up missing Tortosa entirely and beaching us back on Cyprus, where Guy de Lusignan's brother, Amalric, a close ally of the margrave as you may remember, would no doubt take keen pleasure in throwing you into his deepest dungeon, and then entertaining your mistress upstairs while you rot. After all, who can tell if a once-ridden mare has been mounted twice?'

Hartelius reined in his anger. He needed this man. Needed him on his side. And to hell with his insults. 'So what do you suggest? You are clearly a realist. I will not belittle your intelligence by implying that you do not understand the position the princess and I find ourselves in.'

The captain grinned. 'No. I understand it very well. You are between a meltemi wind and a lee shore. It must be excruciating to be in your position. I would not want it for the world.'

'I asked you for your suggestions. Not for your opinions.'

The captain clapped his hands lightly together and smiled. 'My suggestion would be that you compensate me royally for the loss of my ship, and that we scupper her in a bay I know just south of Beirut, from where your horses can easily swim ashore.'

Hartelius shook his head. 'Could you not contrive to put both them and us ashore without the necessity of sacrificing your ship and making us damnably wet in the process?'

The captain shrugged. 'Unfortunately not. The ship must seem to founder naturally. And I must seem to be ruined. Only then will von Drachenhertz believe that I was not instrumental in depriving him of his princess's cunny. It is a tricky time of year. The weather is changing on this coast. And I have always wanted a twin-sailed ship with a central rudder.'

Hartelius closed his eyes. He had never come nearer in his life to hacking a man to death with no warning and with no possibility of mercy. 'How much?'

'Five thousand gold bezants.'

'That is grotesque.'

'So is your tupping of von Drachenhertz's ewe. A man must pay for his pleasures in this world. That is my final price.'

Hartelius turned his back on the captain. It was either that or skewer him to his own mast with a marlinspike. 'I will give you your answer tomorrow. Will that suffice?'

'Well enough. I will try to rein in my excitement in the interim.'

# SEVENTEEN

'Five thousand bezants is an outrage,' said the princess. 'The man is mad. One could purchase a city state for less. What does he want to buy with it? A fleet?'

Hartelius laughed. 'Never fear, my love. He will take less. Far less.'

'How can you know that?'

Hartelius gave a shrug. 'Because I have decided to call his bluff. I have instructed my knights to take over his ship tonight, under cover of darkness. When we have the ship secured I shall offer him fifty gold bezants, which is ample reward for what we need him to do. Which is not to scuttle his vessel, but rather to set us ashore, dry, and with all our goods and horses intact, somewhere north of Tripoli, so that we can make for Tortosa unannounced. After that he can do whatever he wants. Go wherever he wishes. If I were him I would convert to Islam and join the Abbasids. They always need ships. At least he would keep his head that way. For if von Drachenhertz ever gets hold of him, it will end up on a spike on the Acre waterfront.'

The princess shook her head in wonder. 'You really are a warrior knight, aren't you? People always underestimate you, don't they? You have such a quiet, calm exterior. But underneath it all you are a killer. I remember you running at those three *banditti* in the Alps. Sometimes, because you are so gentle with me, I am apt to forget the scars you carry about your person, and that I caress with my fingertips every day and every night.'

Hartelius searched the princess's face with his eyes. Was she faltering? Was she regretting their attachment? When he realized that she was not criticizing him but complimenting him, he inclined his head. 'War has been my profession since the age of fifteen. I pretend to nothing else. The time to be gentle is in the bedroom. Only a fool placates his enemies in the field.'

'I am glad I am not your enemy then.'

Hartelius smiled. 'No. Not my enemy. My only friend.'

That night Hartelius's thirteen remaining knights took over the ship with no loss of life – not even a single injury amongst the crew. Later, Hartelius decided that the captain must have realized this was what he would do, and briefed his men not to resist. That the man's insane request for five thousand bezants had merely represented an amused acknowledgement of their relative positions, and had never been meant to be taken seriously.

'Fifty gold bezants are better than nothing,' said Hartelius, when the ship was secured.

'Indeed they are,' said the captain. 'And more than I had hoped for. I shall use them to have a false head made out of copper to replace the one von Drachenhertz will no doubt deprive me of the moment he sees me.'

'If you are ever foolish enough to pass near Acre.'

'There is that. But I comfort myself with the thought that he will be so busy pursuing you and the princess that he will have no time left to expend on me.'

The offloading went well. Thanks to the shallow draft of the nef, the ship was able to beach itself relatively close to the shore. With the aid of ropes and planks and rafts and rattan mats, all thirty horses were debarked without incident, as were the princess's accoutrements and her two marriage chests. They had been forced to leave her carriage back in Venice through lack of space, but she had been a horsewoman since the age of five, and she found no difficulty in adapting her clothing so that she could sit astride one of Hartelius's spare mounts. She was so early on in her pregnancy that Hartelius decided that no evil could come of it.

Once on shore, he explained to the remainder of the princess's followers something of the quandary they found themselves in. Namely, that from henceforth he would be a marked man, but that he would nonetheless allow them free choice in whether to follow him and his knights northwards, towards Nicaea, the Latin Empire and possible freedom, or to turn south towards Beirut and Acre and whatever that might entail.

All chose to turn south, bar the princess's remaining handmaiden. Hartelius was hardly surprised at the mass exodus. No servant in their right mind would attach themselves to a patron who would very soon be the subject of a royal death warrant both in Outremer and upon the European mainland.

'And why are you, too, not going south?' he asked the girl. 'And please forbear to tell me that you have made your decision out of loyalty to the princess. Because I will not believe you.'

The girl looked down at her feet.

'Is one of my knights your lover?'

She said nothing.

'Ah. So you fear that if the other knights find out, they will turn on him, because he has broken his vow of chastity?'

The girl nodded.

'Then when the princess's tent is set up, secretly point your lover out to me and I will instruct him to be her personal guard. This way you can both meet without causing suspicion. Will that be satisfactory to you? I am doing this not out of the goodness of my heart, you understand, but because the princess will have need of female help at some point in the future, and I might find it hard to recruit a suitable candidate en route to wherever we finally go.'

The girl pressed his hand to her cheek.

'Good. That is settled then.'

Hartelius watched the nef's crew levering their ship back off the strand. Now that the dead weight of the knights, their armour and their horses were discounted, together with the princess's fickle followers and their accoutrements, the ship rode much higher in the water. The captain soon managed to put back to sea, thanks to the adaptability of his single lateen sail. As the nef pulled away, the man raised an ironical fist towards Hartelius from his roost near the stern, and drew one finger slowly across his throat.

Hartelius waited until the ship was out of sight. Would the captain betray them? Would he put into the next suitable port and send word to von Drachenhertz that Hartelius and the princess were heading for Tortosa? Of course he would.

Hartelius abandoned his Tortosa plan without further ado. He would head instead for the Crac de l'Ospital, a Knights Hospitaller stronghold high in the Syrian mountains behind Tripoli. The Hospitallers, he knew, were in open dispute with the Templars, but it was nonetheless likely that, as an expedient nod to the chivalrous behaviour both societies nominally adhered to, they would allow him to borrow against his Templar letters of credit just so long as he accorded them a suitable profit margin.

For Hartelius knew from bitter experience during the Third Crusade, that the quickest way to lose knights – even nominally committed ones – was to fail to feed, fund and re-equip them when they felt it was their due.

# EIGHTEEN

Their first few days on the road were largely uneventful. Hartelius and the princess rode side by side, with the Templar knights spread out behind them, each man leading two laden horses, flank against flank, so that he might rid himself quickly of them in an emergency. Two free-riding knights acted as guides ahead of the column, and two fulfilled a similar function in the rear. The weather, too, seemed with them, with a late summer lingering well on into October.

'Why do we need scouts? This is Christian territory, is it not?' said the princess.

'Nothing is Christian territory out here, bar our fortresses. The Turks range wherever they want, and harry our forces whenever they can.'

'But the peace Treaty?'

Hartelius let out a snort. 'Not worth the paper it is scribbled on. Each side will break it if and when they see fit. That is the way of things.'

The princess looked at him intently. 'But we will be safe at the Crac de l'Ospital?'

Hartelius was only too well aware that the princess, given her condition, craved certainty, but he could not possibly provide it for her. She had abandoned everything to be with him, while he had abandoned nothing. His four children would be secured for life with their mother's dowry, and they would be kept safe by their grandfather, Hugo von Kronach, a man who bowed to no one and acknowledged no other master than himself in his own bailiwick – not even the Holy Roman Emperor. The residue of Hartelius's life meant nothing to him. Only the princess counted any more.

'We will be safe for a short time, yes. But von Drachenhertz will send after us the moment he hears we have absconded. The Crac de l'Ospital is one of the first places his men will make for. So we will be in the unfortunate position of having von Drachenhertz behind us, the Turks to one side, and the Assassins ahead.'

'What do you mean? What assassins?'

'Oh. Nothing. They are nothing to worry about.'

'I recognize that look, Hartelius. You are hiding something from me.'

Hartelius made a silent vow that the next time he spoke to the princess about their situation, he would keep the visor on his war helmet firmly shut. 'The Assassins are Ismailis. Sunni haters. They live in the Jebel al-Sariya, where we are heading. In the castle of Masyaf. The word "assassin" comes from Hashshashin, which refers to the fact that the leaders of the Assassins use the drug hashish to turn their people into mindless *feddayin*.'

'What are *feddayin*?'

'Self-sacrificers. Prepared to martyr themselves for their chief, Rashid al-Din Sinan, the Sheikh al-Jebel, otherwise known as the Old Man of the Mountains. He may be dead now for all I know, but his followers are not. They pay us an annual tribute of two thousand bezants to leave them alone, and we are happy to do so, as their enemies are our enemies. But they are unpredictable. It is impossible to tell what would happen if we ran into them. For they have been told that if they die whilst following the orders of their Imam, they will go directly to Jannah, which is the Mohammedan version of Paradise, where doe-eyed houri maidens await them in a land of milk and honey.'

'Hmm. You are a man, are you not? So tell me. How is it possible to convince men of the existence of such a Paradise as you describe? They can't be such fools as all that. No woman would dream of believing such nonsense.'

Hartelius knew precisely where the princess was heading with her questioning. She took keen delight in enmeshing him in convoluted discussions relating to the differences between the sexes, for she knew full well that he still – in a carry-over from his time as a Knight Templar – found certain subjects difficult to broach. Thanks to her innate capacity for mischief, though, he was fast learning to be less dogmatic.

He manufactured a manly scowl for her benefit. 'Far easier, in many ways, than to convince them of Heaven and Hell.

The hashish drug is so powerful that men will do anything once they are under its spell. Even mindlessly kill. Our people have even used the Assassins for their own ends on occasion. Their imams regularly demonstrate their power over their followers by ordering them to jump to their death over precipices or from castle walls. The *feddayin* seem happy to do so, as they know what awaits them.'

'The houris?'

Hartelius rolled his eyes. 'Indeed. Please believe me when I tell you that houris do not defecate, menstruate or urinate; nor do they have nasal secretions. They are hairless, apart from on their heads and eyebrows, and they have large breasts which are round, and swelling, and pointed, and which do not hang down or sag. Their short pregnancies last only an hour. Their gaze is modest and they are entirely chaste, apart from with the worthy recipient of their largesse. Their bones are transparent and they are eternally young. They also smell like musk.'

'Perfection then.'

'Yes. I am thinking of becoming an Assassin.'

'I wish you joy of it. Although I, too, would like a pregnancy that lasted only an hour. Maybe I should become a houri?'

'You would have to be sixty cubits tall, though.'

'What? How high is that?'

'Around ninety feet.'

'Then how could you reach me to make love to me?'

Hartelius slapped the pommel of his saddle in delight. What had he done to deserve such a woman? No one else spoke to him like this. His beautiful wife, Adelaïde, had been modesty and decorousness incarnate, and he had respected that, whilst occasionally yearning for a fraction more passion in their conjugal relations.

Thanks to the Templar vows imposed on him by his late father when he was barely fifteen years old, Elfriede was only the second woman he had ever made love to. She might have been born a princess, but she spoke like a fishwife when it suited her, and behaved like a tavern wench in the privacy of their chamber. She was utter perfection.

'That is a question I am unable to answer. Perhaps I shall not become an Assassin after all.'

'So you will remain satisfied with me?'

'More than satisfied. Although I regret that you are not transparent.'

'You are, though, Hartelius. I can see right through you.'

# NINETEEN

Seven days into their journey towards Crac de l'Ospital, a cool dry wind, laden with dust and sand, sprang up from the direction of the coast.

Luitpold von Szellen, at more than forty years of age the oldest of the Templar knights under Hartelius's command, urged his horse forward so that he and his spare mounts might ride parallel with their leader. 'We need to find shelter, Commander.'

'Why? This is a simple desert wind. A precursor to winter, surely?'

'Not so, sir. This is a Khamsin. I have seen such a wind before. When it hits us, it will strike hard. If we have not found cover by then, we will be overwhelmed. In spring, these winds can last for three or four days. I have no idea what diabolical form they may choose to take this late in the year.'

Hartelius glanced at the princess. Then back at von Szellen. 'How long do we have?'

Von Szellen wrapped his burnous around his nose and mouth. He looked directly into the teeth of the wind. In the far distance the approaching wall of dust appeared to take on a crimson tint, as if it were a giant vortex of liquid, imbrued with blood. 'An hour. Possibly less. But it will get worse than this before the main storm hits. The horses may riot.'

'What about the princess's pavilion? Could we not shelter in that?'

'Useless. It will simply blow away.'

'What do you suggest then?' Hartelius was shouting now, in an effort to be heard over the wind's wailing.

Von Szellen glanced eastwards, towards the mountains. 'We head for that overhanging cliff edge. At the gallop. If we are lucky we will find a cave there. If not, we may be able to get into the lee of the hill and use that for a shelter. What we cannot do is stay out here.'

'Come then.' Hartelius signalled to his men. He took the bridle of the princess's horse and led it round in a semi-circle. 'You go first, von Szellen. Abandon your spare horses. They will follow the herd. I will bring up the rear with the princess. Use anything you need to construct a shelter.'

'Yes, sir.'

Von Szellen loosed his spare horses and took off at the gallop. The remaining knights fell into column formation and thundered up the hill behind him. Hartelius signalled to his flankers to do the same. One of them – the one he had allocated as the princess's personal bodyguard – broke off from the main formation and took hold of the princess's handmaiden's bridle, before leading her off in pursuit of his companions.

The wind was howling round them now. Clogging their noses. Stinging their faces. Hartelius reached forward and wrapped Elfriede's burnous around her head, leaving a narrow gap for her eyes. Then he took hold of her mare's bridle and led her away at the canter.

'We can go faster than this,' she shouted. 'Give me the reins and I will show you.'

'No, my love. The horse might throw you. And you are with child. Von Szellen has gone ahead. He knows what to do.'

'But what if there is no shelter?'

Hartelius slowed briefly to wrap his battle pennant around Elfriede's mare's eyes, for she was throwing her head about in panic. 'Then we kill some of the horses and shelter behind them. They are expendable. You are not.'

The princess looked at him over her shoulder. 'Would you really do that?'

'I would do anything it takes.'

The main body of Hartelius's knights had already disappeared over the crest of the first hill.

'They are leaving us,' cried Elfriede.

'No. They are Templars. They are doing exactly as I said.'

Hartelius and the princess breasted the crest of the first hill and drove their mounts onwards. The wind bellowed and shrieked around them. The sand pelted their skin with a thousand needle pricks through every unprotected gap in their clothing.

'I cannot see them any more. I can barely see you.'

'I am following the trail of their horses. Look. Down below you.'

'But the wind is blowing it away.'

'No. I can still see it. It is as clear as day to me.'

Hartelius was lying. There was no trail any more to speak of. He was navigating entirely by instinct. He could barely even discern the outline of the sun through the dust storm, far less make out the trail of a herd of horses now five minutes gone. But the sun's glow was enough. They needed to continue east. For that is where the cliff edge would be.

'Please. Can we stop?'

'No. You heard von Szellen. This wind will only get worse. We must ride while we still can.'

'But I cannot breathe.'

Hartelius grasped the princess round the upper body and transferred her across to his mount, so that she was sitting sideways in front of him, with both legs to the left of his pommel, hanging down. When he was certain that she was secure he uncovered her mare's eyes and loosed her, trusting that the animal would have the good sense to follow his stallion's lead.

'Curl your face into me so that you are protected by my body.'

The princess didn't answer. Hartelius could hear her struggling for breath against his chest.

He spurred his horse onwards. Slowly, steadily, he was beginning to lose hope. He had made a grave mistake by underestimating the speed with which the wind would burgeon. He should have called his flanking knights in to him, so that they could have travelled in convoy – it had been wrong of him to send everyone ahead. He had put the princess's life in danger. It was unforgivable.

He was bent nearly double now, with the wind beating at his back and feeling its way through every crevice in his chainmail. The princess was curled unmoving against his chest.

He felt his horse stumble and catch itself.

Please God, Hartelius said to himself. Take me, but protect her. Don't let my horse fall.

Von Szellen burst out of the maelstrom in front of him. He was leading the princess's abandoned horse. 'Follow me, sir. We have found cover. A cave. Large enough for us all to sit out the storm. There is cool water to drink. And paintings. There are paintings on the walls, sir. Of the Christ child. We saw them when we lit our torches. It is a miracle.'

Had von Szellen taken leave of his senses? But no. The man's face was earnest. His expression luminous. As if he'd seen a vision.

Hartelius's mount picked itself up at the sight of the other horses. Hartelius spurred him on behind von Szellen. He had called to God for help and a transfigured von Szellen had appeared from inside the storm, speaking of the Christ child. It was a sign, surely? A sign that what he was doing was right?

'Just over here, sir. The entrance is in the lee of this overhang. It is large enough so that we can ride in without dismounting. But you must duck your head. Then the entrance twists immediately to the right. God's own architect could not have designed it better.'

Hartelius stooped down to protect the princess. He neck-reined his stallion along the inner face of the rock, in the direction von Szellen was indicating. When he was able to look up again, it was as if he had entered the precincts of a cathedral. The roof of the cave soared eighty feet above his head. Its belly extended well beyond his sightline, only to fade away into darkness. The wind continued to howl outside, but inside the cave all was peace.

'God's teeth. What is this place, von Szellen?'

'Look, sir. Look at the paintings.'

Hartelius allowed one of his knights to help him from his horse. He eased the princess down after him. She leaned against him, coughing. Another of his knights brought her a cup of water, which she drank gratefully, one hand resting on Hartelius's shoulder.

'This is a Christian place, sir, predating the Mohammedans. The Holy Spear and the Copper Scroll have led us here. Look.' Von Szellen snatched a torch from one of his subordinates. He raised it high over his head.

Hartelius drew in his breath.

The lower levels of the cave were strewn with wall paintings, as if a madman had been let loose at them with chalk and paint. Some were canted at an angle, as if the painter had been standing on some object while composing them, and had then been forced to use the slant of the wall as part of his perspective. Others were near ground level, with the important figures grotesquely enlarged, and other, lesser figures, made diminutive by contrast.

'Look. Mosaics.' Hartelius dropped to his knees. 'These are Byzantine tesserae, by God. Hold the torch closer, man.' He beckoned to the princess. When she came up beside him he took her hand in his and guided her fingers gently along the ridges of the mosaic. 'See? Feel how smooth these tiles are. I have seen similar things in Constantinople. In the Hagia Sophia. The workmanship is exquisite. Look at the quality of this gold leaf.' Hartelius rocked back onto his heels. 'But what are they doing here? In a lost cave in the mountains? How would the individual tesserae have been transported to such a place? By pack mule? This is utter madness.'

The surrounding knights had fallen silent. All were staring at the paintings and mosaics, which spanned an area thirty feet long by ten feet high, as if at a miracle. The light from the knights' torches reflected back off the golden tesserae with the power of a hundred candles.

'One of our men reports a lake at the rear of the cave,' said von Szellen. 'Fed by an underground spring. Others must have come upon this spot in bygone days and considered it a direct sign of God's Grace. A place worthy of dedication.'

Hartelius took the flaming torch from von Szellen's hand. He swept it across the floor in front of them. 'Look. This floor is beaten down. And these are fresh hoof prints. Are these from our horses, von Szellen?'

'No, sir. We dismounted by the cave entrance. The horses were immediately led away.'

'Then this cave is known about by others. It has ease of access. And it is not far from an established trail. We must be very cautious.'

As if in direct answer to his words, there was a commotion at the entrance to the cave. Five men on horseback entered, brushing the sand from their burnouses. It was instantly clear to the Templars, from the silhouette of the strangers' headgear against the light bleeding through the cave entrance, that the men were Saracens.

Swords were drawn. The Templars instinctively adopted their traditional battle position, in the shape of a narrow V, with von Szellen out in front, and the princess and Hartelius contained within the two outwardly flaring flanks.

The Saracens drew their scimitars also. They formed themselves into a broad line, five wide, their horses still snorting the dust from their noses.

Hartelius forced his way between two of his Templars. He strode towards the Saracens, his sword still sheathed. He raised his right hand. 'Hold fast. All of you.' Still walking, he half turned towards his Templars. 'Put up your swords, you men. We are not at war now.'

He stopped twenty feet short of the Saracens. He laid his right hand across his breast. '*Assalamu alaikum*. Peace be upon you.'

The central figure of the five Saracens hesitated for a moment. Then he nodded his head. He sheathed his scimitar and laid his own hand upon his heart. '*Wa'alaikum*. And on you.' He indicated with his chin that his men must also sheathe their swords.

Hartelius recognized only too well, from the brevity of the response to his greeting, that the leading Saracen had still not made up his mind that he and his men were not about to be set upon. 'Please enter the cave,' said Hartelius. 'You are very welcome to shelter here with us. We have food. There is water. We wish you to share it.'

Behind him one of his Templars muttered, 'But these are only five. We could slaughter them and have done with it. Why feed the swine first?'

Hartelius turned sharply round. 'Enough, Klarwein. We were here first. These men are now our guests. Do you not remember your Bible? "Do not neglect to show hospitality to strangers, for thereby some have entertained angels unawares."'

'How about devils unawares?'

'Enough, I said.' Hartelius indicated with outspread hands that the Saracens should bypass them and head for the underground lake to water their horses if they so chose. Once the Saracens had reluctantly dismounted, he returned to his own men. 'Start a fire, some of you. The sooner we break bread with these men, the better it will be for all of us.'

Three of the Templars unhitched some sheaves of dried sticks from one of the extra horses and began setting a fire, while the princess's handmaiden searched for food in one of the saddlebags.

'And no pork, remember. I don't want my throat cut because of some fool's idea of a bad joke.'

The princess had already laid out a covering for her and Hartelius to sit upon. Hartelius hunched down beside her.

'You understand what just occurred?'

She nodded. 'You stopped a bloodbath.'

'Perhaps. Perhaps not. Until we break bread together, nothing is certain. In Saracen culture you may not harm a man once you have eaten with him. That is why I have ordered my men to start a fire and prepare food. But Klarwein and Nedermann are hotheads. They hate Saracens. I cannot trust them not to do something foolish. Fortunately, von Szellen has a cool head. As you saw just now when he came to find us. And the men respect him.'

'They respect you, too.'

'But I am no longer a sworn Templar. I am their commander, yes. And they have consented to follow me because I am doing what appears to them to be the right thing concerning the Copper Scroll. But that is as far as it goes. If one of them attacks a Saracen for even the most asinine of reasons, they will all do so, regardless of anything I do or say.'

There was a further commotion at the entrance to the cave. Hartelius stood up, masking the princess with his body. He laid his hand on the hilt of his sword.

A seemingly endless line of horsemen began to enter the cave, each one wearing Saracen headgear. When the first man in line straightened up and saw not the five companions he had expected, but the Templars, he reined in his horse so violently that it rocked back on its haunches as if it were about to sit down. The man shouted to his companions and they fanned out behind him in a skirmish line.

Hartelius's thirteen Templars drew their swords as one.

Hartelius strode out in front of them and prepared to fight. There was no help for it now. He and his Templars were massively outnumbered. More Saracens were crowding into the cave every minute, jostling with each other for position, the dust and sand from their clothing rising in great plumes against the light entering from outside.

The Templars drew back towards the apex of the wall containing the paintings. They formed a tight circle round the princess and her servant, their swords pointing outwards. Each man knew that the odds against him were impossible. Mounted men would always win against standing knights, especially if the ratio against them was five or six to one.

'I told you we were entertaining devils,' said Klarwein. 'But nobody would listen to me.'

'You will know more about the devil in a few minutes when you enter hell yourself,' said von Szellen. 'We will all think of you down there.'

'That is very funny. Very funny indeed. And what makes you think St Peter will let you through the Holy Gate? Have you lived such a good life? If you ask my opinion, you will be accompanying me to the underworld.'

'I did not ask your opinion.'

'Quiet. All of you.' Hartelius threw up one gauntleted arm. 'Something is happening out there. But I can scarcely see for the dust. I think the five we first saw are talking to the others. Klarwein, keep your mouth shut from now on. If you interfere in this without my permission, I will consign you to hell myself.'

'But I fought in the third Crusade, Commander. Just as you did. I have earned my exoneration.'

'Enough now.' Hartelius strode into the dust cloud raised by the Saracens' horses. He was instantly cut off from his men's view. 'Von Szellen,' he shouted back, his disembodied voice emerging from somewhere deep within the swirl. 'I am relying on you to keep the men in order while I try to parley us out of this. No rioting. No individual action.'

'It shall be done, Commander.'

Hartelius wrapped his burnous around his mouth and nose. The dust, stirred up by a myriad horses' hooves, was getting worse by the minute. 'I am coming through. My sword is sheathed.' His shout could scarcely be heard over the clatter of unshod hooves, the clank of unsheathed scimitars and the occasional crash as shields smashed together in the churning maelstrom created by the horses.

One of the riders in front of him let out a high-pitched ululation. A number of the other horsemen took it up. The back hairs on Hartelius's head stood up. Was this a prelude to attack? He stopped walking. He allowed the hand that he had been using to protect his eyes from the dust to fall idly to his side, close to the pommel of his sword.

A sudden silence fell over the assembly of Saracens in front of him. Now that their horses were no longer moving, the dust began to settle. Hartelius was soon able to make out the massed ranks of horsemen now clogging the entrance to the cave. It was immediately apparent to him that he was not dealing with a simple scouting party, but a major force.

Already, more than fifty men and their mounts had squeezed into the cave in an effort to gain shelter from the storm. More were no doubt waiting outside, wondering what all the commotion was about, and why their precursors were stopping them from entering. Such a large party of Saracens could do as they wished with him and his men. His Templars might take ten or twenty of the enemy down, but the outcome was foreordained.

As Hartelius watched, the Saracen line in front of him broke ranks. Their horses edged backwards to make way for a lone figure, dressed in a sumptuous blue *thawb*, partially covered by a red *besht* with gold filigree on the collar and cuffs. On his head he wore a mailed turban with a spike protruding from the top. This impressive figure rode slowly through the cave entrance. He was met by one of the five Saracens Hartelius had originally spoken to. The man bent double in his saddle and then offered his commander a right-handed salute which ended, in a sign of deep respect, over the eyes.

Hartelius watched as the man spoke closely to his commander, indicating with one arm the Templars' position, which, now the dust had largely settled, was clear for everyone to see.

The man in the blue *thawb* listened intently to his subordinate. Then he broke away from him and spurred his horse onwards until the animal came to a halt ten feet from where Hartelius was standing.

'*Assalamu alaikum wa rahmatullah wa barakatuhu* – may the mercy, peace and blessings of Allah be upon you.'

Hartelius loosed the burnous from around his face. *'Wa'alaikum salam wa rahmatullah wa barakatuhu* – and may the peace, mercy and blessings of Allah be upon you too.'

'Ah,' said the man, with a half smile on his face. 'It is Johannes von Hartelius of Sanct Quirin, is it not? I thought to find you here.'

Hartelius took a further hesitant step towards the mounted figure. He craned his head forwards and raised one hand to shade his eyes against the dust-laden sunlight entering through the entrance to the cave.

Then he threw back his head and laughed. He repeated the salute he had seen the Saracen soldier give his commander a few seconds before, ending with the very same flourish over the forehead which he knew was the Muslim equivalent of saying 'I place you in an exalted position over my eyes'.

'Amir Maan Ibn Fakhr-al-Din, of Baakleen, in the Chouf. I salute you.'

# TWENTY

At the Amir's suggestion, Hartelius ordered his Templars to set up the princess's pavilion in a far corner of the cave, so that she and her handmaiden would not be subject to the gaze of his Saracen warriors.

'They are not accustomed to seeing uncovered women outside the home, Commander. It is wiser to be discreet.'

Hartelius sat across from the Amir on a series of carpets laid upon the floor of the cave. Outside, the Khamsin was still raging, but inside all was peace. The horses – both those of the Templars and those of the Saracens – were tethered down by the underground lake, and the two forces, thirteen on the one hand and somewhere close to a hundred on the other, had split up and were hunched over their individual campfires, the tendrils of smoke joining together twenty feet over the soldiers' heads, before being swept towards the cave entrance by invisible currents of air.

'And your wound?' said Hartelius. 'It was in your upper back, if I recall?'

'Your administration of moss was most effective. I had no infection. Haly Abbas would have been proud of you.'

'Haly Abbas?'

'Ali ibn al-'Abbas al-Malusi. He wrote the *Kitab al-Maliki*. The *Complete Book of the Medical Art*.'

'Ah. I am flattered.'

'You should be.'

The two men looked at each other for a long time, drinking in each other's faces. Hartelius was the first to break the silence.

'You said "I thought to find you here" after you first spoke my name. What did you mean by that?'

'Can you not guess?'

'I would rather you told me.'

A servant provided water for both men to wash their hands in, and towels with which to dry themselves. Dates were brought, and sweetmeats rolled in honey. Mint tea was served, with the teapot held high above the beakers so that the tea would cool slightly between the spout and the receptacle.

Each man took his tea with the right hand, looking the other in the eye. When the third cup was finished, the Amir clapped his hands together, and one of his Saracens appeared leading Hartelius's stallion.

'You don't mind, I hope? I needed very much to look at him. His father is dead, you see. Killed beneath me three weeks after I left you in that hidden valley where you tended to my wound. I wept long and hard over his body. His was the greatest loss I have ever encountered. Worse even than the loss of my own father, who was a wayward man. To this day I often awaken at night imagining I am riding Antar into battle.'

'He was a mighty horse.'

'He was my soul. He was my heart.'

'And yet you offered to give him to me?'

'You gave me my life. He was my life. The gift was appropriate.' The Amir looked at Hartelius's stallion, his eyes travelling over every inch of the horse. After a while he stood up. He turned to Hartelius. 'May I touch him?'

'Of course.'

The Amir ran his hands across the flanks, then down along the belly and over the hindquarters of the stallion. Then he moved up to the neck and head. He turned his back to the horse, and allowed the stallion to rest his head on the shoulders of his robe. Then he rubbed the horse's chest with both his hands while the horse idly plucked at his *besht* with its teeth. 'He is exactly like his father. Exactly. I prayed so many times to Allah that Antar would be prepotent. For I must tell you this, Hartelius. Your stallion is his only son. His only descendant. I held Antar back from knowing mares while we were at war, thinking that this would weaken him. In this way he was forced to find your mare for himself, while I was injured. I have always regretted my presumption.'

'Have you a mare you would like covered?' said Hartelius. 'More than one, perhaps? If so, Gadwa will be happy to oblige.'

'You call him Gadwa? An Arabic name?'

138

'Yes. Because he was a gift. From God. And from you.'

'Aah.' The Amir closed his eyes and bowed his head. 'In truth I have three mares I would like Gadwa to cover. They are my best girls. Beautiful beyond imagining. But they are back in the Chouf. I would be honoured, therefore, if you and the princess, and any of your knights who may wish to do so, would accept to be my guests in the Chouf for as long as you choose to grace the land of my birth with your presence.'

Hartelius glanced towards the princess's pavilion. 'But to get to the Chouf we would have to return in the direction of Beirut, would we not? Which is towards Acre?'

'This is true. But you would have the protection of my men along the way. And once in Baakleen I would be in a position to guarantee your safety for as long as you decide to reside with me and share my hospitality. No one would dare molest you there.'

'So you know from whom we are fleeing?'

The Amir laughed. 'The entire Outremer coast from Gaza to Antioch knows from whom you are fleeing. The tyrant, von Drachenhertz, has offered a reward for your head and for the return of his intended bride of ten thousand Fatimid dinars. Gold that he no doubt plundered from our people during the Siege of Acre. This man is a monster. Second only to Raynald of Châtillon in the annals of infamy. But ten thousand gold dinars is enough to turn any man's head. Three days' ride from here, in a pass near the Crac de l'Ospital, the Assassins already await you. They know there is no other

139

way for you to travel. That you must traverse this pass in order to reach the Hospitallers' redoubt.'

'So even the direction we are going is known about?'

'It seems so.'

'And you? Is our meeting happenstance?'

'Nothing is happenstance, my friend. All is the will of God. And I wished very much to see your horse.'

Hartelius sighed. He would get no more from the Amir. And further questions would embarrass both of them.

'I cannot speak for the princess, Amir. But I suspect that I already know her answer, which I will confirm presently. My Templars and I accept your kind offer of hospitality. You have no objection to our bearing arms?'

'None whatsoever. You are my guests. We are not at war. Perhaps the enforced proximity between our followers during this Khamsin, and later, when we ride for the Chouf, will serve as a lesson for them both?'

Hartelius threw his head back and laughed. The Amir laughed with him. From all sides of the cave their men watched in awestruck silence.

# TWENTY-ONE

'He is the one, isn't he?' The princess was watching the Amir through a gap in the entrance flap of her pavilion. 'The one you told me about? The one whose life you saved?'

'Yes. It is he.'

The princess cocked her head to one side and narrowed her eyes. 'And he tells you he only came to see your horse?'

'Yes. That is what he says.'

'But you know he really came to save us?'

'Yes. Without a doubt.'

'How do you know this?'

'Because I know him as I know you. Totally. More completely, even, than I know myself. In here.' Hartelius struck himself above the heart with his clenched fist.

The princess shook her head in wonder. 'Men. I will never understand them. Why does everything between you have to be unsaid?'

Hartelius grinned. 'Because all our words are kept for you

women. Then, when the moment comes when men must talk between themselves, there are no words left to be shared. So we are forced to remain silent.'

The princess stared at him, an unbelieving expression on her face. 'Hah. I have heard such silences between men. They are filled with words. They ooze with words.'

'Then I have been misinformed.'

The princess struck Hartelius a glancing blow on the upper arm. 'That is your punishment for teasing me.'

Hartelius bowed his head. 'I accept my punishment willingly.'

'Good. It is only your just dessert. I wish, though, that you would not wear chainmail when I need to punish you. See? I have hurt myself.'

Hartelius took the princess's hand in his and kissed her knuckles, one by one. 'Is that better?'

'Yes. That is better. Much better. Now tell me more about your friend. Not suppositions. Facts.'

Hartelius composed himself. But it was hard. He dearly loved the games he and the princess played, and longed for their continuance. They were his recompense for a youth slipped out of too early and regretted. 'The Amir is a chieftain or commander. You might even call him a prince. Someone exalted above other men.'

'Why is such a man here? Patrolling this benighted desert?'

'For many reasons. His main task will be to scout the lands beyond the thin strip of coast we Christians call our own. To make sure that no one encroaches on Muslim territory. He will have many spies to this purpose. He will know everything that goes on between Acre and Tortosa. I suspect that when he recognized my name, and subsequently heard that von Drachenhertz had put a bounty on my head, he would inevitably have wondered why. Later, perhaps, he might have heard tell of an unattached band of Templars riding through no-man's-land. He would immediately have deduced who we are.'

'So we are his hostages now? Is that what you are telling me? He will trade us for money?'

'No. We are the Amir's guests. He hopes to protect us from von Drachenhertz, whom he hates. Not sell us to him.'

'Why does he hate him?'

Hartelius gave an irritated shake of the head. 'Because your monster of an intended husband raids the Silk Routes whenever the whim takes him. Because he tortures Muslims and forces them to renege on their faith. Because he acts like Raynald of Châtillon used to act before Saladin killed him. Personally. With his own sword.'

'You sound as if you approve of what Saladin did.'

'I do. All sides must strive to behave honourably in a war. Only that way will there be discipline in victory and magnanimity in defeat. Saladin spared Guy de Lusignan for this precise reason. To make a point to his men. That kings do not kill kings.'

'But bestial things do happen. You have told me so yourself. Isn't it true that Saladin ordered all Templar and Hospitaller knights he captured to be beheaded immediately?'

'The exception proves the rule. We are all human. And all humans err when the heat of battle is upon them. Saladin believed us to be cultists who would never cease to make war against him in the Holy Land. He was right.'

The princess closed the flap of her tent, effectively sealing them off from the outside world. She walked towards the area that contained her bedchamber. Without turning her head, she said, 'Do you intend to sleep with your friend then, tonight, Hartelius? Or will you make an exception to your rule and sleep with me?'

'Rule? What rule? I sleep with you every night.'

The princess cast him a coquettish look over one shoulder. 'So. I have your attention again, do I, Hartelius? Listen. You can moon over your new friend during the day, when you are both stinking of horses and ordering people about. But during the night you are mine. Do you understand me?'

Hartelius was already pulling off his chainmail. 'I understand you very well.'

'Good. Ghislaine has drawn us both a bath with water from the lake. She has warmed the water over the fire and had her lover bring it in. I have given her permission to lie with him in my antechamber later tonight as recompense. I suspect that we will have little privacy on our ride to the Chouf. Might we not take advantage of the privacy we have now?'

'Are you suggesting I stink of horses again and need a wash?'

'That, and other things.'

He ran after her and caught her up in his arms. She was already in the process of slithering out of her *bliaut*. 'Hartelius, no.'

144

'Hartelius, yes.' He upended the princess and held her so that her head was just above the bathwater, with her hips on his shoulders and her legs scissoring around his head.

'No. Hartelius. Have some decorum. I am a royal princess. I am with child.'

Hartelius slapped her on the bottom. 'I know. I made you so. But I feel a sudden urge to inspect for myself this extra merchandise you claim to be carrying.'

# TWENTY-TWO

The hawk swung free from the Amir's arm, her jesses trailing. She swept high into the desert air, soaring on the spirals of warm air burgeoning beneath her, her wings working tirelessly. The Amir, Hartelius and the Amir's falconer watched her as if there was nothing more important in this world than the progress of a bird.

When the hawk reached an altitude of five hundred feet, she hovered for a moment to take stock of her surroundings. It was then that she saw the crane.

The falconer looked at his master and grinned. 'She has seen him, Afandi.'

The Amir nodded. 'But he has seen her too. Look. He is veering off his course.'

'Nevertheless. She will catch him, Afandi.'

'No. He is too big for her.'

'Not so, Afandi. She will take him from above, then tear him with her claws. He will have no chance.'

'What do you think, Hartelius?'

Hartelius shook his head. 'I think we are about to receive a visit from the princess.'

All three men turned in the direction Hartelius was indicating. Five of the Amir's Saracens were already riding hard to cut the princess off and escort her safely towards the hawking party.

'Is your princess a hunter then, Hartelius?'

'All women are hunters, Amir. Look at your hawk. She is a female, is she not? And larger than the male of her species?'

They laughed, and returned their attention to the hawk.

The hawk was stooping towards the crane. The crane seemed absurdly lumbering compared to the extraordinarily mobile hawk, which twisted and turned through the air, constantly varying her direction, until she was thirty feet above her quarry, and ready to strike.

Gradually, by increments, the crane had been descending all the time the hawk had been tailing him. Now he threw out his wings, just a few seconds before the hawk was due to strike him, and dropped like a stone towards the ground.

The hawk hesitated, twisting in the air and turning a full circle – even flying for a moment on her back.

The crane struck the earth, its limbs taking the full force of its descent, its wings stretching out to steady itself.

The hawk, too, landed, and stood a few feet away from the crane, studying it, her head cocked to one side. The difference in their relative sizes was now clearly apparent.

The Amir clapped his hands. He struck his falconer lightly on the arm with his riding crop. 'The crane has outwitted your hawk. See. In the air, she is his master. On the ground, he fears no enemies such as her.'

The falconer shook his head. 'But he dare not fly again, Afandi. He is locked onto the ground. If he attempts to take off she will kill him. He has no way of defending himself.'

The princess pulled her horse up near to the Amir's. She was wearing neither veil nor headdress. Von Szellen, who was accompanying her, shrugged his shoulders at Hartelius, as if to say, 'What could I do? She is a princess.'

'So,' said the princess. 'A stalemate, it seems.'

The Amir bowed his head in acknowledgement. 'It would seem so, Princess. At first glance, at least. Do you enjoy hawking?'

The princess threw back her head and laughed. 'I have been contained within the walls of a convent since the age of ten, Amir, and forced to attend only to matters that the mother superior felt were suitable for my limited female mind. Prayer and humility, in other words, alongside chastity, constancy and forbearance. My father, Frederick Barbarossa, took me hawking with him once when I was six years old, and I loved every moment of it. I have never had the opportunity again. When I saw you on the skyline during my early-morning ride, I decided I would invite myself to your hawking party. Please forgive my intrusion.'

The Amir inclined his head. 'It is no intrusion. I am delighted always to show off my hawks. And you are my honoured guest. No doors are closed to you.'

'You are very kind.' The princess allowed Hartelius to help her from the saddle. 'May I ask what occurs next?'

The Amir gave a half bow. 'The crane has won by default. My falconer will lure the hawk back to his glove, and we will strike off in search of further prey. My hawk must taste blood this morning or I fear that she will leave us and look elsewhere for her entertainment.'

'Is this what usually happens?'

'No. My hawk would normally kill the crane with ease. That is the way of things. But this crane was exceptional. He out-thought the hawk. One would have expected him to use his wings. He used his brains instead. He chose the battleground. Turned the thing to his own advantage.'

'Shall I kill the crane, Afandi?' said the falconer, his crossbow at the ready.

The Amir glanced first at the princess, then at Hartelius. He seemed deep in thought. 'I think not,' he said at last. 'No. Such a bird, clearly beloved of Allah, must be allowed to live. Must he not, Hartelius?'

'Yes, Amir. The exception must always prove the rule.'

The Amir smiled, content that Hartelius had understood the significance of his action. 'Just as in the case of our princess. From henceforth she must accompany us whenever she wills. I had heard that the women of the West are unlike those of the East. Now I have proof of this for myself.' He locked gazes with Hartelius. 'I believe I am only now, thanks to the actions of this wily crane, beginning to understand quite what forces have brought us all together in this place.'

# TWENTY-THREE

Barely an hour passed before the Amir's hawk killed a desert hare. The Amir allowed her to taste the liver and pick at the lights. When he was satisfied that she had bloodied herself and eaten her fill, he sent her back with his falconer to roost with her companions. It was then that they saw the scout riding towards them. His red banner was unfurled.

'There is danger ahead.'

'Is that the significance of the red banner, Amir?'

'Yes. If the way was clear it would be blue. The colour of the sea and not of blood. This is why I sent him out.'

They watched the scout approach.

'It is von Drachenhertz, isn't it?' said Hartelius.

'I believe so,' said the Amir. 'I should have expected this. But I did not allow for the days the Khamsin held us up. This has given von Drachenhertz the necessary time to put his arrangements in place. The man bribes half the country to inform him of what is going on. Even those who hate him serve him. That is the way of the world.'

Hartelius stood beside the princess while the Amir spoke to his scout.

'Von Drachenhertz is here?' said the princess. 'He has come for me?'

'Yes. I am afraid so.'

'And will the Amir not give me up? He could negotiate much that was to his advantage if he did so.'

'He will not give you up. No.'

'You are sure of this?'

'Yes.'

The princess nodded. 'Then there will be a fight.'

Hartelius glanced across at her, but she had turned her face away from him and was watching the Amir.

'Yes,' he said. 'There will be a fight. Von Drachenhertz is barring the Amir from returning to the Chouf. Such a thing is unacceptable even in peacetime. The country through which we are passing belongs to no one. It is the mutually accepted no-man's-land separating Saracen from Frank. If von Drachenhertz pitches his camp on the plain leading to the pass, it is an insult to the Amir. An insult no Saracen can afford to ignore without losing face.'

'And your Templars? Men like von Szellen over there? They will not fight alongside the Saracens, surely? They will not turn on their own people?'

'Von Drachenhertz is nobody's people but his own. He will kill us all simply for his own amusement. My Templars know that. There is no law but his out here.'

'Are his people more numerous than ours?'

'The Amir's party consists of one hundred and fifty men. They are tired from the trail. They are armed for skirmishing, not for pitched battles. When they left the Chouf they did so on the understanding that they were a patrol and not an army. Von Drachenhertz's men are fresh. They will be armed to the teeth. He will have offered each man a bounty for my head, and an even greater one for your capture. He set out with the sole intention of finding us and of overwhelming us when he did. He has only this one aim. So yes. He will have more men.'

The Amir beckoned Hartelius to approach. The princess, without being asked, rode alongside him. All four, accompanied by von Szellen and their five Saracen escorts, cantered to the crest of the nearby hill.

The Amir pointed at the plain below them. 'He knows we are here. Look. They have spread themselves like honey. There is no way past them.'

'Can we not retreat?'

'The Assassins are behind us. Von Drachenhertz will have paid them well. The truth is that we are hemmed in both from the back and from the front. Below us is only the sea. And above us are the mountains. If we could fly into the air like my hawk we would be safe.'

'Then hand us over and be done with it. You have no need to be involved in this. The fault is mine and mine alone.'

'You are my guests. A host does not hand his guests over to the executioner.'

As they watched, a detachment of soldiers broke away from the Frankish lines and started towards them up the valley.

The Amir leaned in towards his scout. The two men spoke in undertones.

The Amir straightened up. He pulled back the sleeve of his *besht* and pointed towards the approaching party with his riding crop. 'See? The man in silver armour at the front? With the plumed helm? My scout tells me that this is von Drachenhertz himself. He must be very confident indeed of his position to approach our lines with so few men.'

'You will parley with him?'

'Of course. I am looking forward to seeing the monster for myself.'

'I will come too,' said Hartelius.

'And I,' said the princess. 'I want him to see what he cannot have.'

The Amir threw back his head and laughed, showing all his teeth. 'Come then, both of you. We will ride with my escort to meet him below the skyline. I do not want him to see the paucity of our numbers when compared to his own. That would be to allow the monster too much."

# TWENTY-FOUR

At first it seemed to everyone present as if the Margrave Adalfuns von Drachenhertz did not intend to remove his helmet. The Amir regarded him quizzically – it would have represented an even more studied insult than the man's placing of his troops across the mouth of the one serviceable pass back towards the Chouf.

But even the margrave, it appeared, drew the line at alienating his audience before he had had a chance to influence their way of thinking. He wrenched off his helmet and tossed it to one of his subordinates. Every move he made indicated domination. He had the face of an angry lion and the demeanour of an autarch. His hair hung down in sweaty strands, and there were dark patches beneath his eyes, as if his rage at being defied had been preventing him from sleeping.

'Princess,' he said, with an unctuous inclination of his torso. 'What a joy it is to meet my future bride at last. May I assume that you have been kidnapped, and that the Baron von Hartelius, together with his Saracen subordinates, has come here to negotiate the details of your release?'

'I have not been kidnapped,' said the princess. She took a step closer to Hartelius, as if unconsciously to emphasize her point. 'Your spies will have told you that much.'

The margrave straightened up from his false bow. 'Then you are guilty of treason. The king made me a formal promise. I expect that promise to be kept.'

The princess drew herself up too, her face pallid. 'The promise was made in my brother's name, not mine.'

The margrave sent his gauntlets flying after his helmet. 'They are one and the same thing. You owe a duty both to the king, your brother, and to the king, your sovereign. By whatever name you choose to call them.'

'I owe a duty only to myself.'

Von Drachenhertz shrugged. His mouth twitched as if he were about to laugh. He rubbed his hands down his cuisses to dry them. 'Be that as it may. The end result is the same. It will take months for your brother to send me another wife. And I want one now. So I have decided to forgive your dalliances with this Bavarian upstart and marry you as arranged.'

The princess gave a physical start. 'My dowry and my name are what you want. Not me. We both know that.'

'Amongst other things.'

'The Holy Spear and the Copper Scroll, you mean?'

There was an almost palpable silence following her words. Von Drachenhertz broke the silence with a grunt. He followed it up with a triumphant grin.

'No. I was thinking, of course, of what little I might be able to salvage of your virginity. And musing, too, on what von Hartelius's guts would look like wrapped around my lance – with his rod and testicles riding on top as a pennant.' Von Drachenhertz extended his grin for a second, and then switched expression, so that his forehead creased in a spirit of fake enquiry. 'But what you have just said intrigues me. How do you happen to know of the Copper Scroll? The king, your brother, led me to believe that only he and I knew of its presence amongst your accoutrements.'

Hartelius felt sick. The princess had spent more than half her life in a convent. She was unused to the cut and thrust of male power play. The shattering significance of detail. He was tempted to draw his sword and have at von Drachenhertz without further ado – but by doing this he would simply be heaping insult upon injury onto his host, whose good name would be the one to suffer. An acknowledged parley was sacrosanct. Even a slug like von Drachenhertz would think twice before violating it. 'The Copper Scroll has been stolen from the Templars. It is not the property of the king, and never was. It is not for him, or you, to decide on its fate.'

Von Drachenhertz, like many fundamentally immoral men, was clearly relishing his brief sojourn on the moral high ground. 'Everything belongs to the king. Even you belong to the king, Hartelius. And now you belong to me. The only way either you or the princess could know of the Copper Scroll would be from the breaking of the Royal Seal. And such a thing is punishable by death. But as you are already a dead man, the actual details of what triggers your execution are unimportant.'

The Amir raised one hand. 'This is all beside the point. Both the baron and the princess are my honoured guests. They therefore benefit from my protection, and that of my men.'

Von Drachenhertz started back in mock surprise. 'What men are you talking about, Amir? Not the one hundred and fifty Khamsin-emptied wrecks that await the onslaught of my army? The ones whimpering over the crest of that hillock you have so carefully avoided me broaching? You are joking, surely? You have seen the quality of my host. I have heard reports of the quality of yours. The result is foreordained. Unless, of course, you have a vast force riding to your rescue that I know nothing about?' Von Drachenhertz paused, as if he was genuinely expecting a reply. 'Look. I will tell you what I will do. Give me Hartelius and the princess and I will afford you and your men free passage through to the Chouf. That is a fair bargain, is it not? I cannot now offer you a ransom, because the princess has made it clear to me that she has not been kidnapped. The payment of a ransom would therefore be both insulting and inappropriate. And I am the first person not to wish to insult such a great eminence as yourself. Such a thing would be tantamount to blasphemy, would it not?'

'There is only one blasphemy,' said the Amir, his eyes never leaving von Drachenhertz's face, 'and that is the one that you perpetrate during your forcible conversions of my people.'

'There is only one true faith,' replied von Drachenhertz, 'and that is ours. Those of your people we deign to convert are blessed. I am surprised you don't appreciate that.'

Hartelius stepped between the two men. 'Would you agree to single combat, Margrave? To settle our differences that way?'

Von Drachenhertz roared with laughter. 'And give up the pleasure of killing you slowly? Of monitoring the incremental damage to your nerve endings hour by hour, day by day, and week by week? I have the best torturer in the seven kingdoms, Hartelius. He needs someone new to practise on. Not the dross I am feeding him at present. And I have a perfect audience in the princess. I will tie her to a whore-stool and feed her your tallow like soup. Only then will I marry her. I like my women suitably tamed.'

If von Szellen had not wrapped his arms round Hartelius's shoulders and borne his commander to the ground, the story would have ended there. The Amir's Saracens drew their scimitars and formed a wall round their master and the princess. Von Drachenhertz's men did not even bother to draw their swords. The parley had gone exactly as expected. Strength was speaking to weakness. And weakness needed to assert itself. All present understood the dynamic. It was what informed their lives.

'You have until dawn tomorrow, Amir. I have no desire to fight you. Now is neither the time nor the place. Give up these traitors and you and your men walk free. If you do not give them up I will slaughter you. Then I will hang you and your men upside down on crosses all the way along the shoreline as a warning to your people not to meddle in affairs that do not concern them.'

# TWENTY-FIVE

'This Copper Scroll the tyrant speaks of,' said the Amir. 'It is the one you Templars believe holds the secrets of King Solomon, is it not?'

Hartelius hesitated. But now was not the time to hold back. He and the Amir were alone. Or at least as alone as they would ever be, given the plethora of attendants who catered to the Amir's every whim. 'Yes. The princess's brother stole it from us. He was sending it secretly with her, under cover of the Holy Lance, so that von Drachenhertz could use it to drum up support for a new Crusade.' Hartelius shrugged. 'I am telling you nothing you don't suspect already.'

The Amir allowed one of his servants to slide on his chainmail. 'I will never understand this obsession you Christians have with meaningless relics.'

Hartelius sighed – for he, too, despite his Guardianship of the Holy Lance, instinctively mistrusted relics. 'They are simply a means to an end. They carry messages the way banners carry epiphanies. And your people are the masters of banners.'

'This is true.' The Amir eased the chainmail down over his shoulders and belted it across his hips. 'And you have translated all these secrets? You have them at your fingertips?' The Amir drew on his gauntlets, his eyes still fixed on Hartelius. 'Perhaps your people are, even now, preparing to build your new Temple in Jerusalem, Hartelius, over the dead bodies of their enemies?'

Hartelius grimaced. 'Truthfully? No. More than half the scroll remains to be translated. It is written in a language no one understands. Our scholars have been trying to decipher it for seventy years. Only when this is done will its secrets be revealed and the Temple started.'

The Amir nodded, as if he had been expecting Hartelius's answer. 'Then you must show it to my Sufi master.'

'Why would I do that?'

'Because he speaks every language known to man. If anyone can read it, he can.'

'And he would help us? Even though we are his enemies?'

The Amir smiled. 'He is Sufi. As am I. As, I suspect, are you, although you do not know it yet. We Sufis do not conform to what we are expected to conform to. There are greater things to adhere to in this world than meaningless dogma. Greater passions to be driven by than fear.' The Amir closed his eyes and inhaled deeply, as though he were savouring something only he had immediate access to. 'There is only one truth. And that is God. All else is meaningless. You believe that too, don't you, Hartelius? I am not talking to the air?'

Hartelius gave a brief nod of the head. But he could not quite bring himself to speak – to bring the whole thing out into the open by placing his mouth upon it. The Knight Templar priests who had been responsible for his education had done their work well. Hell was a very real place to Hartelius – and the quickest way to get there, in his opinion, was to betray the dictates of the religion one happened to be born into, even if one did not fully concur with certain of its finer points.

Hartelius watched as the Amir completed his preparations, his face clearly reflecting his reservations about his friend's intended course of action. 'So you really intend to attack? Even though you are massively outnumbered?'

'There is no alternative.'

'You will be slaughtered.'

'That is the will of Allah.'

'You will be slaughtered because of us.'

'No. The tyrant von Drachenhertz has been seeking an excuse to tame us for years. Now he has found one. It is nothing to do with you. This is between him and me.'

'Have you thought about what we shall do with the princess during the fight?'

The Amir refused to meet Hartelius's gaze. 'You and your men are not going to be fighting alongside us, Hartelius. My Saracens would never accept such a thing, despite their utter dedication and loyalty to me. I am therefore sending you and your Templars over the mountains with a guide who knows every defile, every canyon, and every pass. A few well-equipped men may travel where an army may not. My Sufi master I am sending with you also. The death of such a man in a meaningless battle would be a tragedy not to be borne.'

'I will not leave you now. This is an impossible thing that you ask of me.'

'You will leave me because I ask it of you as a friend. The sacrifice of myself and my men is purposeless unless it be in the interests of the laws of hospitality. I gave you and the princess my word that you would be protected. The monster expects his answer tomorrow morning at dawn. He shall have it tonight, while his camp is asleep. I gave my word to no one. It is he who has chosen to bar my way into my own country. We will hew through them like the wind.'

'You know that will not be so.'

'But that is the way it will be written. There are worse ways to die. And tonight there is no moon. And the Franks will be blinded by their campfires. We have a better chance than you are crediting us with.'

'Still. I should come with you. I can understand your reservations about my men. But I could fight in disguise. No one would need to know.'

'Your place is with the princess, not with me.' The Amir touched Hartelius lightly on the arm. 'We will meet again, my friend, if it is written.' He grinned. 'And please remember this. Your stallion still has my mares to cover. That was your solemn promise to me. It is therefore of him and him alone that I am thinking in this matter. I am counting on you to fulfil your part of our bargain by keeping him safe for my girls. You understand me, Hartelius? What happens to you is entirely coincidental as far as I am concerned.'

Hartelius laughed. He knew that he could not counter the Amir's arguments. If their situations were reversed he would have done exactly the same thing. The laws of hospitality were paramount in both of their cultures. Once bread had been broken and oaths taken, there was no possibility of retrogression.

'So,' said the Amir. 'It is settled then. We will meet in the Chouf. Failing that, we will meet in Paradise.'

'Paradise is shared then?'

'There is only one God, Hartelius. We both believe that. Only a rogue or a fool would expect Him to choose sides at this stage of the proceedings.'

## TWENTY-SIX

The Amir ordered his men to cover their horses' hooves with fragments of blanket. The same was to be done with the horses' muzzles, so that they would not cry out or call to each other. Then each man was to coat his face and hands with a paste made of sand, palm oil and charcoal, so that no light would reflect off them.

Night was falling by the time they were finished with their preparations. The Amir led his Saracens wide of the plain and down along the curve of the seashore, so that they would be approaching the margrave's camp in a different direction from the one expected.

Earlier, while it was still daylight, he had had one of his men secretly map the ridges and contours of the land. This man was tasked with leading the Amir's force through the darkness, under cover of the sea's hiss.

The Amir rode in the van, a few feet behind his lead scout. He wore a white covering on his back, as did all his men. In the darkness the white shone out against the black of their fighting clothes, giving each of them a clear view of the man in front as they rode in single file.

One of the Amir's scouts had also done a head count of the margrave's men using an abacus, with the results of his readings recreated on a sand table for all to see. It appeared that there were close on eleven hundred soldiers pitted against them. Not all were knights, however. Some were bowmen. Others were pikemen. These last would surely have trouble in the darkness. They could be discounted, therefore, leaving the odds at about six to one.

But the element of surprise would be on the Amir's side. He would need luck, and the absolute silence of his horses. Added to which there would a period, while his men surged through the camp, where they would be lit up by the margrave's campfires, and would thus be vulnerable. This was their Achilles' heel. The success or failure of the Amir's plan would rest on what happened during this period of the engagement.

The lead scout reined his horse back so that the Amir might approach parallel to him, ensuring that neither man would reveal the white markers on their back to any advance guard. The scout leaned across and touched the Amir's right arm three times, just below the elbow joint. The Amir nodded in the darkness and tapped the man once in return on the right sleeve with his crop.

He eased his horse into an amble. He counted off a hundred paces in his head and then turned the amble into a trot. He counted out another one hundred paces, and now he was able to see the margrave's campfires in a horseshoe curve curling away from the sea, aiming in the direction of where the margrave thought the Amir's most likely line of attack might be.

The Amir felt his heart quicken in his chest. One part of him wanted to seek out the margrave personally and kill him – to punish him for all the horrors he had perpetrated on those of the Amir's people who had had the misfortune to come under his thumb. But another part of him knew that a wise fighter understood when to fight and when to pass up a fight that would bring him no immediate benefit.

He eased his mount into a canter. He counted to fifty in his head and moved into a gallop. If only he had his late stallion, Antar, beneath him. Or one of Antar's progeny. He could hear the thudding of his horse's hooves in the sand. The whisking and thumping of those following behind him. How could the margrave be so stupid as to mount no guards on the sea side of his camp? The man had the strategic sense of an imbecile.

The Amir sensed, rather than felt, the first fall of arrows beside him. He raised his shield and moved it back and forth in front of him, exactly the way his master-at-arms had trained him as a youth – only in this manner, he knew, could one be certain that any arrows that struck the shield would bounce harmlessly off it.

His Saracens began to whoop behind him. The Amir, too, joined in. There was no virtue in silence any more. The more noise the better. Fear was a major factor in victory. Panic was a powerful weapon.

'Unfurl the banners.'

The Amir's bannermen unfurled their great white banners and let them sweep out behind them in the wind of their passing.

This is it, thought the Amir. This is what it feels like to be alive.

It was only when the margrave's men threw off the simmering wooden covers of their hidden bonfires and flamed them with dried brushwood soaked in alcohol that the Amir realized that he and his men were riding straight into a trap.

# TWENTY-SEVEN

Hartelius twisted in his saddle and cast a sidelong glance down the valley towards the margrave's camp. He could see the pinpricks of the margrave's bonfires dotting the distant sand like emerging stars. He turned back and headed up the defile. The prospect of other men fighting his battles for him made him feel physically ill.

The Amir's scout was leading the way fifty feet ahead, with von Szellen, Klarwein and Moberg behind him. The remainder of Hartelius's Templars were bringing up the rear, immediately behind Hartelius, the princess, the princess's handmaiden and Ibn Arabi, the Amir's Sufi master, who was also known as Shaykh al-Akbar, or Al Akbariyya.

Hartelius, on first meeting the Sufi, had been astonished at the man's relative youth. How could a man of a mere forty summers be the master of anything? Most of the priests Hartelius knew were nearer sixty than forty. That was the one major advantage of the priesthood over soldiering, surely? You had a middling fair chance of surviving into old age.

Still, he had finally done what the Amir had suggested and shown the man the contents of the Copper Scroll.

'The Amir said you could speak every language known to man. Can you speak this?'

Ibn Arabi had laughed. 'I can speak Arabic, Berber, Farsi, Spanish, something that passes for German, and a little Catalan. This language you show me is none of these.'

'Do you know what it is?' Hartelius could feel his stomach churn with bitterness. Of course there had never been the remotest chance that this man might unlock the secrets of the Copper Scroll. How could there possibly be, given that a dozen scholars had slaved over the conundrum for seventy years and had seen no daylight? 'Do you have any idea at all of what language this might be written in?'

Ibn Arabi had run his oil lamp back and forth across the manuscript. For a moment Hartelius had feared that he might be about to burn it, or to attempt to damage it in some way, but the Sufi had no such intention. 'This is a great treasure. You realize this?'

'Yes. It is the greatest treasure we Templars possess.'

Ibn Arabi had watched Hartelius for some time. 'If you succeed in having this translated, with or without my help, will you promise me that the truths contained within it will be used for the greater good of everyone? Not just for the Christians that happen to possess it?'

Hartelius had sighed. 'I can promise you no such thing. And I would be a liar if I said I could. The Copper Scroll does not belong to me. I am its temporary guardian through a quirk of fate, that is all, just as I am the guardian of the Holy Lance through a similar happenstance. Anything I discover about the scroll will be handed back to the masters of my Order. That is my gage. It is they who will decide on its future. I will have nothing to do with it.'

'Then I cannot help you.'

'I never expected that you would.' Hartelius took back the scroll. 'But you know, don't you? I can see by your face. You know what language this is written in.'

'I know, yes.'

Hartelius swallowed back his pride. 'The Amir said that you would help me if you could. He said that you Sufis do not conform to what you are expected to conform to. That there are greater things to adhere to in this world than meaningless dogma. Greater passions to be driven by than fear.'

'What else did the Amir say?'

'He said that I am Sufi too. But that I do not know it yet. He said that there is only one truth, and that truth is God. All else is meaningless.'

'And are you Sufi?'

'I am nothing. I am a soldier.'

Ibn Arabi smiled. 'Do you love truth?'

'What is truth? How can I love something I do not understand?'

Ibn Arabi closed his eyes. 'You place me in an impossible position. You realize that?'

'If you tell me so.'

'Impossible, because I am both master and servant at the same time. And because I believe that the servant of whom I am master has shown more wisdom in this than I have.'

'How so?'

'The Amir understands men's hearts. He loves you. Therefore he understands your heart. All loves are a bridge to divine love. Yet those who have not had a taste of it do not know.' Ibn Arabi sighed. He pointed to the Copper Scroll with the tip of his little finger. 'I will say this once and once only. Go seek out the Yazidis in Lalish. They may be able to help you. For I most assuredly cannot.'

# TWENTY-EIGHT

# Shepherd's Bush, London

**FRIDAY 3 MAY 2013**

Amira Eisenberger looked across the kitchen table at her ex-boyfriend, John Hart. This was the first time she'd had the opportunity to study him at close quarters since picking him up at Heathrow Airport an hour earlier. For immediately on his emergence through the Arrivals Gate he had been surrounded by a maelstrom of reporters, most of whom she knew, if not by name, at least by phizog, fighting to interview him.

'Oh come on, Amira. Give us a frigging break,' Martin Halsom of Sky News had called out to her from behind his sound man. 'You can't keep him all to yourself. He's one of us.'

Amira had paid no attention to his plea. Nor to that of any of the others, however friendly she might be with them outside business hours. She had shuttled Hart in front of her and out of the airport as if he were a film star on a lightning visit to promote his new movie.

Once he was in the clear, Hart had shaken his head as if he were recovering from a sucker punch to the jaw. 'I didn't think anybody was picking me up. I was going to take a taxi.' He had snatched another look back over his shoulder at the sad gaggle of newspaper people and TV reporters gathering up their flotsam and jetsam behind him. They all knew better than to argue with Amira. 'Were those people really there for me?'

'No. They were waiting for Justin Bieber. They just thought you were him.'

'Very funny.' Hart had looked across the car roof at Amira as she fumbled for her keys. 'I feel I should tell you that I've booked a room at the Frontline Club. I thought I'd stay there and not at my flat until I found my feet again. At least that way I'd be certain of getting fed.'

'Well, cancel it. You were working for me in Iraq. I've been writing your story while you were banged up. So you are staying with me. Don't worry. I will feed you.'

'In exchange for an exclusive, you mean?'

'Yes. For your exclusive story. What do you think? That I want you back in my life again after your affair with that little fascist in Germany?'

'No. I didn't think that.'

'Thank God for small mercies.'

Hart leaned back in his chair and looked round the room that he had once known so well. The place stank of cigarettes. There were unwashed dishes in the sink. Papers and books strewn across all the visible surfaces. Used coffee cups weighing down the papers. The prospect of eating anything in such an environment appalled him. The place had gone

173

catastrophically downhill since he'd last visited, ten months before, and Amira with it. It could have doubled as one of the Camberwell sets from the film *Withnail & I*.

'You've lost weight.' Amira was watching him as you would a prize steer. 'And you've got a new scar on your forehead.'

'I jumped off a roof and someone's AK47 belted me on the head.'

'I suspected as much.'

They both laughed.

'You're a celebrity now,' she said. 'You do realize that? A star photojournalist. A made man. You'll forever be the guy who shot dead the suicide bomber. It'll be like a travelling footnote. You'll be able to write your own ticket from here on in.' Amira didn't seem particularly happy at the prospect. 'Well. You probably guessed as much when you saw your reception committee at the airport. Those pieces I wrote about you triggered it. There wasn't much other news. So you found the front pages and stayed there. Heroic reporter saves Kurdish girl at the risk of his own life. Takes down human bomb with single shot. "The Templar" strikes again.'

Hart pushed an overflowing ashtray out of the way with the back of his hand. 'That wasn't how it was and you know it. I mostly sprayed the wall above his head because I forgot, in the heat of the moment, that assault rifles throw their barrels upwards when you have them on full auto, and not where you aim. I just got lucky, if you can call it that. And I acted from naked fear, Amira, not heroism. Single shot my arse.'

'But single shot is how it read. And that's what people want in the news. They are sick of downbeat stories. They want triumphs. Good over evil. That sort of crap.'

'I thought you were wedded to the truth?'

'I am. But truth depends on a variety of factors. It's not just someone's opinion. You did do those things I wrote about. And people need heroes from time to time. It amused me to make you one. You can call it subjective truth if you want.'

'But "the Templar"? Couldn't you have thought of a better hashtag?'

'No. You'll thank me one day. People remember nicknames.'

Hart cocked his head to one side and stared at her. 'Amira. . .'

'No. Don't say it.'

'Say what?'

'Whatever you were going to say. How dreadful I look. What a mess this flat is. Why I'm talking to you like this when I should be throwing you out on your ear.'

Hart stayed silent for a long time. 'Why don't I take you out to dinner? The Ivy or Le Caprice. Your choice.'

'Aren't you afraid of being mobbed again, Mr Hero?'

'No. They'll be bored with me already and searching for new victims. Newspaper people need feeding, like guppies. And you just cut them off at the tit. For which I'm sincerely grateful, by the way.'

'You don't like being a celebrity, you mean?'

'No.'

'And you're hungry?'

'Yes.'

'Why don't we eat here then? I've got a freezer. And a microwave.'

'I'd probably get food poisoning.' Hart stood up. 'Jesus, Amira. You can afford a cleaner. Why don't you get one?'

'I like it like this.'

'No, you don't. This is how Wesker used to live. But you're not Wesker. I know he was your mentor, but why emulate his incapacity for housekeeping? He was a disaster in everything bar journalism.'

Amira tapped at her mobile phone. 'Sometimes I wish I was more like him. At least he was able to drown his sorrows in whisky until that fascist thug threw him off the balcony in Germany. But I hate the bloody stuff. And I value my brain too much to fill it full of drugs.'

'I value your brain too. But you don't need to keep it in a skip. Or smoke it to death.'

Amira put the phone to one ear and her finger to another, like a child refusing to listen to its mother's chiding. 'Takeaway Chinese suit you?'

Hart closed his eyes. 'As long as they provide chopsticks. No power on earth will persuade me to eat off your cutlery.'

Amira flicked him a V sign. 'Chinese it is then.'

# TWENTY-NINE

'I want you to look at this for me.' Hart held out the same sheet of vellum parchment he had shown to Nalan Abuna – the one containing Johannes von Hartelius's last words.

Amira spooned some more Dim Sum into her mouth, disdaining the throwaway chopsticks the caterer had provided, and which Hart was manipulating with what she felt was a certain louche dexterity. 'I've already seen it. You showed it to me last summer, remember? Just after your late girlfriend and her tame SS storm trooper had tried to kill me. I don't understand why you're still so fascinated by it.'

'Look again. Hold it up against the light. Better still, play your lighter backwards and forwards behind it. Just try not to burn it, please.'

Amira made a face. She flicked on her lighter and held the parchment against it. She drew in her breath at the mass of additional material revealed by the flame – the dozens of words snaking between the conventionally written lines and up the margins of the vellum. 'I can tell you this much. Your ancestor had verbal diarrhoea. Either that or extreme Asperger's. They say it's genetic, you know?'

Hart pretended he hadn't heard. 'Nalan discovered the hidden writing by torchlight when we were hiding in the cellar in As Sulaymaniyah. She says Hartelius must have done it with urine, or sperm, or some other colourless liquid available to him in his cell. Something that wouldn't show up on a cursory reading, but only when held up against a concentrated light source. Like a candle with a reflector, say.'

Amira shoved the manuscript back across the table to Hart in feigned distaste. 'Nalan?'

'Oh come on, Amira. Nalan Abuna. My guide and translator in Kurdistan. You've already written about her, remember? Not only that, but it was your own bloody newspaper who paid her to assist me in the first place.'

'What? You don't mean that stunningly photogenic twenty-seven-year-old Kurdish woman whose life you so heroically saved and whose photos you've been bombarding my editor with?' Amira raised her eyebrows dramatically. 'The one who was no doubt oozing with gratitude towards you once she'd managed to pull herself together after you shot the bomber. New girlfriend, John?'

'She's engaged to be married. So no. She's not my girlfriend. Nor is she ever likely to be.'

'Not for want of trying, I'm sure.'

Hart slid the parchment back inside its protective cover. 'Not even that. If you knew more about her life, you'd understand. She's got no reason to be grateful to men for anything. And certainly not to me. In fact, to all intents and purposes, it was she who saved my life, and not the other way round. If she hadn't known about the Red Interrogation House, we'd both have been mown down in the street during the first ten minutes of the attack.'

'So why are you showing me this gobbledegook now?'

'Because it's not gobbledegook. Because in it my ancestor talks about a thing called the Copper Scroll. Something historians know for a fact existed, and which was believed by the Templars to hold the key to the secrets of the Temple of Solomon. Also of where to find Solomon's hidden treasure, with which the Temple was to be funded.' Hart jabbed his finger at the parchment in frustrated emphasis. He understood exactly who he was dealing with. Amira put work first and relationships second. In that way she was entirely predictable. And doggedly consistent. 'Johannes von Hartelius knew he was going to die when he wrote this. He had nothing left to lose. So he left this parchment to posterity, knowing it would be sealed inside the Holy Spear by his executioners as a warning to others. In it he tells how he succeeded, where no one else had, in getting the scroll translated by the Yazidis in Lalish. It also tells us how and where he managed to hide it before the Hashshashin got their hands on him.'

'The Hashshashin? Copper Scrolls? The Yazidis in Lalish? You can't be fucking serious?'

'I'm perfectly serious. The scroll, which was considered the greatest treasure of the Templars, went missing in 1198.

Which coincides exactly with the dating of Johannes von Hartelius's deathbed confession. Boreas 1198.'

'Boreas? What's that?'

'It means winter. Boreas was one of the Anemoi. He was the Greek God of the freezing north wind that heralds winter. His other name was the Devouring One. He had snakes instead of feet, and he conjured up the wind by blowing through a conch shell. They say he could turn himself into a stallion and father colts simply by getting his mares to turn their hind-quarters into the wind. Without the actual need for coition, in other words.'

'Sounds ideal. I wish there were more men like him.'

Hart refused to be derailed. 'He lived in somewhere called Hyperborea. Which is the place beyond the north wind. A place of exile. A place beyond the pale. Which also happens to be where Hartelius hid the Copper Scroll.'

'You don't say.' Amira rolled her eyes. 'He hid the Copper Scroll in a place beyond the pale? And it says all that here? On this itsy-bitsy scrap of parchment? Extraordinary.'

Hart threw himself back in his chair. Amira wasn't the easiest person to convince of anything. Her first instinct, when offered unsolicited information, was to doubt it. It was what made her a first-class journalist. 'Not the Boreas bit, no. Frau Erlichmann found all that out for me last year. But listen to this. I emailed a photograph of the new text you've got in your hands to Frau Erlichmann's grandson, Thilo, and he took it straight over to his grandmother's house.'

'Frau Erlichmann?'

'Oh come on, Amira. You remember Frau Erlichmann. The old lady who took me under her wing in Germany last year? The one who gave me her father's malfunctioning First World War pistol? Well, she translated the manuscript for me from the Old German. I received Thilo's reply containing her translation on the plane coming home. If the scroll is still where Hartelius says he left it, its discovery will be the biggest story since the Dead Sea Scrolls were stumbled upon by three Bedouin shepherds back in 1947.'

'And where did Hartelius leave it? I assume he went into a little more detail than simply "beyond the pale"?'

Hart laughed. 'Ah. That's the tricky bit. He left it in a place called Solomon's Prison. The Zendan-e Soleyman.'

'And where's that? No. Don't tell me. You haven't got the faintest idea.'

'Wrong, Amira. I've got a very good idea. It's a hollow mountain in a precise geographical location. Legend has it that Solomon used it to incarcerate his prisoners – one myth has it that he even imprisoned monsters in there. There's no way in but over the lip. And then there's an immediate drop of nearly eight hundred feet to the bottom, which is entirely sealed off by sheer walls. No other way to enter or exit but down the vent. I suppose the prisoners were fed – if they were fed, that is – via a basket let down over the side. I've confirmed from the Internet that the mountain really exists. And hardly anyone ever visits it. And no one, as far as I can tell, has ever been allowed to climb down the funnel.'

'You're joking. A place like that will be oozing with climbers and risk-takers and pot-holers, or whatever they're called.'

'No, it won't.'

'So where is it then? Don't keep me in suspense. North fucking Korea?'

'No. But you're closer than you think. It's on pretty much the same latitude, both politically and geographically. It's in Iran.'

# THIRTY

Amira gave a vehement shake of the head. 'They don't let foreign journalists into Iran any more, or hadn't you heard?' She stared down at her iPad. 'Yes. Here it is. Just as I thought. We kicked the Iranians out of their London embassy in November 2011, after the riots in Tehran in which the British Embassy was ransacked. Now any non-journalistic UK citizen who wants to visit Iran has to apply through their Dublin embassy, where they charge Britons a penalty fee of 180 euros apiece just for being British, and go through every application with a fine toothcomb. And if they can find any possible excuse to do so – like an 'I'm off to your country to plunder the Copper Scrolls from Solomon's Prison' declaration – they refuse you an entry visa. According to gov.uk, individual travel is discouraged anyway – too difficult for the Iranians to police. And I can't see you travelling over there with a tourist party, somehow, and breaking away from your group for the afternoon to go clambering down an eight-hundred-foot-deep pothole.'

'I'm sure I can get around all that.'

'I'm sure you can, Superman. But you're forgetting one other thing.'

'And what's that?'

'You're a celebrity now.'

'You have to be joking.'

Amira struck her forehead with the heel of her hand. 'You know, I always forget that you're not a real journalist, John, but just some snapper who happens to have the word "journalist" tacked onto the end of his job description.'

'Nicely put.'

'Your name and face have just been splashed across half the world's newspapers, or don't you remember? You killed a suicide bomber, John. It's something of a one-off. MI6 will probably be waiting at your flat to interview you. In fact I'm stunned they weren't at the airport to greet you.'

'You probably scared them off.'

'Don't joke about it. It's something people tend to remember. You've no idea of the fuss you caused.'

'But that was in Iraq, not Iran. Why should the Iranians give a shit about what I did in another country?'

Amira rolled her eyes. 'Because it is the Iranians who were almost certainly behind the bombing in As Sulaymaniyah.'

Hart blew out his cheeks. In moments like this he wished he had done his homework a little better in terms of filtering through the news – but his profession consisted in supplying images to other people's content, not in supplying that content himself. That was Amira's job. 'How can you be so sure?'

'Who else wants to undermine the creation of an independent Iraqi Kurdistan?'

'The Iraqi state?'

'Hole in one. And the Iraqi state is predominantly made up of Shia Muslims. Same as the Iranian state. And Shia Iran and Sunni Saudi Arabia are fighting it out to the death on Iraqi soil for influence and control of the Iraqi oil fields. And where are most of the richest Iraqi oil fields located? In Sunni Kurdistan. And what region, beyond Turkey, has the longest natural border with Iraqi Kurdistan? Iran. So it's a welcome player in the anti-independent-Kurdistan league.' Amira drew herself up. She stared across the table at Hart as if she were addressing a madman. 'If the Iranians so much as sniff the fact that you might be entering their airspace, John, they will unleash their dogs of war. You won't even make it past the airport transit bus. In my opinion they'll put you directly on trial as a Western spy. A good show trial always cheers people up. If you're lucky you'll get life imprisonment. But I suspect they'll want to dispose of you quicker than that. Their favourite method these days, as you no doubt know, is hanging enemies of state by crane in a public square.' She moved behind Hart and yanked at his shirt collar. 'Go look on Facebook. Or YouTube. You can see lots of clips of recent hangings. It's not particularly edifying, I can assure you. Wait. Here. I'll even summon one up for you on my iPad. There's nothing like a good execution for livening up one's day.'

# THIRTY-ONE

Hart felt sick. The sequence of public hangings he had just watched had turned his stomach. He'd heard about them of course, but he'd never seen one. A crane hanging wasn't like a conventional hanging, in which the condemned man's neck snapped thanks to the drop. In a crane hanging the victim was slowly strangled by his own body weight. In some of the worst hangings, people from the crowd would run out and grab hold of the hanged person's feet to add a little extra weight to the proceedings. He'd just seen one of those, thanks to Amira's privileged access to some otherwise prohibited websites.

'Then I'll use my Johannes von Hartelius passport. The one I used in Germany last year.'

'But it's a fake.'

'It got me out of England and onto the continent. And no one questioned it.'

'But it's still a British passport, not a German one. The Iranian Embassy in Dublin will check it out big time.'

'What can they do if they find it's a fake? Get in touch with MI5? Hardly. All they'll do is keep it, and I won't be any the worse off then, will I?'

'Oh God.' Amira paced round the room like a lioness in a cage. 'I can't believe you've been in this profession for nearly twenty years and I still have to change your nappies. You're all heart and no head, John. It'll be your downfall one day.' She stopped her pacing and stared at him. 'No. The Iranians won't get in touch with MI5 and hand you in. They're not that stupid. They will okay your visa and lie in wait for you at Teheran Airport. . .'

'Tabriz.'

'Tabriz Airport then, and take you straight into custody, knowing they have a complete fool on their hands whose story they can manipulate in any way that pleases them. You've just been to Iraq, where you killed a man, albeit in self-defence. Then you try to enter Iran using a false passport. Clearly you work for MI6. You will be gifting the Iranians a massive propaganda coup against your own country. Not that I give a damn about MI6, but I do give a damn about you. . .'

'Thank you, Amira.'

'. . .and so I want you to give up on this stupid obsession you have with your family's distant past, and your ancestor's even more dubious role in it, and do something sensible with your life. I've just told you that you can write your own ticket now. Get in touch with my editor and propose something to her. She'll commission you like a shot. Star photojournalists with name recognition are few and far between. Believe me.

I know. We'll even collaborate on something again. You take the shots and I'll write the story. It'll be like old times. Except that you'll get the double-page byline this time, and not me. That should make up for all those years you spent in the doldrums – and pander to your male vanity to boot. A double whammy.'

Hart stood up. He gave Amira an abrupt nod. He felt both angry and subdued at the same time – as if he'd just missed being gored by a wounded buffalo thanks to his own crass stupidity in following it into the undergrowth. 'Cheers for the meal, Amira. And the advice. And the offer. And the fascinating but gruesome PowerPoint presentation. But I'm dog-tired. So I'm going to head back to the Frontline Club, like I said, and use the room I have booked there to get some rest in. I'm due at my mother's tomorrow.'

'And you're not going to Iran?'

'Probably not, if all that you say is true. But I am going back to Iraq. I have unfinished business there. I need to find out, on the ground, if there is still some halfway rational way I can get across the border and check out my ancestor's story about the Copper Scroll.'

There were moments in her relationship with John Hart when Amira felt like wailing out loud. When God invented obstinacy, she decided, He must have used John Hart, or someone very much like him, as His template. 'But the stupid bastard wrote on that piece of parchment eight hundred years ago, John. Eight hundred fucking years. And even a thirty-year time gap would be too long. What do you think this scroll of his will look like now? If you even find it, that is.'

'It was made of copper, Amira, so it won't have rusted. It will only have oxidized and then turned green. And the verdigris corrosion may well have protected it. Look at the Statue of Liberty.'

'The Statue of Liberty is barely a century old.'

'A century and a quarter, actually.'

Amira stifled a groan. 'I can see that nothing I say or do is going to change your mind.'

'Nothing. No. By rights I should have died over there in Iraq. It was a miracle that I didn't. And it's not the first time such a thing has happened to me. I think God may be trying to tell me something. Something important. About priorities maybe.' Hart collected his overnight bag and coat from the one uncluttered table in the hall. 'I need to go back there. I need to work things through.'

'Then at the very least will you promise me that you're not going back there to get inside your cute little translator's pants?'

Hart rolled his eyes towards the ceiling. 'I am not going back to Iraq because of Nalan Abuna.'

'Promise me.'

'I promise.'

'Right then. I don't really know why I'm doing this. But I'll approach my editor on behalf of both of us. See if I can get you on the payroll for a piece about you and your piss-arse ancestor. And we'll interleave the story of your close shave into it. I started this whole thing, so I'll finish it. Do yourself one favour, though. Take some shots of the Red Interrogation House while you're over there. And the place where you killed the terrorist. Bloodstains and suchlike. The shell of the blown-out cafe where you were when the bomb went off. Maybe even the skeleton of the car that contained it if it's still there. Fill the thing in a bit. With you and Miss Dinky-pants in some of the pictures. And when you've got the whole sorry mess out of your system and you're ready to talk to me, call me over, and I'll write your story for you. Do we have a deal?'

Hart hesitated. He knew Amira far too well not to suspect some subtext behind her sudden change of heart. But he also knew that she was first and foremost a journalist, and that this fact coloured everything she did.

He nodded. 'We have a deal.'

# THIRTY-TWO

# Erbil, Iraq

Scarcely six days had passed since Hart had said goodbye to Nalan Abuna for what he had supposed would be the final time. But he had thought about her constantly in the days that followed – days in which he had tried, but failed, to focus his mind solely on the deterioration of his mother's Alzheimer's, and on the increasing mental fragility of her long-time partner and carer, Clive.

His solemn promise to Amira that he was not returning to Iraq because of Nalan had been somewhat cavalier, therefore. But Amira's jealousy made it next to impossible to deal with her rationally. After all, Hart told himself, they'd been living apart for nearly a year now, but Amira clearly felt she owned a part of him. Still tried to punch his ticket whenever she could. It wasn't reasonable. It wasn't acceptable. But it was there. Still. There were moments in life when a man had to move forwards, and this was one of them.

Hart had every intention of searching for the Copper Scroll if it was humanly possible to do so – the very thought of its existence created a void in his stomach that he knew he would need to fill or go mad. But the prospect of seeing Nalan again, even though she was explicitly promised to another man, overrode whatever passed for stable logic in his mind. One thing bled into another, as it were. No Copper Scroll without Nalan – and without Nalan his search for the Copper Scroll would be a pointless exercise anyway. He would as soon be capable of landing unassisted on the moon as he would be of getting into Iran unaided. So, after a certain amount of prevarication, he had phoned.

Nalan had seemed surprised to hear from him again so soon. But he had swiftly reminded her of the manuscript he had shown her in the Red Interrogation House cellars, and explained the bare bones of the translation to her, and of how his newspaper was unexpectedly commissioning him to take the thing a step further. As a result of this he would be able to pay her well above the daily market rate for her continued assistance, with an added bonus at the end of their collaboration if the story actually led anywhere. Surely this would help her with her imminent marriage plans? No? After a little more persuasion, Nalan agreed to go back on the payroll.

Hart's first suggestion had been that she should meet him at Erbil International Airport, but for some reason Nalan had rejected that idea out of hand. They had finally arranged to meet inside the 7,000-year-old Citadel of Erbil, at the place where the guided tours generally started. Nalan was a registered guide as well as a qualified translator, and so this would not seem out of the ordinary. Hart had no idea why she was being so cautious, but he was sufficiently up on Arab and Kurdish customs to know that things were done differently in Iraq than they were in London. There were parameters. Bridges one couldn't cross. Hart sensed that he would need to keep everything on a very formal level indeed, despite the unprecedented intimacies that he and Nalan had shared as a result of the bombing.

He arrived early at the citadel and sat down on the edge of a fountain, near to the tourist office, to await her appearance. When other guides approached him he waved them away, saying that his guide was arriving shortly. After a while they gave up trying and left him alone.

He stood up when Nalan appeared beneath the entrance arch. For a moment she did not see him, and he had the opportunity to observe her afresh. He had forgotten how small she was. Five foot five at the utmost. Her red-gold hair was gathered behind her head, from where it fanned out across her shoulders like a cloak. Her bangles and bracelets flashed in the early-morning sunlight. As she walked she glanced nervously to her left and right, searching for him.

Looking at her, Hart caught himself wondering, yet again, what she had to be so anxious about. He finally decided that it was only a few days since she had been involved in a particularly gruesome car bombing, in which she had come very close to death, and which had been conducted in a place that held abominable memories for her. So it was hardly surprising that she should be suffering from some form of delayed shock. Christ, he was still in shock himself. Only that morning he had woken at 2 a.m. in his transit hotel in Istanbul, bathed in a muck sweat and babbling to himself about hangings. Such things took time to fade away. The memories were way too raw.

Nalan saw him and stopped in her tracks, her face a mass of conflicting emotions. Then she hurried the last few paces towards him and they embraced, much to the consternation of the citadel's curator, who seemed unused to such public displays of affection. When Nalan smiled apologetically at him, however, he smiled right back at her, and flapped a hand in generous condescension.

Nalan stepped back and looked at Hart. 'I'm sorry I hugged you in public, John. But when I saw your face I had to. All sorts of feelings welled up in me about what happened to us in As Sulaymaniyah. And we Kurds are an affectionate race.' She smiled and canted her head to one side. 'Although we don't normally do it out of doors.'

Hart had caught her scent again when he had hugged her – that elusive mixture of musk, jasmine and citrus that reminded him of the very first time he had consciously touched her, when he was dragging her up into the loft above the Red Interrogation House rape room to escape from their pursuers. Then, as now, she appeared to talk one way and act another – her body language, as it were, was out of sync with her words. Hart, inured to the way Western women responded, was unused to it, and it unsettled him.

'No need to apologize. I loved your hug. I think the curator did too. You should have seen his face when you ran up to me like that.'

Nalan turned away and checked out the other guides. Her expression darkened. 'Do you really want to see around the citadel?'

'I thought it would be as good a place as any for us to talk.'

'Yes. It is. A very good place. But there is also the bazaar. Just round the corner. That might be better. I shall have to cover my hair, though. I think we will go there instead. We stand out far too much here.'

Hart had already caught the direction of Nalan's gaze, and the man she had directed it towards. He knew enough about her by now to trust to her instincts. He watched while she tucked in her hair and settled her hijab about her shoulders.

'Why the hijab there and not here?'

Nalan shrugged. 'It is complicated. Sometimes, in Kurdistan, we women are free, and sometimes we are not. It is not as bad here as in Iran, though, where if you do not wear the hijab in public the Ershad – who are their "guidance" or morality police – will intervene and force you to cover yourself after beating you with sticks. Or if you wear too much lipstick, female Basij officers from the Revolutionary Guard will scrape it off your lips with a razor.'

'You're joking.'

'It is true, John. What happens in the house and what happens in public are two different things entirely. Think of it like Britain in the 1950s, when everyone wore hats outside the house, and if you did not conform to this you were worthless.'

Hart had to stifle a laugh at Nalan's choice of example. 'Until President Kennedy broke the taboo at his inauguration.'

'The taboo. Yes. But there will be no President Kennedy here. And certainly not in Iran until the mullahs are gone.'

Situated one block down from the citadel, the Erbil bazaar was a mass of colour, light, and movement when contrasted to the citadel's sand-coloured uniformity. From the moment one entered the main gate each separate sense was assailed – seeing, hearing, smelling, touching. Carpets, rugs and silks hung over the walkways. Gold and silver jewellery glittered behind the windows of shops, where tea-drinking mothers-in-law were busy negotiating the dowries of their future daughters-in-law with hard-faced merchants and their mercurial assistants.

The bazaar was laid out in sections – all the goldsmiths in one quarter, the butchers in another, the spice merchants in another. Over here for carpets, across there for the near-ubiquitous female jeans, which, like the innumerable varieties of hijab, were displayed on semi-realistic plastic dummies that all looked eerily alike. Women in pairs and trios were browsing the stalls – men were going about their business carrying, bartering, or taking their mid-afternoon breaks in the teahouses, smoking their rented hookah pipes. Policemen in bright blue shirts dodged amongst the crowds, checking whilst not seeming to check. The place was run like a well-oiled machine that merely gave the outward impression of chaos.

'Yallah, yallah,' shouted men pushing trolleys piled high with goods. And it was always men. The few women sellers usually sat cross-legged beside their wares, fanning themselves with the ends of their hijabs or khimars, and refusing to meet the eyes of any men but those they already knew, or who formed part of their family. It was alien but not alien – Hart had been to dozens of such places during his career, but each of them had a marginally different dynamic that required both active thought and appropriate response from the bystander.

'Well,' said Hart, 'this place is certainly private. There can't be more than a couple of thousand people filtering through it at any given moment. Tell me, is there any particular reason why we are meeting here?'

'Please keep moving. And when you see police coming, break away from me and pretend you are a tourist.'

'I am a tourist. That much must be pretty bloody obvious to everyone.'

'Still, John. Pretend.'

'Okay.'

Hart walked beside Nalan until they reached a quieter section which specialized in baskets, shoes and swatches of cloth.

Nalan turned to him after one final check around. 'Now. I need to ask you something. And you must answer me truthfully. It is very important.'

'Fire away. I'm all ears, believe me.'

Nalan glanced up at him to see if he was making fun of her, but the serious look on Hart's face reassured her. 'When we were above the rape rooms in the Amna Suraka. Crawling through the attic space with Rebwar. We passed something. A bunch of old metal, you called it. Just some old junk. What was it that you really saw there?'

Something warned Hart that he should no longer attempt to prevaricate. No longer beat about the bush as he had the last time she had asked him the same question, when they had been in fear for their lives. 'It was a Cinestar camera mount. The one we saw used to be state-of-the-art around 1990, when your parents were imprisoned. You often found them in helicopters. A camera mounted on them could move soundlessly. You could roll, tilt and pan with the help of an assistant. Do pretty much anything you liked, in other words.'

'So Hassif was filming what went on in the room below?'

'It seems like it, yes.'

Nalan's face took on a haunted look. 'So he would have filmed all that happened to my mother? Filmed all the rapes? Filmed me having to watch?'

Hart could scarcely bear to meet her eyes. 'Yes. It seems likely. There was a hole in the floor beneath the Cinestar. It was there for a purpose, surely. They probably tricked it up with a two-way mirror, which was taken away when the place was dismantled. I can't imagine why whoever looted the place left the mount behind. It must have been an oversight. Those things are worth good money.' Hart could tell by Nalan's expression that his discursion wasn't working. He tried to sweeten the pill a little. 'Maybe Hassif was required to send the film on to Saddam Hussein to show what was happening in the prison? Maybe he was required to keep records? I should imagine the stock was all destroyed when Saddam's palaces were looted. It is notoriously flammable.'

Nalan's eyes flashed at him. 'No. Hassif was doing it for his own private pleasure. And nothing was destroyed.'

'How can you possibly know that?'

They breasted a corner of the walkway. Three policemen were coming towards them. Hart stopped to look inside a shop which specialized in the repair of electric hairdryers. A flat-screen television was booming in the background. A black-and-white Egyptian musical from the 1960s was playing – the women with heavy make-up and without hijabs, and wearing fashionably short skirts.

Nalan moved on ahead of him and past the policemen, as if she were shopping alone. None of them gave her a second look. When they passed Hart they smiled at him as if to say, 'Well? And how do you like our wonderful bazaar?' Hart smiled back and pretended to blow-dry his hair. The policemen laughed politely, but – and he immediately regretted this – they would remember him now.

He caught up with Nalan round the next corner.

She turned to face him square on, ignoring the few customers hurrying by. 'I know Hassif filmed what happened to my mother, and my own and my father's very private humiliation, because he told me so. What you tell me now only confirms that what he says is true.'

'Says? He is still alive? I thought the Peshmerga got him. I thought they killed them all.'

'Not Hassif. He is like an oily rat that slips out of the hands of anyone who tries to catch him.'

Hart looked around in consternation. 'Is he here? Back in Iraq? Is that why we are being so circumspect?'

Nalan shook her head. 'He is not here. No. He would not last a moment in Kurdistan. We would put him up against the nearest wall and shoot him. He is across the border in Iran. And he wants me to go there and meet him.'

# THIRTY-THREE

Hart and Nalan stood in the entranceway to a shuttered and barred shop. Hart glanced down the passageway between the shops to check if they were being watched or marked out in any way. It was fast becoming a habit. 'If you go to Iran he will kill you.'

Nalan gave a vehement shake of the head. 'No. He is not as powerful in Iran as he was in Iraq. There, he is only a servant. Here, he was the master. He says he must tell me something. About my parents. Something I need to know.'

'You don't believe him, do you?'

'Of course not. He is Hassif. Totally evil. But now I know he is in Bukan I have to go. I need to do this.'

Hart put out a hand as if to stay her from leaving for the border at that precise moment. 'But that's just what he wants you to do. Can't you see? You are one of the few remaining eyewitnesses to the crimes he committed. If the

International Criminal Court ever gets hold of him, your testimony alone could see him imprisoned for life.'

'They will never get hold of him. Iran will protect him. He works for them now. I told you this.'

'Yet another reason why you should not go over there.'

Nalan shook her head. 'He sent me photographs, John. Of men doing things to my mother. He even knew my phone number to call me. Hearing his voice again on the phone made me go weak with fear. It was as if I was a little child again, back in the prison. I cannot understand this man. His given name, Rahim, means merciful and kind. How could God allow such a man to have a name like his?'

'God made a mistake in Hassif's case. A bad one.'

'No. God is not responsible for filth like Hassif. They create themselves. A man like Hassif manufactures his own destiny. He will answer to God, yes. But that will come later. On this earth I want him to answer only to me.'

Hart watched her for a moment, his eyes travelling over the familiar and yet unfamiliar features. 'How can you possibly get into Iran?'

'I am a Kurd. It is easy. I have cousins. Iraqi Kurds travel across the border all the time.'

'Are you serious?'

'Why should I not be serious?'

Hart burst out laughing. It was neither the time nor the place for levity, but he couldn't help it. The expression on Nalan's face when he'd asked her the question had been one of such outraged astonishment that for a moment she had looked like a surprised cat. 'And me? Can I get into Iran just as easily?'

'You? No. It would be impossible.'

'And why, pray?'

'Now you are not being serious, John. You cannot be seriously asking me this question.'

'I am. Seriously.'

She touched his arm and they began walking again. Soon they passed into a courtyard in which carpets were draped over frames and laid out flat on the ground, the better to be admired. They both stood looking at one of the carpets. When the shopkeeper came over to see if they wanted to buy it, both smiled and shook their heads simultaneously. The shopkeeper returned to his game of chess.

Nalan turned towards Hart. 'Any foreigner from the United Kingdom or the United States travelling from Iraq to Iran will be instantly under suspicion of being a spy. The border is very fluid, and many people cross – many, many lorries, and much oil and cement. But few foreigners. And all of these will be in tourist parties, or under special licence, with papers that have already been checked. Visas that have already been issued and certified. It is not a matter here of just turning up at the border and asking to be let through. When they find out you are a journalist—'

'A photojournalist.'

'A photojournalist then. To them this will be even worse. Cameras talk. And cameras can record. The Iranian Revolutionary Guards are not stupid. They will soon discover that you were involved in the recent bomb attack—'

'Innocently involved.'

'This is irrelevant. You killed a man, John. A man who was possibly Iranian. Or at least trained by the Iranians. Although no one will ever be able to prove this, of course. So they will have you on file already. You will be setting your head in the. . .' She hesitated. 'What is it? The French thing they executed people with during the revolution?'

'The guillotine.'

'You will be setting your head in the guillotine.'

This time it was Hart who moved Nalan on. They were already being watched by both chess players, and various other of the shopkeepers. Was he becoming unnecessarily paranoid with all this talk of files and spies and police? 'And illegally? Can one cross the border so that no one knows?'

'Are we talking about you or me?' She raised an eyebrow at him until he was forced to nod in affirmation.

'Me.'

'You do not speak Farsi, John. You do not even speak Kurdish. You are tall. And blond. And pale. A few days ago your face was on all the news programmes. In the papers. On the Internet. For you it would be suicide.'

'But is it possible?'

'Is it possible? Yes. Of course it is possible. People I know do it all the time. But you are not people. You are John Hart the photojournalist. John Hart the British spy. John Hart the Dish of the Day on the Revolutionary Guard menu.'

# THIRTY-FOUR

'And have you met your future husband yet?'

Hart was sitting with Nalan in the back of the taxi which was taking them the ninety-five kilometres from Erbil to the Pank Tourist Village in Rawanduz. Outside the taxi windows the mountains rose up on either side of them in layers, as if some great hand had crafted them out of clay and interleaved them with vegetation and stunted trees, seemingly at random.

'Yes. But I do not wish to talk about him.'

'Oh. Okay.' Hart knew when not to pursue a tricky subject. He looked out at the gorge. An untidy mass of water was cascading down the mountainside, circumventing a projecting rock onto which some madman had constructed a viewing platform. The platform looked in danger of being imminently submerged. 'So why are we going to a tourist village?'

'Because it is the only such place in Iraq. And because these are the Korek mountains, and where we stay in the village it is already 1,000 metres high. And because the

Iranian border post at Piranshahr is only forty minutes further up the road.'

'Shit.'

'It is fine, John. You will be safe here. There is a rollercoaster. And a Ferris wheel. And a dry bobsled run. Bumper cars. A toboggan.'

'Well that's okay then. At least we can have a bit of fun while we wait for the police sweep.'

He lingered in the reception area while Nalan confirmed both their rooms. He was surprised when a golf cart appeared outside and their luggage was piled in the back. They were driven to a pair of bungalows bordering a children's playground.

'I can't get my head around this,' Hart said, when their driver had left them. 'We're up in the mountains, just a few miles from the Iranian border, where some of the worst of the fighting took place during the Iran/Iraq War and beyond, and we're staying in a holiday camp. Which, to my eye at least, seems pretty much empty. What the heck is going on here?'

'Hazem Kurda built this place. He was a refugee from Saddam Hussein. He built this to show his confidence in a free Kurdistan.'

Hart bowed his head in acknowledgement. What else could he do? 'And why are we here?'

'To meet some people. They will come here tomorrow. I owe you my life, John. So I am going to arrange for you to get into Iran illegally. In Iraq, we believe what a man says when he speaks directly to our eyes. You tell me you wish to get inside and find your ancestor's scroll. I believe you. But you must believe me also. I have told you of my reasons for entering Iran. Now we will both do so, but in different ways. When we are the other side of the border we will meet again. Then I will help you go where you want to go. I owe you this. It is not far. Maybe a three-hour drive. There will be checkpoints. But fewer than in Iraq. Still. You will not be able to make such a trip without help.'

'Are you really going to do this for me?'

'Why do you always doubt me?'

'I'm sorry. I don't mean to doubt you. I'm just bewildered, that's all. If we were in the West it would take weeks to organize such a trip.'

'Here, everything is much quicker. There are no rules. No regulations. You see all the cars we passed on the road coming up here? None of them have insurance. Why? Because it does not exist here. If we are ill, there are no Iraqi doctors. We rely on Iranians, who are much better at this than we are anyway. This border area is a fluid place. Sometimes they close it. Sometimes not. Sometimes the lorries are backed up down the road for many kilometres and their drivers take days to pass through. At other times it is all done very quickly. Much is random here. We need to be lucky. If we are, with God's help, it will all pass easily. If we are not, it will be very bad indeed.'

Hart hesitated on the doorstep of his bungalow. 'How are we going to play tonight then? Will you join me for dinner? Are we allowed to sit together here at least?'

Nalan laughed. 'Of course we are allowed to sit together. This is a holiday resort. People can do what they want.'

'Might we even be able to get a bottle of wine? I mean, do you even drink wine?'

Nalan clapped her hands together. Then she unpinned her hijab. 'I am a Chaldean Christian. Of course I drink wine. And beer. Even whisky, although I do not like it. I even go without my hijab in places like this.'

'How about champagne then?'

Nalan frowned. 'Now you are being too much of an optimist even for a Britannia.'

'A Britannia?'

'That is what they call the English here in the local Sorani dialect.'

Hart gave her a mocking bow. 'Then this Britannia invites you for dinner tonight. With or without champagne. But with his deepest thanks.'

# THIRTY-FIVE

Nalan was wearing a floor-length traditional Kurdish-style dress in black silk, with matching silver-filigree jewellery at her throat, wrist and around her waist. The jewellery incorporated dangling silver coins and lapis lazuli inlays in the shape of diamonds. Her arms were bare, but covered in diaphanous gauze, and she had painted her fingernails and was wearing make-up for the first time since he had met her. Imprinted on her dress was a flower design in pearl beads, which was echoed both above and below her waist.

Hart stood at the door of her bungalow and cursed himself for his own slapdash fashion sense. He was wearing a worn pair of black Levi cords, set off by a favourite rust-red Murray's Toggery Shop shirt from Nantucket, which was fraying badly at the collar, and which he couldn't bear to throw away. 'I'm sorry. I didn't realize.' He indicated his own clothes, then spread his hands apologetically to encompass hers. 'You look beautiful. Very beautiful.'

'Thank you. And what didn't you realize, John? You look nice. Like a ruffian. But nice.'

'A ruffian?'

'Yes. Didn't I get this word right?'

Hart coughed behind his hand. 'Exactly right.' He wasn't sure if he ought to kiss Nalan on both cheeks or not. 'How do men and women greet each other here?'

'We do not kiss, if that is what you mean. Not amongst the different sexes. But if we know each other well we sometimes do this.' She leaned towards him and drew his forehead down to touch hers. Hart's had quite a long way to go. 'But this will only be done in private, like here, and not in a public place.'

'Right.' Hart was still breathing in Nalan's scent. He doubted whether in his life he had seen a more beautiful or desirable woman. He fought back a disastrous desire to reach forwards and take her head between his hands and kiss her. 'Shall I call for a golf cart? Or shall we walk?'

'Let us walk through the park. It is a nice evening. The fountains will be playing. And it is too early in the year for mosquitoes.'

She led him along the road and down some stone steps until they came to a parking lot, spanning the main park. 'I want you to look over here.' She gestured that he should walk ahead of her to the very edge of the bollarded area.

The views across the gorge were breathtaking. Pinpoints of light were starting up from some of the houses on the opposite side of the span, and far below them they could hear the snow-swollen river churning past on its way down from the mountains.

'You've been here many times?'

'No,' said Nalan. 'Only once. With a school party I was helping teach English. I had no time to myself. I have always wanted to come back ever since.'

'Probably with someone you love.'

She glanced up at him. 'Probably. Yes.' She turned quickly away. 'You see those mountains? In the far distance?'

'Yes.'

'Iran is over there. And Hassif. But this evening I do not want to think of either. Is this possible?'

'It's possible.' Hart took her arm and they walked through the park towards the restaurant.

As they approached the entrance, and almost without seeming to, Nalan drifted away from him. Hart understood, and did not try to follow her.

They reached the doors to the restaurant with an eight-foot gap between them. They might have been total strangers, with all the unspoken intimacy of the last twenty minutes forgotten. It was another of Kurdistan's paradoxes, Hart decided, this feeling of extreme sensuality followed by an aloofness prescribed by social custom and religious diktat. And for the benefit and protection of whom? The waiters? The maître d'? The pastry chef?

They took a table at the far end of the restaurant complex. The place could not by any stretch of the imagination be termed intimate. There were possibly fifty tables set out in an absurdly well-lit room, which boasted the size and dimensions of a gymnasium. They were the only guests.

'Doesn't look like school is out,' said Hart.

'No. It is not that time of the year.'

Hart glanced towards a central glass-display console. 'Well, they do at least have wine. That much is for certain.'

'It will be very expensive.'

'But would you like some?'

Nalan met his eyes across the table. 'Yes. Very much.'

Hart went across to the console and pointed out a bottle of Lebanese wine he thought Nalan might like to the waiter. There was a part of him that felt like a naughty schoolboy shirking class and out for a lark.

When he got back to the table, he encouraged Nalan to choose their food, and he was glad that he had done so when a succession of wonderful mixed tabbouleh salads were brought for mezza, followed by different kebabs, koftas and kibbeh. He got Nalan to explain every course to him, and what meat or fish they were eating. Soon, almost without realizing it, they had drunk two bottles of Chateau Musar between them – her half bottle to his one and a half – alongside Hart's favourite *doogh* drinking yogurt for good health, or so he insisted. They finished their meal with small portions of *kanafeh*, a form of pastry-like milk pudding made from cheese and semolina, and the near ubiquitous baklava, which they washed down with their Turkish-style coffee.

'You have a good appetite,' Hart told her.

'You think I am fat?' she said.

'Fat? You? There's nothing to you. You'd blow away in a strong wind. When I had to lift you up—' He came to an abrupt stop.

'When you lifted me up into the loft above the rape rooms. Yes. Is that what you were saying?'

Hart watched her from across the table. 'Yes. That is what I am saying. That is exactly what I am saying. When I lifted you up into the loft above the rape rooms, you were so light in my arms I felt you might fly away from me. I even imagined something then. An odd thing.' Hart could feel the wine he had drunk working away inside him. What was he going to say? He didn't quite know. All he knew was that he couldn't hold back any longer. He had to declare himself in some form or another or throw himself under one of the nearby tables and bury himself in a pile of tablecloths and crockery. 'I thought you leaned forwards for an instant and rubbed your cheek against mine. I may have been imagining it. . .'

'No. You were not imagining it.'

Hart felt the muscles around his heart clench and unclench in his chest. 'I wasn't imagining it?'

'No.'

'Why did you do it?'

Nalan looked away from him and down towards the floor. 'I should not tell you this.'

'Please. Please tell me.'

She sighed and turned her head, if that were possible, even further away from his gaze. 'You moved something in me. Something I did not feel could be moved by a man. In the

213

place we were, with the memories it held for me, I found myself wishing to overlay those memories with something better. Something purer. So I touched you. Knowing we would both probably die.'

Hart reached for Nalan's hand across the table, but she evaded him, placing both her hands in her lap.

'I've been thinking about you every day since then,' he said, with the passion of hopelessness. 'You are the real reason I came back here. You must know that. The story is secondary. I came back to see you.'

'I know.' Still she did not raise her eyes to meet his.

Hart felt as if he were climbing high into the rigging of a tall-masted ship – high, high up, with all the world's oceans beneath him. If he fell, all would be taken away from him. If he could simply keep his balance, somehow, by some miracle, and not tip over into the sea, the view would be his for ever. 'I know I should not be speaking to you in this way. I know you are getting married soon.'

'Yes. I am getting married soon.'

Hart flailed around for the right words. The tall-masted ship was tipping, slowly, over onto its side. 'But you are not married yet. And you are here with me. And you are beautiful. When I look at you I cannot believe how beautiful you are. I want to reach across the table and melt into you. . .'

'As if I was a bowl of ice cream?'

Hart's eyes widened in shock. Then he realized Nalan was laughing with him, and not at him. That she was looking him directly in the eyes and laughing with him. In joy. 'Yes. Rum and raisin. Made with real milk and not powdered. And with the raisins well soaked in Bundaberg Rum. And bought on a street in Italy from a travelling gelato salesman who has come directly from his family's house to sell his wares so that they are as fresh as fresh can be.'

'John, you are mad. The things you say.'

'I didn't start this. It was you who brought up the idea of ice cream.'

'I'm surprised you can think of anything edible after the meal we have just had.'

Hart had himself under control again. He had been about to say something stupid – even more stupid than what he had already said – and ruin everything. And Nalan had known it, and had diffused it with her comment about the ice cream. It had been done with such elegance and tact that he felt overwhelmed with gratitude towards her. She had saved him from making a total ass of himself, and allowed him to save face at the same time. His admiration and respect for her was increasing by the minute. 'Would you like to walk back?' he said. 'We could go up to the parapets again. See the gorge at night.'

'How do you see a gorge at night?'

Hart swallowed. His side of this conversation wasn't going well at all. Serve him right for drinking so much. 'Well. Feel it then. Look at the lights across the valley. Listen to the river.'

'I would like that very much.'

It was a lot colder outside, and Hart cursed himself for not having thought to bring a jacket he could have offered to slip over Nalan's shoulders. They were 1,000 metres above sea level, for Pete's sake, and not long out of winter. He was an idiot. 'It is cold. Would you mind if I put my arm round you?'

'No. I would not mind.'

Hart felt as if he were walking on eggshells. What was he to do? How should he play this? Here he was with a woman from another culture to his entirely, and about to be married, and all he wished to do was to take her in his arms and kiss her. But something was atrophying his every movement.

They stopped by the concrete bollards near the parking place, close to where they had stood before supper.

Nalan stepped in front of him and then snuggled herself back against him, so that he would be protecting her from the worst of the wind, which was coming from directly behind them. It was such a natural movement that he did not hesitate. He put his arms round her shoulders and they both stood looking out across the vast black emptiness ahead of them, and towards the tiny pinpricks of light on the other side of the valley. From time to time Hart bent forwards and nuzzled the top of her head with his cheek. But for some obscure reason he still did not dare to turn her round and kiss her full on the mouth. Perhaps he did not wish to spoil the magic?

'I think we must go back now, John. You have no jacket and I have no coat. We have both come ill-prepared for a night up here in the mountains.'

Hart could feel her slipping through his hands.

'Yes. I hope there's some heating in the rooms. An open fire would be nice.'

216

Nalan laughed. She took his hand in hers and they walked back towards their bungalows.

The sudden cold, far from sobering Hart up, appeared to be doing the exact opposite. Why could he never learn? 'And tomorrow?'

'Some men will come here to meet us. To see you. We will speak with them. They will want money from you. But they are honest. You will see. Later, you will go with them.'

Hart could hardly believe they were talking like this. As far as he was concerned, at that precise moment, Iran and the Copper Scroll and his bloody ancestor could go hang themselves. And the rest of the world along with them.

They stopped at the entrance to Nalan's bungalow. Hart saw the night slipping away from him. But he had no idea how to retrieve it.

'Thank you for this evening. And thank you for being such a gentleman, John. You have made it very easy for me.'

'I wish I hadn't.'

'But you did. And I value that. More than you can know.'

Hart bent forwards and they touched foreheads again. She gave him a quick peck on each cheek as a sort of consolation prize. Then she was gone, and he was left standing outside her door, in his shirtsleeves, in a howling gale, and facing the prospect of an evening spent watching CNN or Al Jazeera or whatever the hell else Iraqis received on their satellite dishes.

Should he go back to the restaurant and drown his sorrows? Probably not. He would need to keep his wits about him for whatever occurred the next day. Well, maybe he would go back to his room and send Amira a text in the code they had agreed on back in England. If he succeeded in passing over into Iran, there would be no more communication like that open to him. He would be alone out there in deepest hyperspace.

The story of his life.

## THIRTY-SIX

Hart showered and brushed his teeth. Then he lay in bed with the lights off and thought about Nalan. She had gone as far as she dared go with him; that much was clear. Her aunt and uncle had set her up for an arranged marriage, and she intended to go through with it, come what may. It was the right thing for her to do, he couldn't deny that. For where would an affair with him lead her? Absolutely nowhere. The last thing she needed to be doing at this point in her life was to betray her intended husband and prejudice her future.

There was a soft knock at his French windows. So soft that he wasn't quite sure that he had heard it.

Hart sat up in bed. Something told him not to switch on the light. He moved to the window and opened the curtains. Nalan stood outside. She was dressed in black jeans and a loose brown T-shirt.

He pulled the French windows open and allowed her to slip in past him.

'We need to talk, John. In private. And this is the best place to do it. But don't switch on the lights. It is safer that way.'

As she passed him, her hair drifted across his wrist. Hart was tempted to reach across and take it into his hands – to lower his face into it and breathe in its perfume. Instead he closed the sliding doors and drew the curtains back into place as if it was every night of the year that a desirable young woman entered his bedroom unexpectedly as if in answer to a prayer.

'I'm sorry. You were in bed.'

'It doesn't matter. I wasn't asleep. Just sitting here thinking.'

'Climb back in. I will sit on the other side. We can talk better that way. And it will be warmer for you.'

Hart was grateful, now, that he had decided to go to bed in his T-shirt and underpants, thanks to the cold, rather than in his more usual nude state. Despite this, he found himself utterly wrong-footed by his own prejudices. Nalan seemed perfectly comfortable alone with him in his room. It was he who was attributing some ulterior motive to her every act. It made perfect sense for her to go back to her own room, change, slip out the back way, well protected from the street lights, and come and talk to him privately. Hell, what they were intending to do was sheer madness. They needed to discuss it first. And in the strictest possible privacy. It was only he who was letting other stuff get in the way of it.

He got back into bed and leaned against the headboard. Nalan did the same on her side. She glanced across at him.

Her face was lit up from the reflection of the street lights which leached in through the fanlight above the front door of the bungalow. The light caught the edges of her hair and turned them gold, like an aureole around her head. She looked more beautiful than ever in the half-light. Hart tried to relax, but it was impossible.

'The men coming to see us tomorrow lunchtime are called *kulbar*. They are cross-border couriers. Men who carry tyres and tobacco and textiles and electronic goods across the border illegally. These men are often killed by snipers, or border police waiting in ambush for them. But they know every way and means to cross the border. Every track. How to evade the Iranian drones which pick up the heat of the bodies at night.'

'How is that possible?'

'They travel by horseback. Or with sheep. The drones are not as clever as the ones the Americans have. They find it difficult to differentiate between man and animal. And there are so many *kulbar* and *kasebkar* going across at any one time, what are the Iranians going to do? Massacre them all? Smuggling is illegal, yes. But the normal punishment is usually only a few months' detention or a fine. It is only recently – from 2012 onwards – that the border guards have started shooting. There has been much anger about this. More than one hundred *kulbars* have been killed already. Many others wounded. There is a campaign to stop these abuses. Far less are shot now. Now they shoot mostly only the horses.'

'Mostly? That's encouraging.'

221

'You will go across with one of the *kulbar* tomorrow night. You will dress in Kurdish clothes. Baggy trousers. Baggy shirt. A turban showing to which tribe you belong. White rubber boots.'

'White rubber boots?'

'Yes. Many Kurdish men in Iran wear them. I do not know why. Perhaps it is a fashion?' She burst out laughing. 'I hope they can find some big enough to fit you.'

Hart was having a hard time trying to keep his attention focused entirely on what Nalan was saying. 'And you?'

'I shall be going over by taxi, as I always do. Then my cousin will pick me up on the other side of the border.'

'Does Hassif know you are coming?'

'Of course not. No. This would be madness. I want to surprise him.'

Hart was tempted to say something flip. About how crazy she was to think she could outwit a worm like Hassif. Something along those lines. Then he realized that he was on pretty shaky ground himself.

For the very first time he felt that familiar hollowness in the stomach he'd grown used to when taking photographs on the front line of a conflict. He called it battle nerves whenever he chose to dissect the feeling for himself. Other people, he knew, might call it fear. It was something you had to work your way through. Either that, or give up on your profession.

'Do you have any idea what you intend to do when you find him?'

'I have an idea, yes.'

222

'And are you willing to share that idea with me?'

'No. It is better you have no knowledge of what I am going to do.'

'You're not intending to try and kill him, are you?'

Nalan brushed away his question with a hand gesture. 'I will not talk about it. Much depends on my male cousins. My father was leader of our tribe. He was a respected man. It is not only I who have a score to settle with Hassif. My tribe have a blood feud with him. Now that he has revealed himself to us, everything has changed. Before this, no one knew where he had gone. Even if he was still alive. Now we know. For he has spoken to me in person. This was a big mistake for him. Though he will not realize it. He is an old man who thinks he is young. And such a man is very stupid. Old age should bring wisdom and not vanity. Vanity is for the young.'

Hart turned to her. 'You speak as if you are old yourself. You are twenty-seven, Nalan. That is nothing.'

'One is as old as the things one has experienced. I was old at five. Even older at three. No child should see what Hassif showed me. No child should undergo what he made me undergo.'

'No. That is true. You are right.'

When Hart thought about it later, he realized that he had no clear idea how Nalan came to be lying in his arms. Had he made the first move? Had she? But there it was. Maybe he had reached across to comfort her? He didn't know. But she had curled up in his arms and he had drawn the covers over her and they had lain, entwined like that, and saying nothing.

Once, he had tried to kiss her on the lips, but she had shaken her head, and he had respected that. Some time during the night, though, she had kicked off her jeans and had lain tight against him, half naked now, but seemingly certain by this stage that he would not abuse her trust. This time she had allowed herself to be kissed. Later, much later, he had felt her hand snake down to his groin and hold him. Move a little. Then a little more. He had eased his hand in front of her and done the same thing, brushing her nipples with his free fingers. He had felt her breath fluttering against his cheek. Had heard her cry out in ecstasy, just as he, later, had cried out in his turn.

When he awoke again, around five o'clock, he realized she had gone, like a wraith, back to her own room. He felt her side of the bed for residual warmth, and when he found none, he rolled over and lay where she had lain, with his head in her pillow, drinking in her scent.

He had heard French people speaking of *les nuits blanches*, sleepless nights – nights spent together but without having penetrative sex, perhaps? – but he had never experienced one. Now he had. And it had been the most complete experience of his life.

# THIRTY-SEVEN

The *kulbar* and his son stood incongruously next to the swings in the children's playground near to Hart's and Nalan's bungalows at the Pank Tourist Village. The boy was young enough, in Hart's opinion, to consider playing on them, but the hard lines of his face and the wariness in his eyes suggested that he had seen far too much harshness in real life to retain any boyish outlook at all.

The moustachioed older man was dressed in a blue and white striped collarless shirt with a T-shirt visible underneath, baggy Kurdish trousers and, yes, just as Nalan had forecast, white wellington boots. He wore a red and white turban, or *jamadani*, around his head, indicating his adherence to the Barzani clan, but his son, not being considered a man yet, was bareheaded.

'I cannot tell you this man's real name. But you may call him Ronas, and his son Bemo. They are travelling across the border tonight with a consignment of cigarettes for a village near Piranshahr. They have agreed to take you across with them. You must give them a hundred dollars.'

'A hundred dollars?'

'Is that too much?'

Hart shook his head. 'No. It seems incredibly cheap. Seeing as they will be risking their lives for me.'

'They risk their lives every time they go across the border. Usually for about ten dollars in profits. You will be making their voyage a lucrative one. The equivalent of ten normal journeys.'

'Jesus Christ.'

'This is their reality, John. It is far removed from your own, I think.'

'You might say that.'

'If you are attacked they will leave you. Their only job is to get you across the border. Once you get to the village they will show you a safe place to wait. I will come with my cousin and pick you up.'

'What if you don't show up?'

'Then you will be a blond-haired Britannia sitting in a village in Iran, with no entry or exit visa, and in Kurdish costume.' Nalan started to smile, but stopped herself in time. 'You can still say no to this. Give them ten dollars and they will go away and forget you. This is a good tribe. Very honourable. Not like some.'

'No. If you're going, I'm going.'

Nalan dropped her eyes. But not before Hart saw the echo of their night together flashed back at him.

226

'Please give me the money.'

Hart handed over the hundred dollars. 'Are you sure. . .'

'I am sure. These people do what they say they do.'

The older man, Ronas, gave Hart a low salutation with his hand, but the boy, Bemo, seeing the amount of money his father was pocketing, raised his salutation to above the eyes, which Nalan had explained to Hart meant deep respect.

If a hundred dollars is all it takes to buy deep respect, Hart found himself thinking, it is no surprise these countries are all so corrupt.

The man and the boy walked off. Hart watched them for a while. 'He really takes the boy across with him?'

'It is a spare pair of shoulders that costs him nothing. They can almost double the number of cigarettes they traffic like this.'

'How come they make so little money then?'

'Because another man buys the cigarettes over at the Turkish border and employs them as *kulbars*.'

'So they take the risks and he gets the profits?'

'Yes. That is the way of the world, is it not?'

# THIRTY-EIGHT

That night, Ronas and Bemo were waiting for him three kilometres from the border area, on a stony track leading to a hamlet of partially thatched and partially corrugated houses.

Hart had left his mobile phone, his clothes, and all his cameras – bar one Zeiss-lensed pocket camera – behind at the Pank Resort, in storage, just as Nalan had suggested to him. His passport and his money were hanging from his belt in a leather pouch tucked down inside the waistband of his trousers.

Once the lights of the taxi had disappeared safely down the track, Hart transferred the belt and pouch to the inside of the capacious Kurdish trousers Ronas had brought for him. He slid on a thick woollen shirt over his T-shirt, and wriggled inside the matted shepherd's coat that Ronas had used to wrap the bundle of clothing in. Then the two of them, father and son, grinning broadly as if they were about to play a practical joke on him, placed a conical cap onto his head, and wound a turban tightly around the cap until it was firmly in place. The turban felt fine, but Hart couldn't help wondering for a moment whether he wouldn't get fleas from the coat. In the end he decided that fleas were the least of his worries.

The oddest thing of all was that there was no way that he and the two Kurds could communicate beyond the most primitive of hand signals or the cautious exchange of smiles. They spoke no English and he no Kurdish. Nalan had warned him of this, but the reality came as a shock. He would be entirely in their hands, with no ability to influence what was happening to him. As a means of disempowerment, it was shatteringly complete.

Ronas switched off his torch and hid it deep inside his coat. Then he signalled to his son and Hart to follow him. Hart set off after the two figures in what now seemed to him to be pitch darkness. After a little while his eyes began to accustom themselves to the small quantities of residual light reflecting off the rocks around him. He gradually made out that they were passing down a stony, well-worn track. After about half an hour they came to a clearing. A horse was tethered to the single remaining tree in the centre of the clearing. The horse had been fitted with a wooden frame in lieu of a saddle. Ronas and Bemo began loading the horse with cartons of cigarettes. Hart motioned to them that he would like to help, but they shook their heads.

When the horse was fully laden, and its burden covered with plastic sheeting, Ronas turned to his son. Bemo slung an empty sack onto his back, supported by three ropes – one around the waist and two over his shoulders, effectively turning the sack into a large rucksack. Ronas filled the sack to bursting. Then he beckoned Hart across and went through the same process with him. Before he did so he pointed up at the sky with a warning look on his face. Hart assumed this meant that Ronas was aware of the Iranian drones, and that he felt that carrying the sackful of cigarettes would break up Hart's silhouette and perhaps afford him a little camouflage. But the gulf between them was so immense that, for all he knew, Ronas could have been suggesting something entirely different.

Hart reckoned, by the end of the loading process, that Ronas had burdened him with a minimum of 8,000 cigarettes, or a rough tally of forty or so cartons. They weighed a significant amount. Hart began to dread the walk ahead of him. The sack they had given him was the equivalent of carrying a fair-sized toddler on his back without the advantage of comfortable strapping. The ropes were already cutting into his shoulders – he didn't like to think how he would feel by the time they had completed the border crossing. But he couldn't fault Ronas's logic. If one has to take a Britannia across the mountains, one might as well find a use for the bastard.

They began to walk. Hart started to sing songs in his head. He began with 'Loch Lomond', as that fitted the smart pace the two Kurds were keeping up. He moved on to 'My Bonny Lies Over the Ocean', followed by 'I Want to Buy a Paper Doll' and 'Stardust'. By that time he was pretty much out of songs he actually knew the words to, thanks to his mother's early influence, so he went back to the beginning of his repertoire and started over again. He wondered if this was why US Marines sang so loudly and with such irritating constancy when they were out on exercise.

Three hours into their walk Ronas indicated that they should stop for a rest. They were up high now, on the plateau, and the wind was seeping into every crevice of Hart's coat. He had been sweating, and when the cigarettes were levered off his shoulders, he realized that his back was drenched. He huddled up against a stone and wished he was back at the Pank Resort, in bed, with Nalan lying in his arms. Had she passed through the border yet? He had no watch on him any more, so he had lost any precise sense of time, but his best estimate put it a little after two o'clock in the morning. So yes, she would have passed through a long time ago now.

He accepted some water from Ronas's gourd, and tried to rub a little circulation back into his frozen hands. He was almost grateful when Ronas loaded him up again and they could resume walking.

It took Hart another hour to warm up. Bemo came to him at one point and handed him some dried meat, similar to biltong, Hart supposed, and he chewed on that while they were walking. Everything was done in the strictest silence. The only movement either of the two Kurds made beyond striding ahead of him in single file up the track was to twitch on the horse's halter whenever the animal had difficulty negotiating a stony slope.

About five hours into the traverse, the two Kurds in front of him broke away from the established track and along a small defile. This brought them, after twenty minutes of scrambling, onto a smaller, less well-defined track. Hart suspected that they must already be in Iran, and that Ronas was leading them away from where he knew border guards might be lying in wait.

They followed this lesser trail for another hour, with the sun's rays burgeoning in front of them. Hart was marching in an exhausted rhythm now, like that of a man endeavouring to complete a marathon that has seriously over-faced him – he had given up singing in his head a long time ago. Instead, he plonked his feet wherever the horse's hind legs fell, trusting that the animal, which was more heavily burdened than he, would be far too tired to consider lashing backwards.

The explosion rocked the earth he was standing on, engulfing him in a minor whirlwind, and causing his ears to hiss in protest. Stones and pieces of debris fell around him like solid rain. Hart was cast back onto his rucksack, with his legs flailing in the air like a cockchafer. For a moment he imagined that he was back in the cafe again, in As Sulaymaniyah, moments after the car bomb attack. But this explosion had been a lesser one than that – almost a thunder crack really, more than a bomb. Hart threw off his pack and hastened past the horse, which was frozen to the spot, its nostrils flaring in fear.

Both Ronas and Bemo were on the ground. Bemo was throwing himself about and moaning. Ronas was silent.

His body was in an awkward position, as if he had collapsed beneath the weight of the burden he was carrying.

Hart stopped when he reached Ronas's body. The older man's legs had been blown off below the knee by what could only have been a mine. The body, which was entirely still, seemed almost bled out. Hart suspected that Ronas must have been conscious for some time for the blood to have dispersed like that, which meant that he, Hart, must have been temporarily knocked out by the concussion without realizing it. He'd been mildly concussed only ten days before. Now he prayed that he wasn't double-concussed. For if he had second-impact syndrome, which he knew from his Hostile Environment Training carried with it the danger of brain swelling and cerebral oedema caused by the brain no longer being able to regulate its own diameter, they'd all be left high and dry. He'd never make it down the mountain again.

He turned to the boy. Bemo was holding his midriff and groaning. Hart bent down and tried to get a look at Bemo's wound, but the boy wouldn't let go of his stomach. When Hart tried to prise his hands apart Bemo spat at him. Hart stood up, weaving. He knew what must have happened. They had been walking in single file. Ronas had stepped on a mine – Nalan had warned him that this could happen with mines seeded during the 1980–88 Iran/Iraq War and now partially revealed thanks to precipitation and snow erosion. Ronas had taken the full force of the blast. Bemo, five feet behind his father, had been caught by the residual shrapnel. The horse, eight feet behind Bemo and on a long tether, was unharmed, and Hart, tucked away behind the horse, had been similarly protected.

Hart knew about landmines. He had seen their effects before. This was an old-style anti-personnel mine, designed to maim and not to kill, so that the enemy would be forced into the logistical nightmare of first providing medical aid and then getting the wounded party out of an 'at risk' area. Hart was now faced with a similar dilemma.

He tried again with the boy, but to no avail. Bemo was grasping his stomach almost in anger, his face taut, every sinew on his cheeks and neck drawn tight.

Hart left him for a moment to check again on his father. He bent down and took Ronas's pulse. It was just as he suspected. The older man was dead. No one could survive such a catastrophic loss of blood and live.

Hart cleared the wooden frame on the horse's back of all its cigarettes. The sun was above the horizon now, and the full horror of what had happened was clearly visible to him. He loaded Ronas's body onto the frame and tied it in place with ropes gleaned from the rucksacks. He walked over to Bemo. Bemo was saying something over and over again to him and indicating with his chin. Hart realized that Bemo was pointing to his father's lower legs, which were lying either side of the track, as if dropped there by a passing bird of prey.

Overcoming his revulsion, Hart gathered up the legs and tucked them inside Ronas's coat. Only then did Bemo allow himself to be lifted up and placed against his father on the frame. The boy made no sound during this time. But still he held onto his stomach and refused to allow Hart to look beneath his fingers. Hart decided that there was little use anyway in knowing what lay beneath the boy's clasped hands, as he had neither medicaments nor bandages to offer – he would only be adding to Bemo's discomfort by forcing the issue. In this case the boy's instincts were probably sound.

The sun was well over the hills now. Hart felt furiously unprotected. He started along the track, obsessively searching ahead of himself for the telltale trace of other mines. Whenever he could, he zigzagged from one side of the track to the other – even clambering over rocks, on occasion, using as his logic that thirty-year-old landmines were less likely to be concealed in broken terrain than on a main track.

Behind him, on the horse, Bemo started to groan. Hart stopped what he was doing and searched through Ronas's coat for the gourd that he knew hung there. Thank Christ it was intact. He gave Bemo some water to sip, and then bathed the boy's face with his bare hands in an effort to afford him a little extra comfort. At any moment he expected an Iranian border patrol, drawn by the sound of the explosion, to appear over the horizon and take them in. Either that, or a sniper's bullet. He did not know which would be preferable.

Once, when they reached a fork in the road, he signalled to Bemo that he should tell him which way to go. The boy indicated right with his elbow, and Hart fell into line again, his own stomach clenching and unclenching with fear.

They began a rapid descent on a rocky track, and Hart became more confident that there would be no more mines hidden in such an unforgiving place. He was desperate for a drink of water himself, but knew that he must keep their small reserve for Bemo, who was drifting in and out of consciousness with alarming regularity.

Fearing that the boy would die if he allowed him to sleep, Hart began asking Bemo for directions at every opportunity. Each time the boy signalled right by raising his elbow, and each time Hart began to doubt more and more what the boy was telling him. Was this really the way to the village? Or were they heading in a long looping circle that would eventually take them back up the mountain again? He had no choice but to follow Bemo's lead, as he knew for a certainty that, however hard he tried, he would not be able to find his own way back into Iraq. There was no alternative, therefore, but to go forward into Iran – no option but to trust to the boy's undoubted strength of will, which somehow shone through his dirt-caked face despite the horror of being supported upright on the horse by his own father's dead and mutilated body.

Two hours later, with the sun blazing down on them, Hart began to hallucinate. Ronas had begun to smell, and Hart imagined that it was he, and not Ronas, who was physically disintegrating. A number of times he stopped walking to open his coat to see if he had not, in fact, been wounded himself, and hadn't realized it. Bemo was unconscious now, and Hart forced himself to go back and check on the boy's wound in an effort to break the spell engulfing him. But still, even in this state, Bemo would not allow his hands to be prised apart. Hart moistened his fingers with water and pressed them to Bemo's lips, but the boy would not wake up. Hart imagined himself walking eternally around the Azerbaijan mountains leading a horse with two desiccated bodies attached to it.

He took up the halter and set off again. Once, they came to a stream, and he encouraged the horse to drink its fill. He drank himself, when the horse had finished, and replenished the gourd. In the distance, far across a ravine, he saw two shepherds walking behind an immense flock of sheep, but he was too far away to risk shouting, and he did not wish to draw unnecessary attention to himself. For all he knew the men would turn him and the boy over to the authorities. If that were to happen, Bemo would be in a worse position than the one he was in already. Hart doubted very much whether the Iranian authorities would give the boy any medical attention whatsoever under those circumstances. He would probably be shot outright. And what would happen to Hart himself didn't bear thinking about.

Hart had no idea when he first became aware of the village. He must have been looking at it for some time without actually seeing it. He led the horse, which was limping badly by now, down along a gully and across a small escarpment. One or two people emerged from their houses to watch his progress. They looked like ants. He raised an arm and called out, but his voice emerged as a croak. One of the ant women began running towards him. Then they were all running, old men, women and children. A mass of ants. An ant exodus.

Hart stumbled onwards, an absurd grin plastered over his face. Eventually, beyond his immediate vision, he felt the rope being taken from his hands and the horse led away. He blinked a few times in the sun, then continued his trudging. A hand stayed him. He turned towards the owner of the hand, his face screwed up in mute enquiry.

Nalan.

Now he really must be hallucinating. Yes. That was it. He was out of his head. How could ants run anyway? And what was Nalan doing here?

The hand touched him again.

Then he was enfolded in a familiar embrace and he knew.

# THIRTY-NINE

Hart slept all the rest of that day and half the following night. He awoke in pitch darkness with no idea of where he was. He stumbled out of bed and threw open the door of the hut in which he had been sleeping.

A thin moon lit up the surrounding buildings. Memory came back to him in a rush. He was still in the same village he had entered with the wounded Bemo and with Ronas's dead body maybe twelve hours before. Nothing, bar the time of day, had changed. He was wearing the same reeking coat and the same reeking clothes – only his stubble was a little more pronounced. And that was it. Not even a dog was barking.

He stood in the centre of the clearing and looked up at the mountains. The reality of his present position struck him as crazy. Had he been dreaming that Nalan was there? But no. She had seemed flesh and blood, surely. He remembered her quietly translating all that had happened for the benefit of the head man and his council. She had then led Hart out of the council building and into the dust-strewn square. Everything had been conducted with a curious formality. Hart remembered thinking that this was Iran, and even if these people were broadly sympathetic to him because of his connection to Nalan, and because of what he had done to bring their injured and dead down from the mountain, they were still essentially alien. Nalan could not afford to be seen to be too intimate with him. Not like at Pank. It would only take one person to give him away to the border authorities and destroy them all.

Hart walked over to where he remembered there being a communal well. He unhooked the gourd, scooped up some water from the trough, and drank.

He heard footsteps behind him. He turned. A man he did not recognize was approaching from one of the huts. The man inclined his head and saluted with his hand above his brow. Hart remembered what Nalan had told him and returned the salute.

'I am Elwand,' said the man. 'I am Nalan's cousin. I am pleased you are awake. I am going to drive you to Solomon's Prison.'

'What? Now?'

'Yes.' The word came out as a hiss, as if the speaker was not used to speaking English, and was having to make a superhuman effort to make himself understood. 'It is good time to go. I have rope. You must eat food in car. This way you climb down before dawn, look, and then be away.'

'And Nalan?'

'Busy.'

'Will I see her?'

The man cocked his head to one side like a bird dog. 'When you have what you come for. Then maybe.' Elwand walked towards a battered Peugeot 605 parked at the edge of the clearing. The car was painted such an indistinct colour that it blended perfectly with its surroundings to the point of invisibility. 'Please bring the turban you were wearing on the mountain.'

'But I don't know how to put it on.'

'I shall do it.'

Hart's embarrassment deepened. This was not going the way he had imagined it. Not at all. 'And these people? Ronas? Bemo?'

'Ronas is dead. You know this. Today, when it is light, they will bury him. Bemo has bad stomach. He is very ill. If you leave him on the mountain he die. This village is grateful to you. They will be of service to you. They are happy for Ronas's legs. Now they bury him properly. As Allah made him. They owe this to you.'

Hart washed himself at the well. It was becoming clearer to him by the minute that Elwand was not a man to mince his words. When he was finished with his cursory wash he collected his turban from the hut and hurried towards the Peugeot. Elwand was waiting for him.

'You climb in back.' He pointed towards the boot. 'There is security post ten kilometres down road. You must not be seen. Later you come out.'

'But I can't fit in there.'

'Then you not travel. Stay here. Return to Iraq. Is okay with me. I do this because you pay Nalan and she pay me.'

Hart climbed into the boot. It wasn't quite as bad a fit as he had imagined. Elwand handed him two oranges and a bottle of water. Then he closed the lid.

Hart positioned himself as comfortably as he could against a massive coil of rope and concentrated on controlling his breathing. He wasn't, generally speaking, claustrophobic, but this was an exception. Fortunately, there was just enough air inside the luggage shell to be bearable, as the back seat of the car was broken. If he craned his neck he could even see the left side of Elwand's head round the edge of the smashed seat. It occurred to him that the car may have been used for this purpose before.

The coil of rope soon became his main point of reference. If someone had bothered to procure a few hundred metres of rope, then it was hardly likely that they would betray him, was it? It was clear that they intended him no harm, wasn't it? What he was doing wasn't actually against the Iranian state, of course. He wasn't harming anyone by it. It was just semi-insane. Hart had always known that he was susceptible to women, but this was ridiculous. Thoughts such as these echoed around his head like so many angry gnats. The more he tried to think of something else, the more the thoughts imposed themselves upon him and flooded his mind with trivia.

Twenty minutes into the ride Elwand slowed down and then stopped the car. Hart heard the car door open and

Elwand get out. He heard the crunch of Elwand's shoes across the stone track. Then voices. He waited for the boot to be thrown open and for rough hands to drag him out. Nothing happened.

He heard more voices. Then laughter. Hart was so hyper alert by now that he thought he could recognize the particular sound that Elwand's trainers made as they returned to the car. They were accompanied by the heavier sound of boots. A soldier then. He was lost. What a stupid, bloody stupid way to go. Drifting with the breeze. Not taking control of your own destiny. Just drifting.

The voices started up again close by the car. Hart heard the sound of a match being struck. The sudden catch voices make when their owners are smoking.

He lay in the boot and tried to concentrate on not wanting to cough. A dry cough had been building in his throat for some minutes now, and he had been suppressing it. He felt around for the water bottle but was unable to find it. He began to swallow compulsively, massaging his throat with his fingers. The voices were right beside the car. Almost on a level with where he was lying. If he coughed he was lost.

Hart felt one of the oranges beneath his hand. He tore into it with his fingers, raised the orange to his mouth, and sucked greedily on the liquid. Anything to stop this infernal tickle. But the orange only made it worse.

Someone slapped the car's body shell and Hart almost leapt out of his skin. But it was only a goodbye. Whoever had hit the car had struck it as a goodbye.

He could hear the heavy boots of the soldier retreating back across the stones. The car canted a little as Elwand got into his seat. The engine roared into life. Hart let go of his cough, certain enough, now, that it would be concealed by the engine noise. Christ, though, this wasn't a way to live one's life. What had he been thinking of, coming here? Talk about a wild goose chase. Talk about sheer unadulterated insanity.

The car bumped down the track. Ten minutes into this new journey it stopped. The boot was opened. Hart climbed out. He felt like an old man. 'That was a bit close, wasn't it?'

'Close?'

'I mean dangerous.'

Elwand shook his head. He was busy retying Hart's turban. 'Dangerous? No. This man I know. With another, it would be dangerous. But this man is easy man. I just have to sign register for visit village. I tell him I go courting. He laugh. We share cigarette. Not all like this. Now you sit in front. Later you go back again. Only two more.'

'Two more?' Hart's face must have reflected his anxiety.

'Is okay. Only one in twenty times they check trunk. You have one in twenty chance each time.'

Hart was good at mathematics. There was actually a six in twenty chance that the boot would be checked. And maybe the 'other' man would be on duty then? Maybe they would not get away so easily? But what alternative did he have? He had entered this whole thing with his eyes open, and now he was risking Elwand's life as well as his own. And for what? A bloody Copper Scroll. One man had already died, and his

244

son lay injured. Hart did not feel so good about himself all of a sudden. And the underlying thought of Nalan contacting Hassif without involving him didn't make things any better. Like Amira said, he was all heart and no head. Well. Too late to change things now. He was launched.

It was still dark when they reached the base of the hill called Solomon's Prison. As Elwand had explained, they had needed to pass through two more checkpoints. Lying in the boot of the car, Hart had been comforted to hear the sound of numerous other vehicles on the road. It was clear that there was a great deal of early-morning traffic near the checkpoints – market traffic, or trucks heading for the border, he supposed – and that for this reason alone less attention might be paid to a solitary car. For the past twenty minutes, however, Hart had heard no vehicles passing, which led him to assume that they had turned off the main road onto a smaller highway.

Elwand opened the boot and Hart made his third exit of the morning. He was gradually getting used to the enclosed space, and had even managed to snatch a little extra sleep. Now he squinted up at the outline of the hill ahead of him. It towered up from the plain in the shape of a perfect volcano. But there was something ominous about it. Perhaps it was the association with men being lowered down there and then left to rot? The place had a deadening feel to it, with the plain around it flattened and uncompromising, like the surface of the moon.

Elwand reached into the boot and dragged out the rope. 'This heavy. I need help to carry.'

The two men slung the rope between them and started up the slope. Very soon Hart was sweating. Each step he took meant a concordant amount of descent inside the volcano's shell. Hart had climbed a little as a young man, but vertigo and fear of heights had limited what he had been able to achieve. As with the mild claustrophobia he had experienced in the car boot, he could master his vertigo with discipline and lateral thinking, but the process was an awkward one. The very thought of dropping straight down eight hundred feet, held only by a thin rope and a stranger's hands, was nightmarish in the extreme.

They reached the lip of the volcano and Hart dropped to his knees and crawled to the edge. Elwand, he noticed, had no such reservations. He simply strode to the lip, bent forwards, and stared down.

'Oh Jesus,' said Hart.

'It is far, no?' said Elwand.

'Are you sure there's enough rope?'

'No.'

'What?' Hart cast an appalled look at Elwand.

Elwand laughed. 'I joke only. Yes, I am sure. There is maybe ten metres excess. Easily enough. I use rope from market. Very strong. Strong to tie things.'

'But I weigh ninety kilos.'

'Ninety kilos is nothing. This rope will hold one hundred and fifty easy.'

'You're sure of that?'

'Not sure. Only think. Nothing is sure in this world.' Elwand moved to his left until he reached a hole in the rock.

He reached across, tied a stone onto the end of the rope, clambered onto the top of the rock and started swinging the rope with the stone attached towards the mouth of the hole. 'When stone come through, you catch.'

'I can't fit through that hole.'

'Not fit, no. When you are tied, you climb over, like me. But rock is important to me for putting my legs. Otherwise I will not hold you. I will drop.'

'Christ Jesus,' Hart said again. He caught the stone on Elwand's fifth try.

Elwand unhitched the stone and tied the free end of the rope around his waist. Then he began to unloop the rest of the rope until he found the opposite end. 'You tie this on yourself. Use good strong knot. It break, you fall. Then you climb over rock. I draw back rope to near your end. Let you down slowly. You see? I bring gloves in case you slip.'

Hart didn't dare trust his voice. He simply went through the motions. There was no going back now. It must be like a man on his first parachute attempt, he thought. With people lining up behind you, you simply had to go. There was no possibility of unclipping. No possible turning back.

'Here. Torch. Later, you have daylight.'

'What do you mean, daylight?'

'You loose rope when you are down. I pull up. Later, maybe twenty minutes, I come back with food and water in basket. I send this down too. Then I go and hide rope.'

'You go?'

'Yes. I come back tonight. It is too dangerous to do this

by daylight. People come. They walk up hill. But if anyone come here they will not look down. It is impossible to see in completely unless you are right above. In a balloon. Or plane maybe. Or helicopter. This will not happen. Only a fool climbs to lip and leans out.'

'A fool like me?'

'Oh yes. A fool like you.' Elwand laughed.

'But what if you don't come back?'

Elwand looked Hart directly in the eye. 'Then, my friend, you are in big trouble.'

# FORTY

Hart eased himself up and over the stone. Elwand slid the slack through his hands. To Hart's eyes, there appeared to be an awful lot of slack.

Elwand braced his legs against the rock face and nodded to Hart.

'Are you sure?' said Hart.

Elwand nodded. 'Big advantage for you. If you fall, I don't fit through hole. I stick. You hang.'

'But the rope could slide out through your hands.'

'Might do. Might not. This up to God.'

'Great.' Hart levered himself steadily backwards until he was ready to take up the abseiling position. He could feel his sphincter tightening and his throat clenching. He wanted to mewl like a baby. 'Can you feel me? The weight of me?'

'I have your weight. Now you start. I cannot keep hold too long.'

Hart began to abseil. At first he could hear the rope sliding through Elwand's gloves. Later all he could hear was his own attenuated breathing echoing back from the circle of the rocks surrounding him and the slap of his desert boots against the sides of the chimney.

Each jump bought him maybe five feet. At first, he didn't dare look down. Didn't dare give himself any perspective on his situation. He took on the role of the ostrich – or of a baby playing hide-and-seek under the covers of a bed. He knew what was happening, but didn't dare acknowledge it. If the rope broke, or if Elwand's hands slipped, he'd better hope he died outright. Because the alternative didn't bear thinking about.

Five minutes into his endless swinging, he stopped for a rest. He knew he daren't take too long, because Elwand was carrying the full weight of his body. For the first time Hart really looked around himself. The light was better now, and he could make out much of the detail of the rock surrounding him. There were fissures, yes, but they were interspersed on the way down with long flat slabs which only a man equipped with pitons and a hammer could hope to conquer. The truth was that once you were down there, in Solomon's Prison, you were down there for good, unless someone chose to pull you back up again. Hart had never seen anything like the place. It was terrible.

He recommenced the abseiling motion, and very soon he could see the ground approaching. The base of the extinct volcano measured perhaps fifty yards across. In other words the whole thing was in the form of an inverted cone – wider at the top than at the bottom. Thirty feet from the ground a broad lip shot out – an overhang really – that would have made it doubly impossible for prisoners to escape. The prison, although entirely natural and not man-made, was supremely fit for purpose. A genius could not have designed it better. An evil genius.

The equation was a simple one. You drop a man down here and you begin to destroy him psychologically. Inevitably, during his first day, when he knows he is at the height of his strength, he strives to get out. Finds he can't. Then, as each day passes, he becomes weaker and there is less chance that he will be able to summon the strength of will or of body to climb. It was the most perfect torture imaginable. It worked on every level. The surroundings were so extreme that there was no room for hope. As Hart felt his feet strike hard ground, he wondered how long any prisoner would have been able to withstand the horror or the loneliness. The uncertainty of wondering whether he would be fed or given drink. The uncertainty of everything.

He untied the rope from around his waist and gave it three firm yanks. The rope snaked back towards the surface. Hart switched on the torch. He soon decided, though, that he ought to conserve the batteries in case of emergency, and trust to his eyes in the burgeoning daylight. The sky seemed awfully bright up above him, but it was still very dark indeed down where he was. The contrast sent a chill directly into his soul.

He began by making a tour round the periphery of his temporary prison, hoping against hope that there might be some artificial shelter under the lee of the overhang. But there was none. The only thing breaking the flatness of the base area was a large rock positioned a little off-centre, with a mass of smaller rocks around it. It didn't take Hart long to work out that the rock matched nothing else that he could see, either geologically or topographically. The only possible reason, then, for its presence, was that it had been toppled down from the lip of the volcano for some obscure purpose. Maybe to frighten the inmates?

He looked up again. Was that Elwand's arm he could see briefly against the skyline? As he peered upwards, trying to discern exactly what he had seen, the truth about the single rock came home to him.

It had been sent down against the rains. The motive behind it had to be purely diabolical. Water would naturally stream into the vent during a great storm, and there would be little or no drainage to let it out again – a fact attested to by the paucity of vegetation. So the place would slowly fill up like an old-fashioned wide-mouthed milk bottle under a steadily dripping tap. When the water got too high, the only way for anyone to survive would be to clamber onto the rock. Send too many prisoners down here, and it would be man against man. An interested observer, high up on the lip and anchored by a rope, say, could entertain himself for hours watching his enemies fighting it out amongst themselves for who would be king of the rock castle when the waters finally overtopped a man's head. Later, when the waters did finally subside, the losers in the struggle would be left as mute witnesses, slowly rotting and poisoning the victors' air. Hart shook his head. The place was demoniacal.

He found his first bones fifteen minutes into his search, tight up against the side of the chimney, under the overhang. After that he found nothing but bones. One entire corner was rich with them. They lay scattered amongst the rocks and lichen like the remains of a great battle people had long ago forgotten the name of.

At first he avoided them with his feet as a mark of respect, but, later that day, when he had turned nothing up – no possible hiding place for the Copper Scroll – he found himself kicking them aside in a desperate attempt to unlock the key of the place and discover what his ancestor, Johannes von Hartelius, had been thinking of in using it.

Elwand had been true to his word and had sent him down a basket of food and water some twenty or so minutes after his initial climb. Hart had been briefly tempted to tie himself back onto the rope and shout up to Elwand to haul him up beyond the lip to where he could begin over-arming himself towards normality again. But he didn't. Was it shame, in that he had started all this – drawn all these people into what only he wanted to do – and that he dared not be the one who capitulated to fear? He hardly knew any more.

He spent the next thirty minutes picturing a nightmare scenario in which Elwand concealed the rope, and then hurried back down the slope to his car. The scenario continued with Elwand driving to the next checkpoint, where he would be stopped and found to have infringed some esoteric Iranian law. He would be taken to the local town and locked up. And Hart would have to eke out the water and food Elwand had sent down to him for as long as it took for Elwand to talk himself free.

How long would he last down here? A week? Hardly. He'd heard somewhere, possibly during the Hostile Environment and Emergency First Aid Training – or HEFAT as it was known – that he'd been obliged to undergo as a photojournalist, about the 3-3-3 survival rule of thumb. Three minutes without air, three days without water, three weeks without food. Now, down here, he didn't believe a word of it. He suspected he'd be delusional and gabbling way before the last part occurred. He decided to go easy on the water nonetheless. This wasn't the rainy season. If things went badly wrong he couldn't count on nature to protect him.

Fool. Bloody fool. What was he doing dwelling on this when he should be looking for the scroll?

Hart divided the prison area into four segments. The bone segment. The vegetation segment. The rocky segment. And the cleared segment. He decided to inspect each segment as diligently as he could, and then take a break. He worked out that if he spent around two hours on each, he might reasonably use the time before Elwand came back to the best of his ability, and miss nothing.

He was wrong. Each segment took him considerably less than two hours. It soon became clear to him that there was nowhere – simply nowhere – that anything resembling the Copper Scroll could be hidden.

The few piles of rocks he encountered were easily undone. The ground was bone-hard and unyielding. You'd have needed a pickaxe to make a mark in it, and what would have been the point? A worse place to hide anything could scarcely be imagined.

Hart stretched out on the central rock, making the most of the thin rays of sunshine that descended into the chasm. He might as well admit it. Von Hartelius had intended his secret writing to be discovered by his captors. He'd wanted to send them on a wretched wild goose chase into Persia. He'd probably never even seen Solomon's Prison – only heard of it – and in his desperation for somewhere apparently logical to have hidden the scroll, he'd chosen that. What a bloody fool he'd been ever to have thought that a thousand-year-old message from the dead would automatically tell the truth. People lied in the past just as they did in the present.

Hart ate most of the contents of the basket of food Elwand had sent him, drank thirty per cent of his remaining water, and went to sleep.

# FORTY-ONE

It was after dark when the rope snaked down again. Hart had almost given up any expectation of its coming by that time. He had never in his life spent so much time in such a god-forsaken place. It was enough to drive a man mad.

In reality, of course, he had always had a fair degree of certainty of being able to return to the surface – call it ninety-eight per cent, give or take fifty per cent for nerves and the anxieties of solitude. The men sent down here as a punishment would have had none. It was not the sort of place you would temporarily send a man. This place was an end point. As categorical as execution. As explicit as surgical murder.

Hart was silent as Elwand opened the boot of the car. He lay himself inside as though entombed. The climb back up had been far harder and more taxing than even he had imagined. Elwand had attached the rope directly round the rock, this time, as an anchor. Hart alone was to be responsible for pulling himself up, hand over hand, foot by agonizing foot. This they had agreed beforehand. When Hart was about a hundred feet up, he had managed to jam his feet into a crevice and take a brief, panic-stricken rest. Elwand had taken up the slack at that point and retied the rope around the rock. After that he did this every hundred feet or so as a sort of primitive safety device.

When Hart was close to the lip he had temporarily lost control of his footing and dropped thirty feet, dangling out in space, the rope biting into his armpits and crotch and threatening to overset him. Elwand had shouted down to him. Hart had tried to swing back into the side again, but couldn't get the motion working. Later he discovered that Elwand had eased himself out along the rock and had begun the fresh swinging motion himself, from up above him. If Elwand had fallen then, they would both have died. The difference between life and death was decided by that thin a membrane.

Hart remembered Elwand's face as he breasted the lip of the prison. It was like looking into the eyes of a dead man. Hart supposed his were the same.

Neither of them had said a word to each other on the walk down the slope. Hart had carried his silence forwards into the boot of the car.

The rocking of the car was a comfort at first. Hart lay curled up against the rope, in the foetal position, and tried to close his mind to his own uselessness. But little by little the despair leached through. He almost wanted them to catch him. For the Iranian Revolutionary Guards to throw open the boot of the car and punish him for this crazy exercise in vainglory he had embarked upon without sufficient thought or planning. Who could he now expect to guide him back through the mountains to Iraq? He was a Jonah. No one would come near him any more. He might as well present himself at the nearest security post and speed up the inevitable.

He was surprised, therefore, about two hours into the trip, to hear a mass of traffic around him when there should have been none. Where was Elwand taking him? Because it certainly wasn't back up the mountain towards Ronas and Bemo's village. The quality of the road noise was completely different here. The sound the tyres made on the asphalt was steadier, smoother, as though they were entering a town. At one point, when the car was forced to slow down, he heard people's voices passing close beside him. And these were not guards. These were civilians. He was sure of it.

The car rocked to a halt. Hart waited. The boot was opened and he was blinded by artificial light. He reached out an arm and Elwand helped him struggle out onto what passed for dry land again. He was outside a house, in a courtyard, in what appeared to be the outskirts of a town.

'Hurry now. No one must see you.'

Hart stumbled up the stairs ahead of him and through a half-opened door.

'Where are we?'

'Bukan.'

'Bukan?' Hart tried to summon up a mental map of Iran in his head, but failed. 'What are we doing in Bukan?'

'Nalan. She wish to see you. I bring. She come later.'

Hart felt his anxiety close down on him. He could feel his breathing return to normal. He was out of Solomon's Prison. He was not dead. He was not in an Iranian jail. He would see Nalan soon.

He stopped just inside the door and turned to Elwand. He bowed his head and saluted as deeply as he knew how. 'Thank you, Elwand. Thank you for all of this. And thank you for saving my life today.'

Elwand ducked his head, almost as a child might do when marked out for unexpected praise in a classroom. 'We are lucky. God is on our side today.' Elwand raised his right hand and touched Hart lightly on the shoulder. 'You brave man. You mad man. You crazy man.' He laughed. 'I never do this again. Never. Not for any money. Not for anyone. God help me.' He looked up at the ceiling and crossed himself. 'Never.'

Hart laughed with Elwand, and as he did so, he felt all his remaining anxiety rush away from him like water from a fractured dam.

Elwand put on his serious face again. 'Now, Britannia, you wash. Fresh clothes. Leave beard. Then we eat.'

'And Nalan?'

'Later, I say. She will come later. We need talk. Many things have changed. Please be welcome in my grandfather's house.'

# FORTY-TWO

Nalan sat across from Hart at the kitchen table. Around them sat Elwand and five other males of assorted ages and sizes. Three of them were in Kurdish dress, the other two in what passed for Western dress in Iran – short-sleeved shirts and razor-creased trousers. All had glasses of tea in front of them, served by Elwand's grandmother, who wore a long-sleeved dress in green, with a cardigan over the top, and an off-white hooded snood about her head, tied in place with a red and black tribal bandanna.

Elwand's grandmother firmly refused to sit with the men, but Nalan had no such reservations. It interested Hart that the men seemed to accord Nalan a respect out of all proportion to her age, her sex and her status. Hart imagined this was because of what she and her parents had endured at the hands of the Iraqi Mukhabarat. It was akin to the respect offered in Europe, say, to someone known to have survived Auschwitz.

Nalan spoke in English first, for Hart's benefit, and then translated what she had said into Kurdish. First off, after saying how sorry she was that he had not been able to find the Copper Scroll he had been looking for, she introduced Hart to the remainder of her male cousins.

'Elwand you know. This young one here is Bahoz. This Saman. This Zinar. This Navda. This Elind. All six are my uncle's sons.'

Hart almost said 'what a busy man' out of sheer embarrassment. Looking at the young men around him, he was forced to acknowledge that, despite their shared intimacies at Pank, he really didn't know anything about Nalan at all. 'The brother of your father?'

'Yes. My uncle and aunt brought me up, as I told you when we were hiding in the tank in As Sulaymaniyah. So I do not consider these men my cousins. They are my brothers. Three live in Iran.' She pointed to Elwand, Navda and Elind. 'Three in Iraq.' She waved towards the others. 'This is normal for Kurdish people. During the Iran/Iraq War we supported Iran against Saddam. This is why he was so angry against us. Why he tried to destroy the Kurds with genocide. Why he used chemicals against Halabja in 1988. Five thousand chemical martyrs dead. Ten thousand injured. Our people are still dying of the effects of the chemicals to this day. Halabja is near As Sulaymaniyah, John. In Halabja the Iranians were innocent, and Chemical Ali and Saddam Hussein were guilty. In As Sulaymaniyah the Iraqis were innocent and the Iranians were guilty. This is why life is so complicated for the Kurdish people.'

'And Hassif?'

Nalan bowed her head. 'I talked to him again. On the telephone. This is why I have brought you here. To tell you, before you go back to Iraq, that he hates you very much.'

'Me?' Hart rocked back in his chair. 'Why should he hate me?'

'Please. Be patient. I will explain.' Nalan looked at her cousins. 'Things are not as I once thought them. They are more complicated. I thought Hassif was a civilian. That I could lure him in and that my brothers could seal the trap against him. That we would obtain *qesas* this way.'

'*Qesas*?'

'The right to retaliation. This is a legal right in Iran. You are offered the alternative between *diyeh* – which is blood money – or *qesas*.'

'Ah. The *lex talionis*.'

'What is this?'

'It is written in the Bible. An eye for an eye, a tooth for a tooth, a hand for a hand, a foot for a foot. Burning for burning. Wound for wound. Stripe for stripe. I believe the Koran has much the same thing.'

'Yes. This is the way Sharia is seen in Shia countries like Iran. We were hoping for this for Hassif. Even though we are Christians and he is Muslim.'

'But first you would have to capture him.' Hart was still struggling to come to terms with the fact that Hassif knew about him, and had, seemingly, marked him out for special attention. But he knew Nalan well enough by now to know

262

that she would only tell him what she wanted him to hear when the moment suited her. She was performing in this room for the benefit of her cousins, that much was clear. She had an agenda.

'If Hassif was a civilian, this would be easy. I go to see him. My cousins come. We trap him.'

'So what's changed?'

Nalan looked at Elind, who appeared to be the oldest of her cousins. 'Elind work here for the Iranian government.'

Hart could feel his entire body tense up. Had he walked into a trap? What the hell was going on? He tried not to show his inner turmoil. But it was hard. The palms of his hands began to sweat. So did his head, beneath the turban – he could feel the perspiration trickling down the back of his neck. He was tempted to take the turban off and shake it, but he was worried that this might appear insulting in present company. The last thing he wanted was to alienate his last possible hope of getting out of the country. And he certainly didn't wish to alienate Elind.

'Elind has found out that Hassif now works for an Iranian government agency as well. He is Shia. Like most Iranians. In Iraq he was head of the Northern Mukhabarat – very high in the intelligence services. Here they have made him Deputy Chief Intelligence Officer, Border District. It is a lesser position. But still powerful enough. His office is here. In Bukan.'

'Here?' Hart was feeling more hemmed in by the minute. 'The Iranians must be mad. Why would they employ an Iraqi in such a sensitive position?'

'This is simple. Because he hates the Kurds.'

'But I thought you told me that the Kurds sided with the Iranians during the Iran/Iraq War?'

'They did. But now that the Kurds are more powerful, both inside and outside Iran, the Iranians want to harness them. This is why they employ Hassif. This is why Elind believes Hassif is behind the As Sulaymaniyah car bomb attack. This is why Hassif hates you.'

'What the heck for? Because I killed the suicide bomber? One of his?'

'Yes. You were made a hero by the Western press. You humiliated him in front of his masters. This is why he has made it a condition for me, in order to stop him from publicly disrespecting my mother and father, that I betray you to him. That I somehow lure you back to Iraq and betray you to his assassins there.'

'Is this why you've brought me here? To Bukan? Is that what this is all about?'

Hart couldn't help noticing that Nalan did not translate what he had just said to her cousins. Elwand, who could understand English, half stood up from his chair, and then dropped back again at a sign from Nalan.

'No. I would never do this. How could you think this of me, John, after what we have been through together?' Nalan lowered her eyes. 'The truth is that I had thought not to see you again until I returned to Iraq. That Elwand would return you to the village and that the villagers, grateful to you for what you did for Ronas and Bemo, would guide you back over the mountain. But when I heard the news of Hassif – that he had a high position here, that he had real power – I thought it only right to tell you face to face of what he said to me. To warn you, before you return to Iraq. Before you return home.' She fixed Hart with her gaze. 'Hassif has a long arm. And he is a vengeful man. Listen to me. He will harm you in some way. Maybe not now. Maybe not tomorrow. But some day. When you least expect it. Even in England. You will never be safe.'

'So you knew he hated me before we entered Iran?'

Nalan shook her head in irritation. 'I knew this, yes. But I pay it no attention. Hassif wants me too much to care whether I betray you or not. It was purely a bargaining counter to get to me. He knows he can find you himself when the time comes. You are a photojournalist. A man who seeks out dangerous places. There is no man easier to kill than you.' She half-inclined her head, seemingly aware that Hart was having difficulty following her logic – the logic of a war forever fought within the shifting borders of the mind. 'No. His plan was to put more pressure on me that way. By seeming to relent about you, he counted on gaining better access to me.'

'But why? Why this fixation on you?'

'I am the one he left behind, John. The witness to his barbarities. For him it is personal against my family. He wishes to destroy me, just as he destroyed my father and mother.'

'You knew this and yet you still came? He might have had you picked up at the border.'

Nalan brushed the thought away with her hand. 'Such power he does not have. There is chaos at the border. Hundreds pass through every hour. Trucks, vans, cars, pedestrians, jihadists, refugees from Syria, black marketeers. And I told you already why I come here. We Kurds are tribal. My brothers wish to avenge their uncle and aunt. This is a blood feud with us. And I am the means they can use to approach Hassif. It is my duty to form the bridge they can travel over to take revenge. Even at the cost of my life.' She stood up. 'So. Now I have told you what you need to know, Elwand will take you back to the village. In one day, maybe two, new *kulbars* from the village will cross back into Iraq. You will go with them.'

'What? They'd still travel over despite what happened to Ronas and Bemo?'

'What happened to Ronas and Bemo happens all the time. It was not because of you. It was not because of anyone. It was the will of God. Others will get through where they failed. The village needs to live. This is how they live. You will pay them one hundred dollars again, just as you did last time.'

Elwand interrupted her. 'No. He needs not to pay. I talk to the village. He save Bemo. He bring Ronas back for his family to bury. The Britannia does this when he could have run back to Iraq and saved himself. They guide him back as honoured guest to Iraq. No payment.'

Hart was feeling more bewildered by the minute. He had somehow managed to stumble into a culture that appeared to take part of its ethos from the Middle Ages, and part from an equally unfashionable sense of chivalric morality. The result was unsettling in the extreme. It made him feel powerless. And guilt-stricken for his mistake in treating everything as a sort of game. It was definitely no game for Nalan and her cousins. 'And Elwand is to take me back to the village now? This minute?'

'Yes. What you needed to do here is done.'

'And how do you intend to get close to Hassif, Nalan? With this new position you tell me he has, he will have bodyguards. Protection. There's not a chance in hell that you will get near him unless he wants you to.'

'This is what my brothers and I are deciding now. How I should sacrifice myself to give them access to Hassif.'

'Sacrifice yourself?' Hart shook his head in despair. 'Sacrifice yourself? And you seriously intend going through with this?'

'I can never forgive this man for what he did. For what he made me watch. For the injury he did to my parents. And for the injury he still intends doing to their memory.'

Hart looked around himself. At the faces of Nalan's cousins. At her face. At the faces in the family photographs hanging on the wall. He could feel everything he had gone through in the past few weeks needling through his body like the prelude to a particularly pernicious form of blood poisoning. 'Tell me this much then. Am I right in thinking that Hassif is a greedy man? An ambitious man? A man who will care very much what his new masters think of him? Is this a fair summing up of his character?'

At first Nalan hesitated, as though Hart had gone too far. Then she shrugged her shoulders. 'Oh yes. Very much. He will care very much what his new masters think of him. This goes without saying. He will not be strong in this. They will be watching him. Weighing him up.'

'And he hates me? Wants revenge on me? You're sure of this?'

Nalan frowned. It was clear that she did not understand why Hart was persisting with his line of questioning. But still she translated everything that Hart was saying for her cousins' benefit. 'Yes. This surprised me too. But he hates you for what you did. Made my betrayal of you a condition of whatever we could agree about my family. I told you why.'

Hart laid both hands on the table, as a man will do when he wishes to demonstrate that he holds no concealed weapons. 'Then I have a plan. A way for me to pay back some little part of what I owe you.'

Nalan shook her head. Her brow cleared, as if everything had been magically explained to her. 'No, John. It will not be enough for you to sacrifice yourself on my behalf. This will not satisfy him. It is me he wants.'

Hart opened his hands. He looked round the table. 'Then let's give him both of us. With a little cream on top for good measure.'

# FORTY-THREE

Rahim Hassif watched the prisoner's hands being tied behind one of his legs, high on the upper thigh. Despite the man's pleas, he was brusquely upended on the ground and his shoes and socks taken off. A pole, maybe three inches thick, was brought in from outside the room and the man's bare feet tied to it, their soles facing outwards. The pole was then raised by two guards, one on each end, until the man's legs were at waist height to the guard holding the rubber piping – the man's head, too, was forcibly raised off the ground, thanks to the position of his bound arms behind his thigh.

The prisoner was now effectively pinioned, with the main part of his body on the cement floor, and his feet vulnerable. It was a position Hassif had studied scientifically, and which was designed to cause its victim maximum discomfort and apprehension. The guard with the rubber hosepipe stepped back and looked at Hassif. Hassif nodded.

The guard began to beat the man's feet. The man screamed.

Then screamed again. Soon the screaming and the beating became one. A continuous loop.

Hassif watched for a little while, but his heart wasn't in it. He turned away from the beating and lit a cigarette. He had missed a trick with the Abuna girl, and he knew it. He had ordered all borders watched for a woman with her name, but no one had paid him any attention. He still had no real clout with the Iranian military hoi polloi – or not remotely what he had had in Iraq. Underlings nodded, said they would do what he asked, and then ignored his requests in favour of their own agendas.

The Abuna girl had actually phoned him from somewhere inside Iran. That much was certain. The telecommunications people nominally under his command were far more effective at gathering intelligence than the border people, who were corrupt worms, more interested in squeezing blood out of a stone than in serving their country. He would hang them all out to dry one day. That much he promised.

The man being beaten stopped shrieking. Hassif walked round the sweating guards to check on the condition of the prisoner's feet. The guards were sweating because it was hard work holding a pole with a man's legs attached, and acting at the same time as shock absorbers for the blows he was receiving.

'Twenty more.'

'But he is unconscious, Effendi.'

'Then he won't notice the extra blows. But he will feel them later when he tries to walk. In this way we will mitigate the advantage he has taken over us in falling unconscious.'

'Yes, Effendi.'

The beating continued. Hassif thought about Nalan some more. He wanted her now very much. The smell of blood always had this effect on him. It went straight to his crotch. He threw away his cigarette and strode out of the cell.

In ten minutes he was back at his office, sorting through his videos of Nalan's mother being raped. He slid one into the machine and ran it. He began to masturbate. Then his phone rang.

Hassif almost didn't take the call. But it might be his boss, inquiring after the prisoner being beaten. The man had insulted a senior official in some way. His boss had asked Hassif, as a personal favour, to humiliate the man, and cause him to be punished. Hassif hadn't hesitated. The senior official in question had serious clout. Hassif never ignored men who had clout. It was the way he had made it to the top in Iraq. Why shouldn't the same work here?

'It is I. Nalan Abuna.'

Hassif sat up in his chair. It was a long time since anyone had spoken Kurdish to him. He was almost tempted to do up his trousers, but some perverse streak caused him to leave them open. 'I was hoping to hear from you. I am looking at a video of your mother right now. I am sorry the sound is muted, or I would play it to you over the phone. But for this I would need to stand up and go over to the player. And I cannot be bothered.'

The truth was that Hassif was still not sure of the people working for him in the anteroom situated directly outside his office. He assumed that half of them had been ordered to spy on him – this much was a given. It simply wouldn't do for him to be heard watching the equivalent of loud porn videos in his office during working hours. The truth was that he hid his whisky drinking, also, and used a powerful fan to mitigate the scent of his Havana cigars. These Iranian cocksuckers were up their own arses when it came to religious practice. Until he was more secure in his position, it behove Hassif to at least seem to toe the line in terms of the Five Pillars.

'I know you are in Iran,' Hassif continued, still in Kurdish. At least his use of the language might make any eavesdropping that much more difficult. 'So I also know you have decided to come to see me, as I requested. There is no danger for you. I merely wish to show you certain things pertaining to your parents. Have you the Britannia for me? Or have you thought of a way to discredit him? Perhaps if you accused him of rape? This would be satisfactory. English people seem to take rape very seriously. Far more seriously than your mother or father took it. I am looking at your mother now being raped. It makes me very nostalgic. I am sorry she is dead. She was such an accommodating woman. I caused her to believe that if she volunteered herself, we would spare you, her daughter, from a similar fate. She found this difficult in the extreme. But she managed it. I have the proof here in front of me. I would very much like to share it with you. In fact I would like to share it with the world. But I realize that this may seem unreasonable from your perspective. So. Do we have an accommodation like the one

I entered into with your mother? Your father, I fear, never appreciated the value of compromise. It was a shame. He studied in the same university as me, you know? We were fellow students. It hurt me very much, all that he did.'

Hassif waited. He could pick up the tension at the other end of the line. He was good at picking up tension. It was his stock-in-trade.

'John Hart is in Iran.'

Hassif set the video player to pause. The action he was watching was distracting in the extreme. How strange to be talking to the daughter while watching the mother being raped. And more than twenty years after the event had happened. Hassif felt absurdly pleased with himself. He had engineered this whole process from the beginning. It was outrageously beguiling. Just the sort of situation he most relished – one in which he enjoyed all the power, and his victim had none.

'In Iran, you say?'

'Yes. He is here in pursuit of something of great value.'

Hassif's ears pricked up. 'What, of great value, could a Britannia hope to find here? Except his death, of course.'

'If I tell you this, and cause you to secure this object, together with the Britannia, will you agree to hand over to me all the material you hold in your possession concerning my mother, my father and me?'

Ah. Barter. Hassif understood this so well. Barter was at the essence of being Arab. He could feel the blood pulsing through him again. This time in different directions.

'How valuable is this object the Britannia wants?'

'So valuable that the Jews would pay nearly anything for it.'

'The Jews?'

'Yes. The Jews.'

Hassif did some quick mental calculations. Deputy Chief Intelligence Officer, Border District, was all very well. The bribes were good, although the pay was non-existent. But it was not the sort of sinecure he had become used to in Iraq. No. He would never reach those heady heights again. He was sure of it.

'The Jews would buy this thing?'

'Yes.'

'And it is easily portable?'

'Yes.'

'And the Britannia has it?'

'No. Not yet. But he knows where to find it. It is for this reason alone that he has entered Iran illegally. And I know when and how he will go to where it can be found.'

'And you wish to tell me this?'

'Only if we can come to an accommodation.'

Hassif thought for a moment. But it was only a moment. He had not achieved all he had in this world without knowing when to take risks. When to plunge. He could happily leave the Iranian government out of this. Hire himself some thugs – he knew just where to find those. Secure the Britannia and whatever he was looking for. Or, more likely, already had. Then dispose of the Britannia and the Abuna girl as and how he saw fit. And if the object was as valuable as the

274

Abuna girl declared, he could negotiate with the Jews and get them to fill up his foreign bank accounts for him. Then he could show Iran and the fucking Iranians a clean set of heels, have his face and passport fixed, and live a new life. In South America maybe. Or the Caribbean. Some place where everything can be bought, if you know how power works, and if you are sensible enough to keep the bulk of your money tied up safely elsewhere.

'What is this object?'

Nalan told him.

At first Hassif was tempted to laugh. But something halted him. This idea of the Copper Scroll, and how the truth of its location was found – the Holy Spear, the concealed parchment – all this was far too outlandish to be a trick. Nobody would think this nonsense up and expect a man like him to be gulled by it. Hassif was a trained interrogator. When people made up stories, they made up stories they thought you would believe. As Nalan spoke to him he fiddled with his mouse and did some furtive checking on the computer. The facts he found tallied with what the Abuna girl was saying. If it was a honey trap, it was a very elaborate one.

'And you can prove that this is what he is after? And that he knows exactly where to find it? And then you can give him to me?' Hassif could feel the laughter urge beginning to overwhelm him, but still he forced it back. How naive this silly little girl was to think that she could trick him. Copper Scroll or no Copper Scroll, he would emerge the victor from this trade he was about to undertake with her. Revenge.

Riches. They were all the same in the end. They weighed up similarly in the great scales. Both were equally sweet.

'Yes.'

'You will come here to my office, of course. With the requisite proof.'

'I cannot do that. You know I cannot do that.'

'Then I will release film of your mother and father on the Internet.'

'I don't think you will. I know of your position now in the Iranian government hierarchy. I think we are both after different things. But we both need to protect our backs. I want what you have. You want what I have.'

'But I do not know what you have.'

'If I cause the Britannia to be held? And for you to come and see him?'

This time Hassif did laugh.

'Then what?' said Nalan. 'What do you suggest?'

'Where is he coming to collect this scroll? And when? This is what I need to know.'

'Do we have a deal?'

Hassif made a fluttering motion with his hand, which of course Nalan could not see. He was enjoying this process immensely. 'You know I will come with many people. You know that he will have no chance of escape.'

'I know that. Of course I know that. But I need bona fides.'

'What?'

'I need proof that you will do what you promised.'

'Give you what I have, you mean?'

'Yes.'

'Okay. I tell you what. I will put some videos in the post to you. By courier. You will get them later today.'

'You are joking.'

Hassif shrieked with laughter. Then he remembered the people outside his office. It wouldn't do to sound as if he was enjoying something outside of official matters. Someone might start asking questions. These Iranians had no sense of humour. 'Yes. I am joking. I am testing you. To see how stupid you are. But you are oh so clever. Like your mother. She knew what to do. Who was boss.'

'You are the boss. I know it.'

Hassif nodded his head. 'Good. This is an improvement. Now we are getting somewhere.' He thought quickly. Maybe someone was taping this call. Maybe all his calls were being taped and he didn't know it. He was receiving this on a personal pay-as-you-go mobile phone. One not associated with his office. But still. He had already prejudiced himself by asking the border area guards to look out for the Abuna girl. In his opinion it had been a risk worth taking. The request had been buried amongst a dozen others. Which was why those lazy corrupt bastards had not prioritized it. But the communications people were a different matter entirely from the border guards. They were hardline servants of the state. He had made one call to the Abuna girl on his office phone. Just one, before he had been able to pass her his mobile number. Maybe this had been a mistake and maybe not. It was too soon to tell.

'I will send a man. In a car. One man. To Kitakeh. He will leave a parcel. Wherever you want. A present from me. Then you will phone. Tell me where the Britannia is going. You will be there too. This is essential for me. I have things I need to show you. You will be in no danger. I am a kind man. Although you may not think so. But much has changed. I knew your father well. I liked him so much before he betrayed me.' Hassif stopped. He listened hard for any sounds at the other end of the line. Maybe he had gone too far. Maybe he had curdled the milk with his lies.

'We will both be there. If what you show me has any value to me, that is.'

'Oh yes. Believe me. It has value to you. Much value. And value to me. I am a sentimental man. I honour the past. It will cost me much to part with it. Do we have a deal?'

Nalan held her silence for the count of five. Now Hassif was doing the asking. This was how it should be. 'Yes, Hassif. We have a deal.'

# FORTY-FOUR

'But what if he comes with many men, as he says? He could surround the place. Bring in helicopters. Seal every road. None of us would stand a chance. He'd just sweep us into his net.'

This was the first time Hart had been alone with Nalan since his return from Solomon's Prison. Her cousins had dispersed. Her grandmother had grudgingly left for the market without being able to persuade her unmarried granddaughter to accompany her. Hart was meant to be resting in his room. But, glory be to God, Nalan had come in to tell him about her call to Hassif.

'This area around the volcano cannot be sealed, John. You have seen it. You have been there with Elwand. One road in and one road out. But around it, mountains and plain. Hassif would need a thousand men to secure it.'

'Still. He has every advantage. We will have none.'

'We have his greed.'

'Are you sure of that?'

'I remember him.'

'Three- to five-year-old children, as you were at the time you were imprisoned at Amna Suraka, don't remember such things.'

'I remember.'

Hart shook his head. 'You remember what you have been told since. Or what you imagined when you revisited that place a few years ago.'

'No. I remember everything. When we were freed by the Peshmerga I was nearly six years old. I remember Hassif drinking whisky while my mother was being raped. And eating *kleicha* and *qatayef* so greedily that the cheese ran down his beard. I remember him pretending to offer me some, and not knowing whether to take it or not, as I was so hungry. I remember my mother weeping in humiliation as he offered them to her, and then weeping more when he raped her himself and wiped his fingers down her face and breasts to clean them. This man is greedy. He wants things for himself. Now he wants me and the scroll.'

Hart could feel the blood draining from his face. When Nalan spoke to him like this, it was as if he was talking to a stranger. She was somewhere else. Somewhere he couldn't hope to reach her. 'He wants me too, remember that. Are you sure that the kudos of catching a British spy on Iranian soil – because that's how he'll spin it – won't outweigh the rest? I'll be bait enough, surely. You have no need to risk yourself.'

Hart's interjection had allowed Nalan enough time to compose herself. She sat down a few feet away from him on the bed. 'Elind knows for whom Hassif works in the government. He is not in a strong position there. They will distrust him because of who he is and what he was. They will use him, but they will distrust him. We are offering him a way to get out of the country. A way to get significant money. You are the cream, as you say. You are his security if things go wrong. He will have something to show his bosses. A reason for his apparent misbehaviour. But it is me he really wants. I know this in my bones. He will only agree to come for the two of us.'

'You know he will not come alone.'

'This, too, we understand. It is a risk we must take.'

Hart hunched forwards on the side of the bed. He stared at Nalan. 'This thing with Hassif was always on the agenda, wasn't it? Even before I met you? You and your family have been waiting all this time, haven't you, to get your revenge? And the bombing triggered it. It brought him out into the open.'

Nalan shook her head. 'This is not true. We thought he was dead. We thought someone had killed him when Saddam was brought down, that maybe he was the unknown man who died with Saddam's sons, Uday and Qusay, at the final shootout. When they were betrayed for the Yankee blood money. The truth is we did not know what to think. Hassif had disappeared into thin air. Now we know he was in Iran all this time. This has changed everything.'

'But you still think my plan can work?'

'Only God knows what will work and what will not. God placed us here to make our own decisions. You came here for the Copper Scroll. It was a dead end. Your ancestor misled you. But your presence is a gift to us. To me and my family. You can still say no, John. Still go back to the village. You will be back in Iraq in a couple of days. Back to your old life. As if nothing had happened.'

'You know why I will never do that.'

'Do I?' She looked at him.

Hart raised his hand, intending to cover hers. He ended up by placing it on the bed between them. 'Yes. For you. I will stay for you.'

# FORTY-FIVE

Rahim Hassif was not a man to take risks lightly. His entire life was premised on weighing up the advantage and disadvantage of any action, and basing any future course he chose to take on the outcome of his cogitations. So he had made some calls. Privately. On a newly bought phone that was untraceable. He had used a pseudonym too. He had chosen the name of a Lebanese Christian. He could manage the accent. No Jew would be able to pick it apart.

First he had called the Israel Museum in Jerusalem. The one which housed the Dead Sea Scrolls. He had been very cautious. He had talked only generally. But it soon became apparent that the Copper Scroll, if it did indeed hold the secrets of King Solomon's plans for the new Temple of Jerusalem, and the location of the lost treasures of Solomon – to include the Ark of the Covenant, the Tabernacle and the wherewithal to rebuild the Temple to a preset design – would be cheap at any price. The Jews would mortgage half their state to get their hands on it.

Next he had telephoned Bernhardi, Tauschwitz and Seeligman in New York. During his time as head of the Mukhabarat, Hassif had had occasion to buy certain artefacts for Uday Hussein, who had been an avid collector and hoarder of valuable items. Uday was in the habit of helping himself to articles, too, from the Iraqi National Museums collection, on what might charitably be called a permanent loan basis, and then selling them privately, via amenable dealers, to generate a little ready cash with which to fund his pleasures and his own private collections. BT&S had been Hassif's first port of call whenever one of these eventualities had happily presented itself.

Nothing had changed. Yussuf Bernhardi recognized his voice immediately. He had shown no surprise at Hassif contacting him from, as it were, beyond the grave.

'I won't tell you where I am,' said Hassif.

'And I won't ask you.'

The conversation had gone on from there, taking pretty much the same line as the conversation with the custodian at the Israel Museum had taken. But this time Bernhardi had talked real money, as Hassif had known he would.

'We would pay ten million dollars.'

'That does not seem a lot, in the circumstances.'

'But we would be taking all the risks. These things take time to certify. The item or items will have to be authenticated. Politics will be involved. There will be much publicity. We will be forced to operate in its full glare. Not to speak of the perils of attribution.'

'There will be no attribution problems. The object will have been found on land I own in the Lebanon. On this land there are caves. It will be found in there.'

'But your name. . .'

'Is not on the deeds. Another name is. A name I will be using from the day after tomorrow.'

There was a heavy silence from the New York end of the line. 'And where will you be based for this transaction?'

'Bermuda.'

'Ah. Good choice. An excellent climate. Easy access to the USA.'

'I will not be going to the USA.'

'But your representative will?'

'No. You will be coming to Bermuda.'

'I see.'

'And you will be bringing twenty million dollars with you. In bearer bonds.'

'Twenty million? That is impossible. And bearer bonds are far too dangerous now. Our government has clamped down on them since your time.'

'I have spoken to the Israel Museum. The Jews will pay anything you ask for this scroll. And there are one hundred million dollars' worth of bearer bonds still in circulation. It is those or nothing else.'

'But I've told you about the risks.'

'Then I will phone London. You know exactly who I will call.'

'No. No. Don't do that. I'm sure we can come to some accommodation.'

'Yes. A twenty-million-dollar accommodation.'

The conversation had continued along those lines for some little time. The final sum agreed had been fifteen million. In bearer bonds. Five per cent on delivery. Residue on authentication. Hassif liked dealing with professionals. And he had a track record. Nothing he had ever traded had proved a fake. BT&S must have made a fortune out of him in the past. They would make one again from the scroll. But fifteen million was fifteen million. It was enough, with what he had salted away already, to allow a man to live out his retirement in luxury. And it never did to be too greedy. Leave that to the man you were dealing with.

Hassif made some more phone calls. For a long time now he had been in the habit of weighing up the prisoners who fell into his hands to see if any might, one day, be of service to him. These lucky few, once certain undertakings and safeguards had been put into place, he agreed to let go. It was to these men he now addressed himself. They were the lowest of the low, of course, but they would do the trick. They feared the Iranian state – and they feared the things Hassif had on them. It was the perfect position to be in. And the ultimate beauty was that if things went wrong, the recidivists were guaranteed not to hang about and tell tales out of school. They would disappear into thin air. Back to the sewers they sprang from. Because if the authorities ever got hold of them, and if Hassif was forced to declare all he knew, which was a given, they were all doomed.

Over the next two days, Hassif smuggled all his videos and secret files out of the office. It was easy enough to do. No one knew they were there. He had not left them in his house because it went without saying that the Iranian Security Services would have conducted a thorough search of his premises at some point during his tenure of office. It was what he would have done himself in similar circumstances. No. Hiding them in his office had been a stroke of genius. The best place to hide something was always in plain sight.

Now he took them all out in a series of journeys and hid them in a Mercedes he had bought privately at the same time as he had bought the unmarked Mercedes his martyrs had hidden their car bomb in. Mercedes were far and away the best receptacles for car bombs, because they were made entirely of metal and not of plastic, and the fuel tank was located behind the rear seat, making for a more concentrated explosion. The fuel tank and the attached air-storage unit for the vacuum pump were also ideal places to hide stuff in if one didn't wish to be caught with one's trousers down at unfriendly borders. Hassif was a past master at this sort of engineering. He didn't get his own hands dirty, of course. But he knew exactly what to ask for from his mechanics, and how to ensure the job was done to his entire satisfaction.

When the car was ready, and loaded with all his necessities, Hassif signed off for the Iranian weekend, which always fell on a Friday. It was a one-day weekend, which was entirely typical of the cheeseparing motherfuckers who ran the country – but it would be more than enough for his purposes.

He did not have far to go. The Abuna girl had received his sample video in Kitakeh. He, in turn, had received photographic proof of the parchment rescued from the Holy Spear, which clearly spoke of the location of the Copper Scroll. Once again, only a fool would fabricate such an elaborate and unnecessary device for entrapment purposes. The parchment was original. There were enough clues for the trained eye to pick up to confirm that fact. Hassif had not wasted his tenure in Iraq all those years ago. He was something of an expert on ancient artefacts. He thought with nostalgia of some of Uday Hussein's collections, which he had facilitated, and of what must have happened to them after the overthrow of Saddam Hussein. Such a waste.

Fifty kilometres outside Bukan, on the road to Shahin Dezh, Hassif stopped at a Kurdish teahouse, sat on one of the raised carpets inside the glass interior, and drank three glasses of tea. He also ate half a dozen potato pancake patties called *kuku-ye zibzamini*, drenched in Iranian *shahde golha* honey. Most Iranians would have considered pouring honey over such a savoury dish sacrilege. Hassif didn't care what they thought.

Twenty minutes after his arrival a minivan with six men inside it turned into the gravel parking space. Hassif got up, licked his fingers, and then accepted the bowl of scented water and the towel the owner of the teahouse was holding out to him.

When the man requested payment, Hassif produced his identity card and was gratified when the man bowed and ushered him to the entrance without further ado. Hassif never paid for anything if he could avoid it. It was a habit he had got into years ago in Iraq, and which he had no intention of changing. Why carry money when you can put the fear of God into people, and earn yourself a free ride instead?

When he left in his Mercedes, closely followed by the minivan, Hassif did not see the owner of the teahouse, who was wearing a red and black turban and traditional Kurdish men's clothes, run to the telephone to make a call. Three minutes later, the woman who had been posted on the highway to watch in case Hassif's car came past the teahouse without stopping, also came inside.

'Six, no?'

'Six men, yes, Father.'

'Armed?'

'I could not tell. But yes. Of course they will be armed.'

'I have phoned already. Hassif is on his way.'

'You are sure it was Hassif?'

'Totally sure. The damned fool even showed me his identity card so that he would not have to pay. The bill was for a few thousand rials. Hardly enough to get his shoes polished. But still he is greedy. What do they say about such men? "May God strike the rich man blind by his own gold."'

# FORTY-SIX

John Hart stood at the base of the slope that led up to Solomon's Prison and cursed whatever evil cloud had caused him to venture into Iran. Each minute he lingered on Iranian soil made it that much more likely that something would happen to bring him to the attention of the authorities. And maybe it had already happened? Maybe Hassif was gathering his forces together at that very moment to apprehend him?

He glanced across at Elwand. Elwand looked as sick as a dog. He gazed at Nalan. She looked poised and decisive. Excited even. Hart forced a smile onto his face. He slipped out his pocket Leica and took a few shots. His battery was close to zero.

Elwand nodded to him and pointed to the rope. Hart heaved it out of the boot of the car and he and Elwand looped it about their arms and began the ascent. Nalan followed along behind, talking all the while on her mobile phone, whether in Farsi or Kurdish, Hart could not tell.

'Hassif is coming,' she said to him at last, in English. 'With six armed men. They left the Darvish Teahouse ten minutes ago.'

'Six armed men?' said Hart. 'How can we deal with six armed men? Hadn't we better get out of here while we still can?'

'It's too late for that. The teahouse is only twenty minutes' drive from here along a single-carriage road. We are committed.'

'Where the hell are your other cousins then? I thought they were coming here to protect us?'

'Where they must be. Do not worry, John.'

'Worry? Me?' Hart shifted his end of the rope to his other arm. It weighed as much as a dead man. He stared up the slope ahead of him. Solomon's Prison was the last place on earth that he wanted to revisit at that particular moment. In fact it was the last place on earth he would ever want to revisit. 'Perish the thought.'

'Britannia. Look.' Elwand was pointing away into the middle distance.

Hart squinted. He could just make out a trail of dust on the road leading in from the main Bukan highway.

'This is them. Two cars.' Elwand held up two fingers.

'Two. Yes,' said Hart, for want of anything better to say. He felt like dropping the rope and legging it round the mountain to the safety of the other side. He looked down at Nalan behind him. She was making light going of the climb. To look at her, he decided, you would think that she was setting out on a bracing after-breakfast walk in a comfortable old democracy like Switzerland – not an assignation in an alien totalitarian state with the man who had tortured and brutalized her parents.

Three hundred metres up the slope Hart began cursing the weight of the rope. Then he cursed Hassif. When he was through doing that he cursed his ancestor, Johannes von Hartelius, and then he cursed the stupid Copper Scroll and his gullibility in believing the thousand-year-old message that had caused him to come all this way looking for it. Now he was merely the bait in someone else's trap. The jam in their sandwich. And what if these very same people decided that the odds against them were no longer worth the candle? He would be dangling by his neck off an Iranian cargo crane before he knew what hit him. Bloody, bloody fool.

Soon, he and Elwand were up near the lip of the volcano again, just as they had been two days previously. Hart could see the hole through which they had sieved the rope the last time they had visited the ill-begotten spot. He remembered the nightmarish climb down inside the funnel, and the even more nightmarish climb back up again. What crazy brainwave had caused him to suggest this location to Nalan in the first place? He had vowed never to come back here. Not for a thousand Copper Scrolls. And yet here he was. With the Deputy Chief Intelligence Officer, Border District, following half a kilometre behind him, and with a vanload of armed men in his train. Christ, maybe the Iranians would send in helicopters? What was to stop them doing that? Elwand and his buddies would be okay. They knew where to go. Where to disperse. But he and Nalan would be sitting ducks.

Elwand eased his way out over the rock face and started to swing one end of the rope back and forth. 'Catch it, Britannia. Just like you did the last time.'

Nalan drew in her breath as she peered over the lip of the volcano. 'This is a terrible place. Your description did not do it justice, John.'

Nalan's horror at the prospect below her pleased Hart. He had started to feel isolated in his reaction to the place. 'You can't describe places like this. You can only feel them. It's like a tomb down there. Believe me. A living, open tomb.' He caught the rope Elwand threw him and slid it through the gap in the rock.

This time Elwand had brought a steel crowbar with him. He climbed down from the rock and attached the rope to the crowbar with two half hitches, then jammed the crowbar against the base of the hole. They had no intention of using the rope, of course, and were simply going through the motions in case anyone was watching them through binoculars, or, God forbid, via a drone. This, at least, was what Elwand had assured him back in Bukan. Now Hart was not sure.

Seven hundred metres below them the two cars carrying Hassif and his men pulled into the parking lot beside Elwand's car. Six men piled out of the minivan, and a single stout figure climbed out of the accompanying Mercedes. Hassif. Hart noted that the men surrounding him weren't carrying any obvious weapons.

There was a lot of shouting and gesticulating, followed by much pointing up the hillside. Then Hassif barked out some orders. Hart suspected that Hassif had simply been ensuring that no casual visitors to the site were to be seen, because the six men now threw open the back of his Mercedes and helped themselves to the automatic weapons secreted there.

'Shit. Look at that. He's got an armoury in there. I hope they don't open up on us.'

'We are not yet within range,' said Elwand.

'Well, that's a comfort,' said Hart. He watched the six men begin their climb up the hillside towards them, with Hassif puffing along behind. 'Maybe he'll have a heart attack?'

'God is far too just to let someone like Hassif die of a mere heart attack,' said Nalan. 'Come. We need to move round the lip of the volcano to the eastern rim.'

'I really hope you know what you are doing,' said Hart.

'My cousins know what they are doing,' said Nalan. 'We are the bait, remember. You must look as if you are running now.'

Hart found that bit the easiest to mimic. He broke into a run, alongside Elwand and Nalan, just as if they had found themselves surprised by Hassif and his men and were trying to get away.

'Go on. Faster. Run ahead of us. He must think you feel that I betrayed you.'

There were a few scattered shots from the hillside below them. Hart could hear the spent bullets fizzing through the air above him. One or two ricocheted off the rocks below. Hart heard a distant shriek, which he assumed was Hassif telling his men to cool it, and not risk hitting anyone valuable.

'Quickly, quickly,' said Nalan.

Hart had little idea of what plan, if any, Nalan had hatched with her cousins. Everything had been conducted in far too much haste, in his opinion, and there had even come a point, early on in the proceedings, when Nalan had given up translating everything for him and had simply left him to stew in his own juices. Elwand had attempted to take up the slack in terms of Hart's understanding of the situation, but his efforts had fallen largely by the wayside. It had been extremely humiliating. As if they had purposely left him out of the loop.

Hart was astonished, therefore, to see close on a dozen men, armed with assault rifles and telescopic sights, emerge like ghosts from the cover in front of him.

'Now we get down. Here. Behind these rocks.'

Hart spreadeagled himself beside Nalan in the lee of a jagged outcropping of rock. His new position gave him a superb view of the six now struggling men accompanying Hassif, a hundred and fifty metres below them down the hillside. He began to understand why, throughout the entire history of warfare, enlightened combatants had always sought to defend and hold the upper ground.

The trap had been well sprung – the outcome a foregone conclusion. Hassif's six armed men were caught way out in the open, already exhausted from sprinting up the hillside, and therefore sickeningly vulnerable. The dozen rested men who passed him by, and amongst whom he recognized Nalan's five remaining cousins, dispersed themselves behind the ample cover at the top of the hill. Hart expected someone to call out to Hassif's men to give themselves up, but this did not happen.

What followed was as close to a clinical execution as Hart had ever witnessed. Hassif's men were systematically picked off by men occupying the higher ground and benefiting from the immense advantage of telescopic sights. It was a massacre. Each approaching man was targeted by at least two shooters. If he tried to fire back, he stood no real chance of hitting anything because of the upward arc forced upon him by the contour of the volcano. It was all over in under a minute.

Hassif was left standing alone on the hillside, his hands at his sides, his mouth hanging open in disbelief. As Hart watched, Hassif dropped to his knees and fumbled for his mobile phone. Or it might have been a pistol.

Nalan stood up from where she was sheltering and shouted down to him.

Hassif raised his hands above his head and waved them to show that he was not holding anything. Then he sat back in the dirt like a child in a sandpit. Hart felt almost sorry for him.

Nalan's cousins dispersed like chamois down the hillside. Ignoring Hassif, they set about collecting the dead men scattered around him. When this was done, they carted them the remaining distance to the edge of the volcano and tumbled them over the lip.

Nalan and Elwand started down towards Hassif. Hart followed them. Bahoz, Saman and another man, whom Hart did not recognize, moved across to meet them.

Only now was Hart able to see Hassif clearly for the first time. The man was unutterably nondescript. Hart had been expecting a monster. A man with the wages of sin stamped across his features. Instead he saw an elderly, overweight man, with dyed hair and a dyed beard, sucking air in through his teeth and close to hyperventilating.

The five of them accompanied Hassif to the top of the hill. The remainder of Nalan's cousins and kinsmen came to join them.

Nalan was the first to speak. She pointed to the lip of the volcano, and then down at Hassif's car. Hassif answered her. Nalan spoke again.

Hart edged his way towards Elwand. 'What is she saying?'

Elwand leaned towards him. 'She is asking if he has brought all the film with him in his car, as agreed. If he has not, she will throw him personally into Solomon's Prison after his men.'

Hassif was nodding vehemently now. Throwing his arms around. Selling himself dearly, thought Hart. Trying to cut a late deal.

Bahoz, the youngest of Nalan's cousins, broke away from the others and sprinted down the hillside. Everyone watched him. When he reached a patch of scree he began a skiing motion with his feet, negotiating the broken rock as if he were surfing on snow. In five minutes he was at the bottom of the hill.

He disappeared inside Hassif's car.

He emerged after two minutes and squinted up towards them. Nalan's phone rang. They could all see Bahoz talking into his phone, and hear Nalan replying to him nearby. Bahoz was making the universal symbol of empty-handedness.

Hassif said something to Nalan, and Bahoz disappeared back inside the car.

Hassif was grinning and smiling now, his expression that of a man who feels he will soon have fulfilled his part of the bargain, and who is confidently expecting his competitors to fulfil theirs. If it wasn't for the neat pile of weapons stacked about thirty yards down the slope, thought Hart, it would be impossible to believe that a gun battle had taken place here a mere ten minutes before. Or that anything untoward had happened. Maybe Hassif really did have the measure of it after all?

Bahoz re-emerged from the Mercedes far below them and a further conversation took place by phone. At the end of the conversation Nalan nodded at two of the men waiting beside her. These were men Hart did recognize. Hart assumed that everyone would now make their way down the hillside and clear the area, and that these men had simply been detailed to collect up the fallen weapons. But no. The men came towards him, smiling. Hart smiled back.

The two men caught him by the arms and wrenched them behind his back. Hart cried out, but another man he had not noticed slipped in behind him and gagged him before he could speak.

Hart tried to struggle but it was impossible. The three men were bearing down on him with all their weight. His arms were soon secured and his pocket camera taken. One of the men took out the camera's memory card and crushed it beneath his heel. Then he tossed the shattered SIM card over the lip of the volcano, after the dead men. He slipped the now useless camera into his side pocket.

Hart was forced back against a rock and left there, half sitting and half lying. Hassif clapped his hands together. He was sweating and smiling at the same time. Even though things suddenly appeared to be going his way again, he still looked sick.

Hart tried to bypass the gag with his tongue but it was impossible. How could this be happening? He had offered himself as bait alongside Nalan to trap Hassif. Were her people now about to hand him over to Hassif in exchange for the film of her parents that Nalan wanted destroyed?

Hassif indicated Hart with both hands, and made as if he intended to start down the hillside back towards his car. He was clearly expecting some of the men present to drag Hart to his feet and accompany him.

Something closed down in John Hart's chest. Had this been on the cards all the time? Had he simply been the most perfect sort of patsy imaginable? He could feel the sense of outrage consuming him. He had even, God forbid, travelled into Iran under his own steam, risking none of Nalan's family in the process. What an ass. What a consummate ass he had been. He lurched to his feet and aimed a kick at the man nearest to him, but he only succeeded in twisting round on the spot and falling down again. He lay on the ground and waited for what was about to happen to him. One thing he knew. He would sell himself dearly from here on in. He wouldn't go to his fate like a lamb to the slaughter. They'd have a fight on their hands.

As Hart watched, lost in his own sense of high dudgeon, four of Nalan's cousins bore down on the leering Hassif. They took Hassif's arms and legs and pinioned him to a flat rock. Hassif began to scream. One of the other men walked behind Hassif's head. The man felt about in the pockets of his baggy *shirwal* trousers and brought out a black leather box, about the size of a large book. He opened the box and took out a syringe. Hassif shrieked some more.

Hart tried to rock himself sideways and onto his knees, but someone was pinning him down with their foot. The gag in Hart's mouth was tight and getting tighter. He tried to signal Nalan with his eyes, but she refused to look at him. All her concentration was on Hassif.

The man with the syringe threw something silver to one of Nalan's cousins – Hart could no longer remember exactly who was who any more, but it might have been Elind. Elind placed the object in Hassif's mouth and began to screw it open. Hart realized that it was a mouth clamp. The sort of thing that might once have been used for dentistry, or as a prelude to take out someone's tonsils and adenoids. Hassif ululated through the opened aperture.

The first man now indicated to the others that they should support Hassif's head. When this was done, he sat himself astride Hassif's chest, aimed the syringe inside his mouth, and injected him a number of times. Then he waited.

Hart closed his eyes. Were they intending to torture Hassif? Punish him in some way by extracting his teeth? Was this some weird sort of Kurdish blood revenge? Then what were they going to do with him? He could feel the bile rising in his throat.

The man sitting astride Hassif's chest bent forwards again. This time he was holding a scalpel in his right hand. Hart could see Hassif's feet drumming on the ground.

The man made a series of quick movements, and then stood up. He was holding something bloody in his hand. He moved towards the lip of the volcano and tossed it into the void.

The dental gag was unscrewed and Hassif was dragged to his feet. His hands were untied. His knees immediately gave way, but four men were supporting him now and he remained on his feet. His mouth was rimmed with blood.

Elwand tied the end of the dangling rope about Hassif's waist. Hassif began to kick and fight. He was making gagging noises, but no real sound was emerging from his mouth. No human sound, anyway. Hart realized that it was Hassif's tongue they had cut out. The man who had done the cutting shook a jar of pills in front of Hassif's face. When he was sure that Hassif had registered the fact of the pills, he shoved them into Hassif's pocket with a flourish.

Hassif was manhandled to the edge of Solomon's Prison and held there, looking down. Nalan approached him. Hart expected her to say something to Hassif, but all she did was spit in his face. The men surrounding him levered him over the rock ledge and took up his weight on the rope. Then they began lowering him. It took four of them to do it.

Nalan watched the action of the rope with a frozen expression on her face.

Hart shook his head and looked up at the man who was pinioning him. The man seated him upright again and left him to his own devices. But he did not untie him, nor did he take out the gag.

Elwand circled his hand when he saw that Hassif had reached the bottom. He pointed to the tension of the rope against the crowbar and twanged it with his finger.

The man who had cut out Hassif's tongue handed Nalan the scalpel. Nalan crawled to the mouth of the hole and began sawing at the rope.

Hart threw himself forwards, but it was a pointless gesture. All he succeeded in doing was to ensure that he was even further from standing up without someone's help.

The rope parted and fell into the abyss. The crowbar clattered to the ground. The swish the rope made as it looped into the void merely added to the unholy silence left after its landing. Elwand picked up the crowbar and turned to go.

The man guarding Hart reached down and untied his gag. Then he freed him from his bonds.

The other men were all starting down the hillside as if nothing had happened. Nalan followed them.

Hart hurried to the lip of the volcano. Despite his vertigo, he managed to ease himself as close to the edge as was humanly possible. He stared down.

Hassif was standing on the 'king of the castle' rock eight hundred feet below. He was alternately waving his arms and holding on to his face. No sound came from him. No sound carried up the dead vent of the volcano.

Hart realized that Nalan and her tribe had devised, in their own eyes, the most perfect punishment imaginable for a man with whom they shared a blood feud. They had not killed him. They had even anaesthetized him during the surgery to his tongue, and given him further analgesics to deaden the pain afterwards. But they had condemned him to eternal silence. No water. No food. No possibility of ever calling for help. Even if people visited the site, which they only did on occasion, they would not be able to see him unless they risked their lives by leaning far out over the precipice. And who, bar a maniac, would ever do that?

What had Hart remembered while he had been down there? The 3-3-3 survival rule of thumb. Three minutes without air, three days without water, three weeks without food.

He looked one final time at the man standing on the king-of-the-castle stone and then slid his way back from the lip and followed the others silently down the hillside.

# FORTY-SEVEN

Hart was silent in the boot of the car going back to Ronas and Bemo's village. He had been given some water in a plastic bottle, and this he drank to prevent a recurrence of the coughing fit that had nearly given him away the last time.

He could make out the back of Elwand's head again round the broken back seat, but he couldn't tell if anyone else was in the car with him. Only when Nalan spoke, about twenty minutes into their journey, did Hart realize that she was sitting ahead of him in the passenger seat.

At the village he waited patiently for Elwand to open the boot. When his way was clear, he clambered out. He could smell his own stench mixed with that of whoever had originally owned the Kurdish clothes that he had been wearing for three days now.

He glanced across at Nalan. She was watching him, a sad smile on her face.

Hart walked across to the well and spooned up some water. He rinsed his face and scrubbed his teeth with his fingers. Then he drank some more.

When he straightened up he realized that Elwand had left the two of them alone and was talking to the head man. He was gesticulating up the mountain, and the head man was smiling and nodding his head.

Hart walked back towards Nalan. 'He won't be dead, you know. Not yet. There is still time.'

'No, there is not.'

'He will already have suffered a nightmare beyond your imagining.'

Nalan shook her head. 'No. Not beyond my imagining. He made my mother and father suffer a far worse nightmare, and for far longer. My own nightmare was nothing in comparison to theirs. What we have done is only just.'

Hart fixed her eyes with his. 'What? Cutting out his tongue? Abandoning him to die of thirst in the most godforsaken place on earth?'

'Yes. This is just.'

Hart shook his head. 'I cannot accept that.'

Nalan touched him on the arm, very lightly. 'This is because you have never suffered, John. Not in any real sense. You have lived surrounded by your cocoon of comfort, and you have taken pictures of the suffering of others. History afforded you the luck to be born in a peaceful country. Amongst your own people. If you had been born here, or in Iraq, you would have been a different man.'

'A man whom you might have married?'

Nalan hesitated. But only for a moment. 'Yes.'

'But you will not marry me now.'

'No.' She touched his cheek with her hand. 'But you always knew this. I always told you this.'

'Yes. But I didn't believe it.'

'That is your problem, John. You do not believe.'

Hart drew in his breath. He could see Elwand and the head man approaching. 'The man you are going to marry. He was one of those on the mountain, wasn't he?'

'Yes. He is the doctor.'

Hart threw his head back. 'The doctor? You call that a doctor? A man who cuts out people's tongues? I suppose you'd call a man a doctor who conducts amputations on thieves?'

'No. I would not.'

'Then how is this different?'

'If you do not know, I cannot tell you.' Nalan stepped back a pace. 'Goodbye, John. Elwand has arranged for you to pass back beyond the mountains. Now he is going to drive me to Bukan.'

'And I suppose you won't be there to greet me when I arrive in Iraq? No more passionate nights at Pank?'

'That is not worthy of you.'

Hart shook his head. He felt sick to his soul. 'Tell me something. One last thing. Before Elwand gets here. Why did you give me that night? Why did you risk everything to be with me?'

Nalan cocked her head to one side, so that her hair fell heavily onto her right shoulder. 'But I thought this was obvious. Because I love you.'

'Because you love me? But what about your husband-to-be?'

She tucked her hair back inside her scarf. 'There is no question of love for me with him. But respect? He has all of that from me. He has protected his family and his kinsmen. He has acted on my behalf in the punishment of the man who shamed my parents. I owe this man everything.'

'And you owe me nothing?'

'Only love, John. Only love. But that is my curse, and I shall have to live with it.' She touched her heart with her hand. 'Go back home. Find a woman of your own race to be with. Then think of me in quiet moments, when you are alone, just as I shall think of you. And do not grieve for me. As the poet Rumi says, anything you lose comes around again in another form. You will dance for ever in my breast, where no one but I can see you.'

# FORTY-EIGHT

# The Lebanon Mountains

### EARLY AUTUMN 1198

On the evening of the third day of their trek through the mountains, Hartelius and the princess returned early from their customary walk. The princess had been feeling unwell, and Hartelius had recognized this, from previous experience, as the customary affliction women experience during the early stages of their pregnancy. He had insisted that Elfriede return with him to their lean-to, and he soon had her comfortably snuggled in beside him, sipping a herb tea made from lemon and ginger that her handmaiden had brought her. Before long they were talking quietly together, with much caressing of hair and face, their eyes never leaving each other, their bodies touching along their entire length beneath the talismanic fur blanket Elfriede had brought with her all the way from the Rupertsberg Convent, and which she had possessed ever since she was a child.

It was then that the Amir's Sufi master, the Shaykh al-Akbar, also known as Al Akbariyya or Ibn Arabi, chose to approach them. The Shaykh was dressed for the first time in his *khirqa*, or Sufi mantle, which was multicoloured, with many patches, and made of a mixture of ram's wool and goat hair. It most resembled a shepherd's cloak, and bore no embroidery of any sort, being of the utmost simplicity in design. Above this the Sufi wore a turban, with one end hanging loose down the front of his clothing. He gave both Hartelius and the princess a deep salute above the eyes, which they immediately returned.

Hartelius could see his thirteen remaining Templars watching their unlikely new grouping with interest. This was hardly surprising, since Hartelius had explained to his men, three days before, that the Shaykh had immediately recognized the unknown language in which their birthright, the Copper Scroll, was principally written, as being that of the Yazidis of Lalish, and therefore a variant of Kurdish – but that the Shaykh had refused to discuss the matter further due to the conflict of interest the scroll posed for him. As it was common knowledge amongst Templar Knights that generations of their Order's scholars had been trying, and failing, to decipher this part of the written scroll for the past seventy years, the Shaykh's extraordinary revelation had come as a shock to them all.

The Shaykh, for his part, once he had vouchsafed this momentous information to Hartelius, had chosen to keep himself to himself, a fact noted and resented by the men, some of whom had even advocated taking the Sufi by force and torturing the truth out of him. Hartelius had felt obliged, not for the first time, to explain the unwritten laws of hospitality to his men.

When things were at their bleakest, with his men seemingly prepared to mutiny over the matter, Luitpold von Szellen, at rising forty years of age the oldest and most respected Knight Templar under his command, had, to Hartelius's relief, come out into the open with his backing for his commander's position. The Shaykh's reappearance now, and the depth of his salute towards Hartelius and the princess after three days spent ignoring everybody, came as something of a surprise.

'Let me tell you about the Yazidis,' the Shaykh said, squatting on his haunches and picking through the fire with a stick.

Hartelius sat back, astonished at the Shaykh's seemingly innate ability to read his mind. 'The Yazidis. Yes. The princess and I were just discussing them. I would obviously appreciate any further insights you may feel able to give me.' Hartelius hesitated, still a little unsure about the Shaykh's unlikely change of mind. 'Their true location, for instance, which I personally believe to be somewhere along the Southern Silk Road near Mosul, in Upper Mesopotamia. Which is at least twenty days' ride from here. If I am not mistaken, that is, for the map I possess of the Silk Route is an old one, and somewhat misused.'

The Shaykh flapped his hand. 'You are intending to travel there, are you not? To leave your princess behind with me, her handmaiden, and two of your knights, and take the remainder of your Templar Knights with you? This is why you are resting your horses here. Is this not so?'

Hartelius sat back on his haunches. He gave the princess a guilty look and then nodded. For how could he do otherwise? Everything the Shaykh said was true. 'How can you possibly know this?'

The Shaykh shrugged. The vestige of a smile, part hidden by his beard, played across his features. 'A man who keeps himself to himself is eventually ignored by everybody. Then he may hear things that others wish to keep secret. Voices carry in these mountains, Commander. I have been listening to you and your men very closely over the past few days. I know, for instance, that you have argued many times to save my life. That those two. . .' he pointed across to Klarwein and Nedermann '. . . would have taken and tortured me to give up any further information about the scroll I might carry in my head.'

'I would never have allowed this. You are my guest.'

'I know, Commander. I know.' The Sufi was smiling broadly now. 'Still. It is true what I say.'

The two men watched each other across the fire. The princess took Hartelius's hand in hers. Hartelius could feel the intensity of the look that she gave him, but he found that, despite all his efforts, he could not turn his gaze away from the Sufi.

'I have rarely in my life seen so great a love as you and the princess show to each other,' said the Shaykh, inclining his head towards the princess. 'And I have never known my pupil, the Amir, to love a man as he loves you.' This time

311

the Shaykh's eyes focused on Hartelius alone. 'You are much loved of God to be so loved in this life.'

Hartelius bowed his head. 'I know it.'

The Shaykh smiled an even broader smile. 'But do you acknowledge it?'

Hartelius glanced to his right, where the princess was watching him, her eyes sparkling with anticipation. For Hartelius never spoke openly of his personal beliefs – or only in the most general terms, when he was telling her of his Templar upbringing and its extraordinary strictures, perhaps, and comparing them to what she had experienced at the Rupertsberg Convent. Or merely in jest.

'I do. Yes. Each day I thank God for the princess, and the child of ours she bears. For the love I bear her and for the love she bears me. And each day I thank God for the Amir, and the love he bears me, and the love I bear him.'

'And you are overwhelmed?'

'Yes. The emotions that I feel when I thank God, and do not ask for his favour, overwhelm me.'

The Sufi bent forwards, as if he was listening to the meaning behind the meaning of Hartelius's words. He grasped Hartelius's free hand between both of his and held it, just as the princess was doing. 'And you do not ask for His favour? That is interesting. And hardly Christian.'

Hartelius closed his eyes. He felt an extraordinary surge of energy pass through him, as if both the Shaykh and the princess were somehow meeting in him through the simple touch of their hands. He suspected that what he was about to say might be construed as blasphemy in some quarters. He lowered his voice so that his men might not hear him – or, at the very least, not be entirely certain of what he said.

'What is Christian and what is Muslim? There is, and can be, only God. When I was drowning in the Saleph River – when I was trying to rescue the princess's father – I had a vision.' Hartelius caught himself mid-stride. 'No. It was a presence rather than a vision. Well. . .' He shook his head dazedly. 'I do not rightly know what to call it.'

'Yes, you do.'

Hartelius let out his breath. 'Yes, I do. It was a direct experience of God. From that moment onwards, everything in my life, everything I did, was focused directly on Him.'

'To the exclusion of all dogma? To the exclusion, even, of your own faith?'

Hartelius no longer even cared who might be listening to him. He was overwhelmed by the need to describe what he felt. To describe it for the very first time, and out loud. 'To the exclusion of everything but God.'

'And what is God?'

Hartelius smiled. 'God is everything. We are all within God as He is within us.'

'And you love God?'

'Totally.'

'And you came to this love yourself? Not through any human vessel?'

'I did not come to this love through any volition of my own. Nor through any human vessel. It just is.'

313

The Sufi remained silent for a long time. Hartelius, too, stared into the fire, as though its energy might feed his emotional exhaustion. He was profoundly aware of the princess beside him – of her stare – but he could not bring himself to raise his head. He had opened his innermost heart to a stranger. Why had he done this? And in front of his men? But it could not have been otherwise.

'Give me the scroll.' The Shaykh held out his hand.

Hartelius rose to his feet. He walked towards his saddle bags. He felt inside one of the satchels and returned with a package wrapped in sheepskin. He handed it to the Shaykh. He could hear murmuring from his men, but he ignored them.

The Shaykh offered him another salute. 'Thank you. Thank you for your faith, Baron von Hartelius. I shall translate these and then return them to you.'

Hartelius was fleetingly tempted to ask, 'Why? Why will you translate them for us?' But he did not. He sat down beside the princess and laid his head in her lap. He lay like this for a long time, with his eyes closed.

When he awoke it was to his Templars telling him that the Shaykh had gone.

# FORTY-NINE

At Hartelius's insistence they stayed on the mountaintop for a further three days, just as they had agreed with the Amir. The men were restless, and eager to set off in pursuit of the Shaykh, but Hartelius forbade them. And the habit of discipline was so strong in them that they obeyed him.

For each man knew that something had changed in their commander since the night he had communed with the Sufi mystic over the fire. They had not heard his words, nor understood fully what had gone on, but the act of handing over the Copper Scroll to one who might be construed as their enemy appeared significant to them in a way beyond their immediate understanding.

On the evening of the third day the Shaykh returned. He handed the sheepskin package back to Hartelius.

Hartelius acknowledged the transfer with a bow.

'It is done,' said the Shaykh. 'Poorly, but it is done. Do you still intend to send it back to your Templar masters?'

Hartelius shook his head.

'I thought not. You will send it to the king instead?'

'To the true king, yes. To Frederick.'

'The infant nephew of your princess?'

'Yes. I will have von Szellen take it to Sicily, with ten Templars to protect him. I will send the remaining two Templars to speak to our Grand Master. When he hears that it was the upstart Philip of Swabia who stole the scroll from them, he will understand my actions. He will acknowledge the real king and place the Templars at Frederick's command, and not at the command of his uncle. The scroll will then be returned to its rightful owners.'

'And yet you have not read my translation of the scroll.'

'And neither shall I, for my life is forfeit. If I am taken and tortured, I would rather know nothing. In this way I will not be brought to a betrayal of my Order.'

'Yes,' said the Shaykh. 'You are wise in this. But let me tell you this much. All that has been said about the contents of the scroll is untrue. It does indeed speak of the building of a mighty Temple, and where the wherewithal to build that Temple may be found. But the Temple will not be built in Jerusalem.'

'It will not?'

'No. It will be built in the north. Far in the north. Where it is needed most. At a site on which a temple already stands. A temple that will be dismantled to make way for the new Temple.'

Hartelius turned to the princess. 'You are fresh from the convent, Elfriede. Have you heard of such a place? A place

316

in the north where an old temple is to be dismantled and a new one built to replace it?'

'By temple, do you mean a cathedral?'

'Yes.'

'Then it can only be Chartres.'

'Why is that?'

'Bishop Fulbert's cathedral was burnt down four years ago. It was one of the greatest tragedies in Christendom. Even rustics such as you in Bavaria must have heard of it,' she added with a smile. 'Everything bar the crypt, part of the west façade and two towers is gone. A great new cathedral is to be built on the spot after the dismantling is complete. The greatest of all cathedrals. But there is no money. No will. No possibility of this coming to fruition.'

'Now,' said the Shaykh, 'there is.'

'And with no danger to Islam,' said Hartelius, with a smile. 'Let us not forget that.'

'None,' said the Shaykh, echoing his smile, and toying with his Carnelian prayer beads.

'But you would still have given me back the scroll if there had been.'

'Yes,' said the Shaykh. 'It formed part of an unspoken contract between us.'

'And what was my part of the contract?'

'This, you know.'

'Yes,' said Hartelius. 'This I know.'

# FIFTY

Hartelius watched von Szellen and the nine Templar Knights who were to accompany him, including the troublemakers Klarwein and Nedermann, mounting their horses. At the very last moment he brought the sheepskin package from its hiding place and set it firmly in von Szellen's hands.

'You understand why this has to go to King Frederick's court in Sicily? And not to that of his uncle, King Philip, in Mainz?'

'I know that King Philip stole the Copper Scroll from our Order and that you are returning it to the Grand Master, via our rightful sovereign.'

'Yes, together with a request to him, as King of Sicily and true head of the House of Hohenstaufen, that I might be allowed to marry the princess, his aunt, by the left hand, in a morganatic marriage, as she is to bear my child.'

Von Szellen drew in his breath. 'I did not know.'

'It is best that no one else knows either. For I intend to prejudge the king's permission and marry the princess anyway.

The king, after all, is only four years old, and Pope Innocent III is his guardian. I do not have high expectations there.'

Von Szellen threw back his head and laughed. 'And who will you get to witness the *verba de praesenti*? This Sufi? The princess's handmaiden? I know why you are staying behind, Hartelius. What chance do you think you have? The Amir and his men were due here two days ago. They have not come. Which means that he has fallen foul of von Drachenhertz and has been killed. Every man and woman between here and Constantinople will be out looking for you now in search of the reward. And you have given me all your letters of credit to furnish my men. How long do you think you will last in these mountains with the little gold you have left? Best come with us and take your chances. At least we have numbers on our side.'

'I cannot. And you will be safer without me and the princess along.'

'I know that too.'

Von Szellen eased his horse away from Hartelius's side and raised his arm. Both men had learned on campaign not to waste words once things were decided. Von Szellen's men fell in behind him. 'It has been an honour to ride with you, Commander,' he said over his shoulder.

'And I, you,' said Hartelius.

After that von Szellen did not look back.

Hartelius paused, watching the Templars until they disappeared from sight. Then he strode across to the two men who had elected to make their way back to Germany

319

on his behalf. 'Now. You go too. I am relying on you both to recount, fully and impartially, all that has taken place here to the Grand Master.' He handed them a purse. 'And that I am fulfilling my role as Guardian of the Holy Spear by keeping it safe from the tyrant von Drachenhertz.'

'It shall be done, Commander.'

The one remaining Templar, Aludo von Eisenbrand, had asked if he might stay with Hartelius in order to protect the princess. The truth was that he was in love with the princess's handmaiden, and when it was made clear that she could not accompany either of the Templar parties as she would only slow them up, he had elected to remain behind also. Hartelius was grateful for his presence, as this would give the princess and the Shaykh at least some protection whilst he was away.

'But why do you have to go?' said the princess. 'The Amir may still come as he promised.'

'No. He will not. But if he does, you will be here, as arranged, to meet him.'

'But why you?'

'Because the Amir is my friend. And the Shaykh and I have a contract.'

'Unspoken.'

'But still a contract. Both of us knew it when I let him take the scroll. He has fulfilled his side of the bargain. Now I must fulfil mine.'

'But you will be killed.'

'Perhaps not.'

'I know you will be killed.'

'That is God's will.'

'And still you will go?'

'Yes, my love. Would you have me be an unworthy friend?'

'For unworthy friends make unworthy lovers? Is that what you are saying?' The princess was smiling through her tears.

Hartelius knelt in front of her and kissed both her hands. Then he placed his head against her stomach and she held him there, lightly, while he communed with his unborn child.

# FIFTY-ONE

Hartelius retraced his steps at perhaps twice the speed in which the original journey had been conducted. He was travelling downhill for the most part, and along already blazed trails. He slept and then rode in two-hour stages to rest Gadwa, his stallion, and his relief horse, an Arabian gelding called Ishan. He continued like this throughout the night, relying on the horses to pick their way along the tracks and byways as much by scent as by sight. The air was clear and each breath he took was a joy.

But as he approached the place of the armies, his spirits lowered and he began to doubt his mission. What could a single man do in such circumstances? How could he have left the princess with only one knight, an unarmed Sufi and her handmaiden for company? What if he never came back? What then?

Time and again he thrust these questions from his mind, but always they came back to torment him. Privately, he had spoken to his last remaining Templar, Aludo von Eisenbrand, and agreed with him that if he were not to return or send word within a period of ten days, he too must make for Sicily with the princess's party, where Hartelius had every reason to believe she would be safe.

If von Szellen had done his work well and prepared the ground, it would be acknowledged by all that he and the princess were, by convention at least, married. The young king's express permission would then turn an informal, albeit legal, convention into a formal Muntehe binding – one in which Elfriede's child would stand to inherit his or her part of Hartelius's estate, alongside his four other children, together with any title of nobility that might accrue from their mother or their father's line. If either estate or line were left, that is, after news of Hartelius's betrayal was carried back to the false king in Germany.

To this end Hartelius had brought everyone together, before leaving, and had conducted a *verba de praesenti* ceremony in which he had uttered the words 'I do, here present, receive you as mine, so that you become my wife and I your husband' – words then mirrored by Elfriede. He had then transferred his family ring from his hand to hers, in a further token of their arrangement, and to mark his formal acquisition of tutelage over his bride, the ring being worn on the fourth finger of her right hand, which traditionally possessed a vein that carried blood directly to the heart.

Elfriede, for her part, presented Hartelius with a wreath made from flowers, which she placed on his head in honour of fertility. The presence of three witnesses was enough to legitimize the ceremony, which, again according to convention, stood in no need of a priest's attachment to make it legally binding. In this way, at least, Hartelius had managed to lay his own and the princess's mind at rest.

But, as Hartelius slithered towards the edge of the escarpment overlooking von Drachenhertz's camp, marriage, and the creation of dynasties, began to seem the least of his worries.

Nothing had changed. The camp still spread the width of ten cathedrals across the plain. To Hartelius's mind this could only mean one thing. That the Amir and his men had not succeeded in breaking through von Drachenhertz's defences, and had been either killed or captured.

That night Hartelius muzzled Gadwa and Ishan and rode down to within a few hundred yards of the enemy's skirmish lines. He tethered the horses behind a dune. Then he stripped himself of all unnecessary accoutrements beyond his sword, his dagger, and his hauberk, and began his slow crawl towards the nearest campfire.

Three times he was forced to stop and bury his head in the sand as guards passed. And three times he continued with his relentless crawling.

After the last guard party passed, he stood up, brazenly, and strode past the outer boundaries of the first campfire he could see, knowing that in the darkness at the periphery of a fire, all faces look the same.

His one advantage now was that he was amongst his own people. He wore the same chainmail as they did, and carried the same sword. His hair and beard were shorn in the same manner. His bearing was the same, together with his size and shape. He even spoke their language. All things that would stand him in good stead if he were stopped.

He picked his way towards the centre of the camp, striding confidently when he saw men approaching him, and walking with more caution when he was alone.

No one challenged him. No one called out to him. Thus it soon became clear to Hartelius that the host spread out around him was no longer on the alert. It was only when he saw the great mound of abandoned Saracen weapons piled in the rough centre of the encampment that he realized quite what a disaster must have happened to his friend the Amir and his men.

Hartelius was now faced with a dilemma. He needed information. But that information would only be available by asking. And any man asking would instantly fall under suspicion, as who but an enemy spy could not possibly know everything that had occurred without the need for words?

Hartelius passed one campfire with only Knights Hospitaller gathered round it. Another with Teutonic Knights. He avoided these. Any Templar Knights, he knew, would be keeping themselves to themselves at the far edge of the camp, where they would be the first into danger and the first into battle, as was their custom. He would avoid these too, for fear of being recognized by former crusading companions. No. What he must find were mercenaries. Men who gathered together in disparate gangs and who fought purely for gold. Here, only, would he have a chance of gathering information.

As fate would have it, he chanced upon none of these. Instead he saw the figure of a man limping in front of him. A man who walked with a hunched back and one leg thrown out to the side. A man who wore a white surplice with a red Templar cross on the front and back.

Heilsburg. It must be Heilsburg. No one else walked as he did. His nickname during the third crusade had been 'half man half frog' – shortened to 'frogman' or *froschmann* amongst his friends. It had been he who had first found Hartelius on the desert road after he had plucked the Holy Lance from Frederick Barbarossa's saddle. He who had explained away Hartelius's deplorable condition to Frederick Barbarossa's mourning son, the Duke of Swabia, triggering Hartelius's unexpected rise to the nobility.

Hartelius was now faced with a terrible dilemma. If a committed Templar such as Heilsburg was still here, it must mean that formal word had not yet come through from Germany of the annexation of the Copper Scroll from the Templars by the king. If that were to be the case, there was no reason to suppose that, beyond the conventional bounds of a long-standing friendship, Heilsburg would in any way be minded to show favour to him. In fact Heilsburg being Heilsburg, he would no doubt act first, out of instinct, and ask questions later. When it would already be far too late.

Hartelius shadowed Heilsburg as well as he was able, but he soon began to fear, given the complete set of armour

Heilsburg was wearing, that his friend must be returning from some duty or other, and would soon lead him directly to the Templars' encampment, which was the last thing that Hartelius wanted.

So he picked up a stone and threw it at Heilsburg's back. The stone struck Heilsburg on his neck mail, high up on his left shoulder. Immediately upon throwing it, Hartelius ducked into the lee of a tent and waited.

He could hear the crunch of Heilsburg's sabatons approaching, and the muttered curses his friend was uttering. Something about children and their lack of respect for authority.

Hartelius crossed himself and waited for Heilsburg to come parallel to him. His one advantage was that he knew on which side Heilsburg was invariably thrown when he limped. As Heilsburg rounded the corner of the tent, Hartelius grabbed him by the collar and jerked him violently in the direction he was already veering.

Heilsburg lost his footing and pitched into the sand. Hartelius fell upon him and raised a warning hand. Heilsburg's eyes widened, but he did not cry out.

Hartelius sat up and flipped his dagger round. He touched the point to his throat and forced the haft into Heilsburg's hand. 'I am in your hands. Kill me if you will. I ask only, as your friend, that you give me five minutes to explain myself before you hand me in to your new master.'

Heilsburg spat the sand out of his mouth. 'My only master is God. You should know that as well as anybody.'

Hartelius let out a sigh. 'I was hoping you would say that.'

Heilsburg dropped the point of the dagger and embraced Hartelius. Then the two men sat side by side in the sand for a moment, like small children.

'You must come with me,' said Heilsburg.

'Where?'

'I owe you five minutes, remember. Here, you are on a major thoroughfare through the camp. Do you want to be caught?'

'No.'

'Then come.'

Heilsburg led Hartelius to a tent. He tipped the flap and checked inside. 'Good. Still gambling.'

'Who is still gambling?'

'Fournival.'

'But gambling is illegal for Templar Knights.'

Heilsburg snorted. 'Much has changed since last we met. But then, why am I telling you this? You already have intimate acquaintance with our margrave. And with his bride-to-be, as I understand it, also.' He ushered Hartelius ahead of him inside the empty tent. 'I can only tell you that everything you have heard about the man is true. And more besides. Everything is slipping. There is no morality any more. He will be the death of us all.' Heilsburg turned to Hartelius, his eyes dancing with mischief. 'But I rather suspect he will be the death of you first.'

# FIFTY-TWO

'It was a massacre.' Heilsburg finished his beaker of wine and held it out for Hartelius to refill. 'The Saracens rode in from the sea, thinking they had outwitted us. But the margrave, for all his sins, is nothing if not a tactician. He had caused deep bonfires to be built in every part of the camp. With sundried kindle wood laid near them, soaked in tar. And then he ordered the bonfires covered. In this way, in a matter of seconds, the fires could be uncovered and any part of the camp could be lit up as in a festival.'

'What happened?'

'The Saracens came howling and yodelling in from the sea, all banners unfurled, as is their wont. It was a fine sight. They broached the edges of the camp in darkness and thought to ride on through and out the other side, like a scimitar slicing through silk. But the bonfires caught them out. Then it was only a matter of numbers. They were surrounded and slaughtered by von Drachenhertz's mercenaries. Even the idlers and malingerers dipped their swords in Saracen blood that night. It was disgusting to see. These men were not our enemy. It was the margrave who challenged them and barred their legal way. Many of us felt the shame of it. But there was little we could do but watch the massacre from a distance.'

'And the Amir?'

'Their leader, you mean?'

'Yes.'

'He is a prisoner. Men such as he are worth a fortune in ransom. And the margrave clearly hopes the Amir's presence will lure you out of hiding and give you into his hands.' Heilsburg grinned. 'And he was right yet again. I am almost beginning to believe in the man myself.'

'And you. You believe all you hear about me?'

'Me?' Heilsburg shrugged. 'I am a Knight Templar first and foremost. I do what I am told.'

'What if I told you that King Philip of Swabia stole the Copper Scroll from our Grand Master? That he sent it, as part of his sister's wedding portion, for the margrave to use as he saw fit? And that I stole the scroll back, had it translated, and it is now on its way, with von Szellen, to the true king's court in Sicily.'

'If you were any other man I would call you a liar.'

'But you know I am not.'

'I have never known you to lie. No.' Heilsburg bent forwards from the hip, his trunk and one arm canted sideways, his other hand holding his wine. 'This is true, what you say? The scroll is translated at last?'

'By a Sufi, yes. One of the enemy. Who trusted me enough to give it back to me.'

'Why did he trust you?'

'Because he knew I would come here and try to save his pupil, the Amir.'

Heilsburg shook his head. He did not even laugh. 'This is impossible. Even for you, Spear-Saver. I have just come from guarding the man. There are twenty other knights guarding him at any one time. And a thousand knights guarding those knights. And a thousand further knights guarding those. No one man can get through. It would take an army.'

'Still. I must try it.'

'Then you will be caught. And I shall be forced to watch your execution, which will be most objectionable to me, and which will probably cause me to miss my breakfast. Or to throw it up, given what methods the margrave will doubtless use on you.'

'I have walked through this camp already unchallenged.'

'That would end the closer to the Amir's prison tent you came.'

'And there is no other way?'

'Bar giving yourself up in exchange for the Amir? None.'

'Giving myself up?'

Heilsburg rocked his head back and forth. 'If you knew how the margrave longs for your head, you would not seem so astonished, my friend. He would free the Amir, as you call him, in two shakes of a rat's tail if you were to offer yourself in his stead. Don't you think he knows what a hornet's nest he has stirred up with his massacre of Saracens during a time of peace? Even the margrave is not immune to this one. If he can save face by freeing the Amir – under certain conditions, that is – he will do so. The margrave may be a monster. But he is not mad. But what am I saying? Why would a man deliver himself up to another man who has promised to castrate him, torture him, hang, draw and quarter him, and then leave the residue to the fire ants?'

'Will you act as my intermediary?'

'You are not serious?'

'If you agree, I will leave the camp again, and wait for a pre-arranged signal from you that all covenants are in place.'

'Hartelius, this is mad.'

'I owe the Amir my life, Heilsburg. He is a captive and his men are dead because they tried to guard me and the princess. The princess is waiting at a pre-arranged place for the Amir to come and offer her his protection. If my sacrifice can ensure his freedom, then the princess will also be safe, and my child with her.'

'Your child?'

'Yes. The princess and I are married.'

'Holy Mother of God. You cannot be serious.'

'I am deadly serious.'

Heilsburg looked long and hard at his friend. Then he shook his head. 'This is too great a sacrifice you are making. Think of it, man. Think of what von Drachenhertz will do to you.'

'I am thinking of it. All the time I am thinking of it. But I don't know what else to do. I can hardly charge the Amir's tent and free him that way.'

'Then ride to the place he comes from. Tell his people what has happened.'

'They would spit my head onto a pole and roast it over a griddle.'

Heilsburg sniffed. 'You may have a point there. They would certainly not be well disposed towards you.'

'So you see? I have nowhere else to turn. You can say that an arrow was fired into the Templar camp carrying a parchment with my conditions on it. That you picked up the arrow. Together we can write something out that will make sense to von Drachenhertz. From what you say, he is so consumed with hatred of me that he will agree to almost anything to have me in his hands.'

'There is that.' Heilsburg looked up at his friend. His features were thrown into deep contrast by the oil lamp separating him from Hartelius. 'But you know, if I were you, I would leave the camp as you say. Then I would ride. As far and as hard as my horse could take me. And I would not stop till I reached the ends of the earth.'

'But I am not you, Heilsburg. Unfortunately, I am me.'

# FIFTY-THREE

The moment Hartelius left Heilsburg's tent it was clear that something was amiss in the camp. Men were running to and fro, calling to each other. Fires were being added to. Hartelius knew that he had only a certain amount of time left before the atmosphere inside the camp would come to resemble day.

He began to run too, as running seemed the only sensible thing to do. For he could hardly remain in place when all about him was in flux. And neither could he remain in the tent. Fournival was no Heilsburg. Fournival would give him in as soon as look at him, in the hope of some advancement for himself. The man was a gambler. What more needed to be said?

Hartelius had almost made it to the outer periphery of the camp, near to the point where he had entered it, when he saw Gadwa, his stallion, and Ishan, his gelding, being led in by a squire. Both had their muzzles off. Someone was shouting that they had found the Holy Lance in the stallion's saddlebags, and others were responding that this meant that Hartelius and his Saracen allies were already in the camp. Hartelius now understood what had initially triggered the alarm.

Each man now began looking around himself. Everyone became a potential Saracen. The camp went from being sloppy to alert in the twinkling of an eye.

Hartelius forged on towards the outskirts of the encampment. For what else could he do? One of the horses must have slipped its muzzle and begun calling. Hartelius guessed it was Gadwa, who had probably caught the scent of a mare as the wind changed. He ought to have thought of this eventuality. Gadwa lived through his loins, as all stallions did. Why expect him to be any different? And now he was lost. Hartelius felt as if his heart had been torn in two inside his chest.

'You. Who are you with?' The captain pointed at Hartelius with the tip of his sword.

'The Templars.'

'Why are you heading in the opposite direction to their encampment?'

'To collect my armour from the smith.'

'You should be searching for von Hartelius. Not running errands.'

'I am sorry, Captain. I will begin searching immediately.'

'What is your name?'

Hartelius could feel the portcullis closing down on him. 'Szabo.'

'Szabo. I know of no Szabo. I have never heard of any Szabo amongst the Templars.'

'I am new. I only got in three days ago. After the battle.'

'But we have had no fresh Templar recruits from Acre.'

'I came from Tortosa.'

The captain moved towards Hartelius. Hartelius could only wait. He could feel the hand of fate grasping him by the shoulder. It was at this moment that Gadwa saw him and began nickering.

The captain turned round. 'Do you know this horse?'

'No, Captain.'

'But the horse knows you, it seems. Look at him pawing the ground trying to get to you.'

Hartelius tried to break away, but there was not the remotest possibility of escape. He was instantly surrounded and borne to the ground, where his weapons were secured and his chainmail lifted from him.

'If I have made a mistake,' said the captain, 'so be it. But we shall take you to the Templar encampment and confirm your identity. If you are recognized, and your story confirmed, you shall have a cup of wine on me. If you are not, you die.'

# FIFTY-FOUR

It was Himmelstreich who turned Hartelius in. It was inevitable. Himmelstreich had loathed Hartelius from the moment Hartelius had presented the Holy Lance to Frederick of Swabia, eight years before, and been exonerated from his Templar vows – illegally, as Himmelstreich saw it – and allowed to marry.

'It is he. Johannes von Hartelius. The false Templar. I would know him anywhere. Look at the scar on his face where the Saracen quarrel cut him.'

Hartelius could see Heilsburg amongst the crowd of Templars surrounding him. His friend was talking urgently to Fournival. Explaining things to him. Probably telling him what a fool Hartelius had been ever to come calling at his bitterest enemy's camp.

Someone held a burning brand close to Hartelius's face. Other Templars began adding their Groschen-worth of opinion to Himmelstreich's outpourings. Hartelius tried to shake off the arms that held him, but to no avail. He was borne bodily back towards the centre of the camp.

Is it to be now? he said to himself. Is it all to end here? Far from my love and my child, in this benighted desert, under an alien moon?

He came to his senses again when they stood him outside von Drachenhertz's tent.

The man will gut me in front of everybody. He will have my entrails out and leave me for the ants, just as Heilsburg says. And I will have deserved it for my stupidity in taking God's mantle for my own, and challenging fate.

Hartelius could hear the margrave's personal guard whispering to the captain. 'The margrave is with a new woman. I cannot disturb him. He will have my ears cut off.'

'I will cut your ears off now if you do not call him. And your nose. And your tongue. Then I will start on your feet and travel upwards again until I reach the crown of your head.'

The guard turned pale, saluted, and slipped in under the tent flap. There was a loud shout, as indeed of someone being obnoxiously disturbed. Then a rustling and a crashing.

The next thing Hartelius knew, von Drachenhertz was standing in front of him, half naked, his penis at half mast, his eyes alight with victory.

'So. You came for your friend the Amir. I knew you would. Idiots like you sicken me. You are so predictable. For you, friendship counts over common sense.'

Von Drachenhertz looked back over his shoulder towards the tent. His mind, it seemed, was still partially on other things. Some of the men around him exchanged knowing glances.

'I am far too busy to torture you now. Virgins like the one I am just about to deflower do not grow on trees.' Von Drachenhertz laughed at his own joke. 'Shall I have you castrated straight away?' He looked down at Hartelius's midriff and then at his own. 'No. You shall think about it for a night. About everything I intend to do to you. And before I destroy you, you shall write out your apologia for our king. While you still can. It shall be sealed inside the Holy Lance and sent back to Mainz, alongside your skull. When I have made enough play with it, that is. I shall drink out of your eye sockets, Hartelius, and suck jelly from your pate. Dwell on that for a few hours. For now, I am otherwise engaged.' Von Drachenhertz turned back to his tent. He snatched open the flap and peered inside. He looked back at Hartelius. 'I am about to do something you will never do again, Templar. Now who is the cuckold? Now who is the fool?'

'Where shall we put him, Lord?' said the captain.

'Give him pen and paper and throw him in with the Amir. I want them guarded by a thousand men. They can bugger each other to their heart's content if they so choose. Far be it from me to deprive a man of his final fling with anyone other than my intended bride. Tomorrow, at dawn. . .' He hesitated, his eyes still on the inside of the tent. 'Tomorrow at midday we begin the torture. Arrange a feast. We shall eat while Hartelius screams. There will be no need for other music.'

# FIFTY-FIVE

'So you came.' The Amir watched Hartelius from across the tent. His guards had chained him to a neck collar, which was, in turn, chained to a pillar.

Hartelius was chained on the opposite side of the room. Both men's chains measured approximately five feet from haft to lock. Even placed end to end they would not have allowed the men the possibility of anything other than a distant nod to each other.

'I came. Yes,' said Hartelius.

'I knew you would.'

'I, on the other hand, did not. I am a surprise to myself.'

Both men laughed.

'I had thought they would at least have disembowelled you by now. Von Drachenhertz's threats are seldom plucked from thin air.'

'He has a virgin to deflower. He wished to prove to his men that he has his priorities right. That he does not attach much importance to me.'

'But he does.'

'Yes. You know that and I know that. But the margrave is a man who likes to grandstand. The night is not good enough to do what he wants to do to me. It must be done in broad daylight, with a few thousand men watching. And a party alongside. That's how von Drachenhertz does these things.'

'And yet you don't seem scared.'

'Why should I be? I shall be dead long before his torturers get to me.'

'How, may I ask?'

'You will kill me.'

The Amir sat back on the floor of the tent. He pointed to his chain. 'But I can't get to you.'

'But you will. Von Drachenhertz will insist that you watch what he does to me. I have a stiletto concealed in my boot. Small, it is true. But still sharp. As we are taken outside I shall leap on you as if we are in some way enemies. I shall have the stiletto in my hand. I would appreciate your using it on me.'

'Why don't you do it yourself?'

'My faith forbids it. But neither your faith nor mine forbids you killing me. Will you do it?'

'Of course.'

'Thank you. I should not like to be made a public spectacle of by a man I despise. And now, Amir, I must write my apologia to the king.'

'And you will do this thing? You will write an apologia for something you are not responsible for?'

'Yes. To disguise something else.'

341

The Amir smiled. 'Ah. The Copper Scroll. My Sufi master, Ibn Arabi, translated it for you, did he not?'

'You knew he would.'

'I did. Yes.'

'This was a great gift you gave me.'

'And this is why you came back for me? To repay him?'

'No. I came back for you because I love you as a friend. My love for you is beyond explanation. I could not have done otherwise.'

Both men fell silent. After a little while, Hartelius began scratching out his apologia on the parchment he had been given.

Ten minutes later, he looked up. 'Amir, what is the wildest and most absurd place that one might hide something? The most likely, and yet the most unlikely?'

The Amir sat back and stared at Hartelius as if his friend had temporarily lost his senses.

'Imagine, for a moment, that I have sent my Templars to hide this thing. Within, let us say, a month's ride from here. Somewhere that might seem logical to a man obsessed with his own greatness. And a place that would cause him the maximum amount of inconvenience to approach.'

The Amir thought for a while. 'The scroll tells of Solomon's Temple, does it not?'

'It does, yes. And the key to the treasure that will fund its building.'

'Then have it hidden in Solomon's Prison.'

'Where is that?'

'Near a place called the Takht-e-Soleyman – Solomon's Castle. It is beyond Arbil. Beyond Bukan. And near Takab, in Persia.'

'This is a real place?'

'This is a terrible place. A place where monsters were once imprisoned. All know of it. The Kurds who live there guard their lands very diligently. Whoever goes to find it will have their work cut out. They will likely not return.'

'Good. This strikes me as the perfect hiding place. Forgive me while I urinate into my hand. I need to inscribe this into a poor, but almost invisible code. After you have killed me, I want von Drachenhertz to discover it. I want him to set off in pursuit of my Templar Knights. The imagined ones I will have sent to Solomon's Prison, of course. It will amuse me, while I pass my time in purgatory, to know that this man is ordering his men off on a wild goose chase to the east, while my true knights head for Sicily and the west.'

The Amir remained silent while Hartelius wrote. And then, at last, he spoke.

'I am not sure I will be able to kill you.'

'Yes, you will. You have killed many men. I am a man like any other.'

'You are my brother. You are more than my brother.'

'For that very reason you will kill me. No man can bear what von Drachenhertz has in store for me. I have lived my life according to certain principles. I do not wish to fail those principles at my death. Not in front of men I have fought with.'

'Will they not try to save you?'

343

'No. There is no chance of that.'

A guard came in and held his hand out for the parchment and quill that Hartelius had been using. Hartelius gave them to him. The guard watched him for a moment, and then shook his head.

Hartelius looked up at him. 'Do I detect sadness in your gaze?'

The guard nodded. 'Yes, Commander. Many here are uncomfortable with what will happen to you tomorrow.'

'But still. It will happen, will it not?'

'Yes, Commander. There is nothing that I, or any man here, can do about it.'

'Then thank you for your courtesy in telling me of your feelings.'

The man touched his chest very lightly with his fist, as a Roman soldier might. 'They say wine helps. If I smuggled you in a flagon, would you drink it?'

'Assuredly.'

'Then I shall do so.'

'Thank you again.'

The guard left.

'Was he one of yours? A Templar?'

Hartelius shook his head. 'No. A simple soldier. But he will know that I retrieved the Holy Lance from Frederick Barbarossa's knapsack on the Saleph River. Frederick Barbarossa was their beloved king. The Holy Lance was Barbarossa's symbol. A little of Barbarossa's glory, might, in their eyes, have rubbed off on me.'

'But still they will not help you.'

'No. A soldier is a soldier. He does what he is paid to do. And von Drachenhertz pays them well.'

The Amir looked at his chains. 'Is it possible that you could open these chains with your stiletto? The locks are simple. Then I might embrace you for a final time.'

Hartelius looked down. 'Yes. It is possible.' He waited for the guard to return with the wine. When the man was gone he slipped the stiletto from his boot and began manipulating the lock. In a little while it fell open. Hartelius walked across to the Amir and did the same for him. Then they embraced and waited together for the dawn.

# FIFTY-SIX

At first light Hartelius returned to his corner of the tent. He snapped the lock back so that it appeared to be shut. He had left the stiletto with the Amir, on the understanding that, as soon as they were taken outside, the Amir would kill him.

But it was not to be.

At a little after ten in the morning the guards returned. Hartelius was unclipped and led outside. The Amir was left where he was.

As Hartelius walked alongside the guards, he knew that he had left his one possible means of exit back in the tent. Could he have killed himself? Everything that he had ever been taught mitigated against it. Suicides were buried outside consecrated ground. Could he have forced himself to overcome this taboo and hasten his own death? Yes. He probably could. But now there was no option. His one comfort was to know that he had left the Amir with the means, at the very least, to defend himself.

'What is to happen to me? I thought this farce was due to start at midday?' Hartelius said to the guard who had brought him last night's wine.

The guard shook his head. It was clear that he had been ordered to maintain strict silence in the face of any of the prisoner's questions.

Hartelius could feel the eyes of the camp upon him. He looked here and there for familiar faces, but saw none. Maybe they were keeping the Templars away from the execution in case they attempted to rescue their old comrade-in-arms? A likely story. Most would spit on his unmarked grave.

Hartelius was forced to mount a platform that had been erected at the exact centre of the encampment, near to the pile of discarded Saracen weapons. Hartelius looked with longing at the abandoned scimitars and crossbows. Just one was all that he would need. But he was not even able to attempt a run. His guards held him fast. And he was surrounded by a phalanx of them. He would not manage a single yard unmolested.

He submitted to being chained at the very centre of the platform. The guards dispersed. Hartelius sat down and waited.

He forced himself to drift inside his head. To clear his mind of what was about to happen and to concentrate on the princess. There was nothing any longer he could do about the position he was in. Last night, when he was briefly free from his chains, had been the last time he might have actively influenced his fate. But he had not done so. Why?

Because there is always hope.

He fixed on this, and tried to conjure up a picture in his head of him meeting the princess once again. Embracing her. Drawing her to his chest. Drinking in her fragrance. Touching the gentle swell of her stomach where his child quickened inside her.

His one comfort was that no one knew where to find her. And that when he did not return, von Eisenbrand would do his duty and conduct the two women under his tutelage – one of whom he loved and one of whom he served – to the court of King Frederick in Sicily.

Hartelius returned to the present moment. He looked around himself. Men were seating themselves in tiers ranging back to fifty yards from where he sat on the platform. None bore arms. Hartelius managed a smile. So von Drachenhertz distrusted his own people, did he? Thought they might riot if the Guardian of the Holy Lance, a former comrade-in-arms, was publicly and humiliatingly killed in front of them?

Hartelius watched as a man mounted the platform. Was this the torturer? But no. The man held the parchment he had written his apologia on the night before. He also held the Holy Lance, secured from Gadwa's saddlebag. Well. This had been inevitable.

The man raised the parchment and began to read.

'In his own words the Baron von Hartelius condemns himself as a traitor to his king and station. Here. Listen all of you. And weep.'

'I, Johannes von Hartelius, Baron Sanct Quirinus, hereditary guardian of the Holy Lance, lawful husband of

348

Adelaïde von Kronach, lawful father of Grimwald, Paulina, Agathe, and Ingrid von Hartelius, former Knight Templar, exonerated from his vows of chastity and obedience by Frederick VI of Swabia, youngest son of the Holy Roman Emperor, Frederick Barbarossa, acting lawfully in the name of his brother, Henry VI Staufen, do dictate this letter on the very day of my execution, to be placed inside the Holy Lance as a warning to all those who may come after me. Swayed by my unlawful love for Elfriede von Hohenstaufen, former lawful sister of the king and former intended wife of Margrave Adalfuns von Drachenhertz, military governor of Carinthia, I turned against my king and misused the Holy Lance which had been placed in my care. In doing this I refused to heed Horace's warning, passed down to me with the guardianship of the Lance. *Vir bonus est quis? Qui consulta patrum, qui leges iuraque servat.* Instead, I purposefully misunderstood the words Catullus handed down to all unvirtuous men – *Mulier cupido quod dicit amanti, in vento et rapida scribere oportet aqua.* I thus deserve my fate. May God have mercy on my soul.'

Well, thought Hartelius, if they wanted the job done correctly, who better than the condemned prisoner to do it for them?

It was at this point that he watched in dismay as the parchment was formally sealed inside the Holy Lance so that everyone present might witness the act of concealment. Clearly the idiots who had read it had not discovered the hidden writing – or had chosen to overlook it or not draw attention to it. Or had chosen to copy it privately, and use it later. Any of these was possible. What had he been thinking?

Hartelius felt the dismay of a man grasping, and failing, to reach the final straw.

The sun was now beating down on the top of his head. It was midday. He waited. The men around him were drinking and feasting, just as von Drachenhertz had ordered. Pitchers of wine were being handed down the lines. He could smell the odour of roasting meat. Very soon that roasting smell will be me, he thought to himself. And I will have been entirely responsible. I will have acted as my own nemesis.

The noise emanating from the thousands of men surrounding him was rising in volume by the minute. Hartelius could now make out the Amir, in the very front row, held between two guards. As he caught the Amir's eye, the Amir raised one hand in salute, and then opened both his hands in the universal sign of powerlessness. Ten rows back he could see Heilsburg and Fournival, unarmed like everybody else. Hardly a threat. An entire unarmed army, watching him. Surely this said as much about von Drachenhertz as it did about Hartelius's nominal crime?

Hartelius waited some more. Three hours had now gone by since he had been brought to this place. Was this all part of the plan? Part of the torment? This uncertainty? Hartelius was almost relieved when von Drachenhertz himself mounted the podium. The monster had timed it well. His men were mostly drunk. The volume of noise near its peak. Von Drachenhertz smirked at Hartelius and turned to address his army.

'Men. Men. Am I carrying out a justified execution?'

350

There was a roar of approbation. By that point, thought Hartelius, the men would have approved anything. Even their own excommunication, if it coincided with the appearance of more drink.

Von Drachenhertz motioned to a man, dressed all in black, who started up the steps to the podium.

Ah, the torturer. Hartelius could feel his innards liquefying in fear. He swallowed back the bile that was threatening to rise into his gorge and overflow. Damn the wine the guard had brought him. And damn him for drinking it. But still. He was relieved that von Drachenhertz was not going to conduct the preliminaries, in terms of torture, himself.

'I demand the right to trial by combat.' Hartelius's voice was drowned out by the howls of the melee. 'As the Guardian of the Holy Lance I am still the king's representative. As such I have the right to such a trial. I demand trial by combat.'

No one took any notice of him.

Von Drachenhertz leered at him. He leaned close, so that Hartelius could smell his sour breath and see the vaginal secretions encrusted on his beard. 'Did you really think I hadn't thought of that one? Why else do you imagine I have wasted a fortune on feeding wine to this mob? No. You will not have your trial by combat. You will have your trial by me. And I pronounce you guilty.' He stepped back. 'Do your duty,' he said to the torturer. 'As from now your payment is doubled for each and every time you make him scream.'

Hartelius attempted to draw himself back, but there was nowhere left to go. Four soldiers vaulted onto the podium and took his arms. He felt himself being stretched out. He felt the sun warm on his face. In the distance he could hear the gentle plashing of the surf. He tried to imagine the princess, but he could not. He was too scared to think clearly any more.

He heard shouts from the crowd of soldiers surrounding him. What sounded like howls of glee. Then all fell silent as if in the prelude to a storm.

# FIFTY-SEVEN

For some time now, the Amir had been watching the soldiers around him. Judging their lack of sobriety. Noting their absence of arms.

Before he had begun his disastrous attack on von Drachenhertz's camp, the Amir had sent messengers back to the Chouf by every route he could think of, each bearing the same message. 'Your Amir needs you. At Uluzia Pass. Come swiftly. The tyrant von Drachenhertz has broken the truce. Your Amir will try to break through. But if he fails, you must become the backbone of your people. You must clear the Franj from our lands. You must take revenge for the dishonour done to your brothers.'

It should have been enough. But nothing had happened. And now the Amir was about to see his friend tortured and shamed in front of a gang of drunken ruffians.

He looked to one side and noted that none of the Templars had been drinking. Was this part of their culture? Or were they preparing to rescue their commander? But no. When he looked closer he saw that they, too, had been disarmed.

So where were his people? What better moment to attack a camp? When its entire host were at your mercy. Surely his scouts would have seen what was happening?

The Amir struck the guard to his right full in the throat with his stiletto. In the confusion caused by the sudden spray of blood, he ran forward and vaulted onto the podium. The torturer turned to face him.

The Amir feinted to the right, and as the torturer shadowed his movement, the Amir sliced through the man's doublet and emptied his stomach contents onto the stage.

It was only when he withdrew the stiletto that he realized the point had shattered. He searched for the torturer's dirk with which to kill Hartelius but it was too late. The guards were upon him.

The Amir cursed the futility of his action as the guards bore him down. He should have made straight for his friend, and not dallied with the torturer. But the man had been in front of him. Standing like a dam between him and Hartelius.

There was uproar in the camp. Men were running in every direction. Shouting. Screaming.

The Amir fought his way to the surface of the men weighing him down as if he were fighting his way back from beneath the waves.

He felt his arms being pinioned. Saw von Drachenhertz approaching him with sword unsheathed.

And then the arrows started to flow. Like water they fell on the unarmed host. Like a great curtain, blotting out the light of the sun.

The Amir lay and watched the slaughter, his eyes alight with joy.

Drunken men ran for their weapons and tripped over each other, offering even larger targets for the descending quarrels. Men started fighting each other for possession of a weapon. Any weapon.

Von Drachenhertz stood at the very edge of the podium, his sword tip lowered, his mouth open as if frozen in the very act of speaking.

As the Amir watched, von Drachenhertz abruptly returned to his senses. He pointed to the Amir and signalled to his men to bring him. They grasped the Amir by the shoulders and upper arms and dragged him to where von Drachenhertz was standing. Von Drachenhertz put his sword to the Amir's throat, but there was no one to see him do it.

All was flux around him, his men decimated three times over by the arrows falling upon them. Those not killed were being herded together like tuna fish by black-clothed Saracens on horseback wielding mighty pikes.

Von Drachenhertz waited. On the podium everyone waited. The guards surrounding him and the Amir. Hartelius, hunched forwards under his chains. The still-twitching torturer, with his entrails hanging out like the tentacles of a squid.

An unarmed and drunken army cannot stand firm against sober, well-armed men. Von Drachenhertz had been the author of his own misfortune. But still he stood, his sword against the Amir's throat, his few men backing him as if, via this thin lifeline, they might seek to turn the tide of the fiasco facing them below.

Saracen crossbowmen ran forwards. First they picked off all the soldiers surrounding the margrave and his prisoner. To men used to firing at moving targets from horseback, this was child's play.

Still the margrave stood stock still, his sword never wavering from the Amir's throat.

The Amir called instructions to his captains. Men darted to and fro, clearing the podium of bodies, releasing Hartelius from his bonds. Still the margrave did not move. Still he stood over his prisoner.

Hartelius staggered to his feet. He walked towards where the margrave and the Amir were perched.

'Stop. Stop there,' said the margrave.

'My life for his.' Hartelius held out his hands. 'I am unarmed.'

'The king will ransom me,' said the margrave. 'I have no need to barter.'

'We want no ransom,' said the Amir. 'We will call for no ransom. Your name is lost for ever, Margrave. No one will know of your end. Only of the ignominy of your actions.'

'And if I kill you, Muslim?'

'Another will take my place. Nothing will change for you.'

'And if I fight you in single combat and win? As you suggested?' The margrave was looking directly at Hartelius. At the state of him. At his lack of chainmail. At his obvious exhaustion.

'If you win, you may go,' said the Amir, noting his friend's brief nod. 'Freely and without hindrance.'

'And my men?'

'They too. What is left of them. Without arms. But freely.'

Von Drachenhertz stood up and lowered his sword. The Amir moved away from him. The Amir signalled to one of his men to throw up a sword to Hartelius. At first the man raised his scimitar to throw, but the Amir shook his head and pointed to a Templar sword, abandoned near the stage.

Von Drachenhertz was already circling Hartelius, his own weapon at port arms, his gaze unwavering. Hartelius stooped to pick up a spent arrow with which to defend himself, but von Drachenhertz darted to the right and cut him off.

The Amir slid the Templar sword across the floor of the podium to Hartelius's feet. Then he jumped down and ordered his men to fall back, so that all could view the combat.

Hartelius could feel the strength slowly returning to his limbs. Could feel the blood infusing him, as if it had been lying in wait, or skulking somewhere deep in his recesses, as far from the torturer's knife as it could get.

He felt the sun on his head as a blessing now, and not as the penance he had before. He breathed the air in through lungs unpunctured and unburned. His limbs responded in their entirety, without let or hindrance. Without intercession from alien interests.

Von Drachenhertz had little to lose. His nature was one which did not indulge in retrogressive thought. He ran directly at Hartelius and the two men set forth at each other. Hartelius was shocked at the sheer brute strength that von Drachenhertz showed. The absurd power he wielded at each blow.

Hartelius found himself being forced back to the edge of the podium. There, he knew, lay disaster. Once he lost his footing, he was easy meat.

He tried, by sudden movement, to speed up the return of blood to his body. To restore his lost energies. But fear had sapped him. The deep fear that a man cannot show, but that is still there nonetheless. The fear of losing one's dignity. Of finding oneself bereft of courage after a lifetime in which the manifestation of courage is the one defining marker by which a man is judged.

Hartelius had not lost his courage, of course. But he would have. He knew that only too well. Ten minutes into the torment he would have been screaming and begging the torturer to stop. He had seen other men, braver than he, succumb to the knife.

Von Drachenhertz sensed that his opponent's mind was wandering and made his move. He feinted to the left and then, when Hartelius responded clumsily to the feint, he struck right. Hartelius had been expecting this. He dropped to the ground and rolled, just as he had done with the final Italian *bandito* who had attacked him all those many months ago in the Alps. Von Drachenhertz, his weight dispersed far beyond his right leg's capacity to carry it, pitched to the ground on top of Hartelius's upturned sword.

This time Hartelius was wearing no mail. As von Drachenhertz fell, Hartelius dragged wildly at his sword to clear it from landing back onto his own chest. Von Drachenhertz cried out and fell upon him, his sword arm clear.

Hartelius thrust back in, catching von Drachenhertz beneath the ear, a little above his chainmail's upper curtal.

Von Drachenhertz's eyes widened, just as his bodyweight fell dead. Finally, after a series of convulsive movements, he lay at full stretch on top of Hartelius's prone form, his eyes turned inwards, his mouth drooping open like that of a sleeping cat.

Hartelius could feel the Amir's Saracens lifting the margrave off him. He stood up, the blood streaming from him like liquid mercury.

'Your blood or the margrave's?' said the Amir.

'In truth I am not sure,' said Hartelius. He stared at the carnage around him. 'It is one of many things I am no longer sure of.' He limped to the edge of the platform and looked out over the camp. 'My Templars?'

'Yours to command. They held back from the slaughter of my men when ordered to participate by von Drachenhertz. I have given orders that they are to be spared. I shall have their arms returned to them.'

'And my stallion? Gadwa?'

'Look,' said the Amir. Gadwa was being led through the wounded and the dead towards them.

'He is yours, Amir. I return him to his rightful master. Please honour me by accepting my gift.'

The Amir saluted Hartelius from high above his brow. Then he clapped his hands together like a child who has just been given a much wanted toy. 'Be assured, my friend. Your gift is

359

my joy. This one thing I swear to you. That the very first of my maidens who has a colt by Gadwa, it shall be yours.' He canted his head to one side and contemplated the stallion. 'The pleasure, of course, will be Gadwa's.'

# FIFTY-EIGHT

# Millook Haven, Cornwall

**WEDNESDAY 14 MAY 2013**

'You look like a blind man who has lost his guide dog.' Amira crunched down the pebble-strewn beach towards Hart, who was sitting on a rock, staring out at the sea.

Hart half turned towards her. Then he turned back again. 'Isn't that rather an inelegant way to begin a conversation?'

'To hell with elegance.' She sat down beside him.

The sea churned back and forth along the length of the shore. Both of them watched it, mesmerized.

'How did you find me?' Hart said at last.

'You brought me here once. For a dirty weekend. Remember? Three years ago. When you still liked me. One night we went to the pub. Actually had a good time for a change. There was a local man there. Wanted to become a journalist. He gave me his card.'

'And?'

'I finally called him. Yesterday. Asked if he would drive down and check if you were here. He did. You were. I came.'

Hart shook his head slowly. 'You are something, Amira. I'll give you that.'

'I'm your friend. That's what I am.' She hunched herself more closely inside her coat. 'Now tell me what happened out there in Iran.'

'What do you mean?'

'I know you, John. I know what it means when you hide yourself away like this. You're hurting. Like a little boy who's been bullied in the playground.' She lit a cigarette. 'No one's been able to contact you. Even that idiot man-friend of your mother's didn't have a clue where you were. Oh, and he's clamouring for more money, by the way. I hope you discovered Solomon's treasure while you were out there, because you're going to need it.'

'Fuck off, Amira. You're the one who's doing the bullying.'

'Well, at least you're getting your sense of humour back.' She sniffed the air a little, as if she might be able to detect something significant through the cigarette smoke she was allowing to pass through her half-opened lips. 'Buy a girl a drink?'

Hart sat up straighter. 'This is about the story, isn't it? You want your pound of flesh. And sod friendship. Why not come clean for a change?'

Amira groaned. 'The story is part of it. Yes. You promised it to me. But I could still do with a drink. I've just spent five hours in a car with no air-conditioning and with Rider driving. He could probably do with a drink too after the tongue-lashing I've just given him.'

'Rider?'

'He's waiting back there in the car. And let me tell you. Sterling Moss he isn't.'

'Your conversation on the way down must have been scintillating.'

'Yes. He depressed me about the prospects in the Middle East. Then he depressed me about the UK economy. Then he depressed me about you. When he started depressing me about all his aches and bloody pains I drew a line in the sand and told him to belt up. Washed straight over his head, of course.' She made a vague gesture with her cigarette towards the sea, as if she needed to illustrate her point with something concrete.

'So it is about the story? My first instinct was dead on, as usual.'

'I suppose.'

'Because you're a journalist over and above everything?'

Amira hesitated. 'But that doesn't make me any the less your friend. You just happen to be the sort of man stories stick to, John. You're like a roll of human flypaper. I just trail along behind and pick you up when you're down.'

'And I'm down now?'

'Well? Aren't you?'

'At which point you swan in and strip the flypaper of its stories?'

'Something like that.'

Hart looked at her for a long time. Then he laughed. 'Okay, Amira. Where do you want me to start? At the fact that there was no Copper Scroll to begin with? That I was sent on a wild goose chase by a desperate man, facing certain death, who cast around for the most unlikely place on earth he could think of to pretend to have hidden something, and I, his distant descendant, fell for the story nine hundred years later – hook, line and fucking sinker – and ended up with egg all over my face? Or do you want me to start with last week? With the bad guy who had his tongue surgically removed and was then lowered eight hundred feet down an extinct volcano to starve to death? He's still down there. Probably only been dead a couple of days. The Iranians could find him easy-peasy and martyr the people that did it in revenge for the years of rape and murder and torture he inflicted on them in Saddam Hussein's Iraq. Or do you want me to start a few days earlier, when the father of an Iraqi *kulbar* boy who was guiding me across the border for the princely sum of a hundred bucks stepped on a landmine, twenty feet in front of me, which blew both his legs off and injured his son so badly that I had to cart them both down into Iran on the back of a donkey, with the father's legs tucked inside the pockets of his coat so that he could be properly buried?'

'Christ Jesus.'

Hart turned back towards the sea. 'Well, you wanted a story. Reckon you can write that, do you? Do it justice?'

'You know I can't. You wouldn't last a week out on the streets.'

Hart stood up. 'Well, all right then. At least we've got that straight.' He hitched his chin towards the road. 'I'll take you and Rider for that drink now.'

# FIFTY-NINE

# Post Scriptum
# Chartres Cathedral

### JULY 1250

The princess allowed her son to take her arm and lead her across the sward towards the main entrance to the newly finished cathedral. She still retained much of the beauty of her youth, although her auburn hair had long ago turned white, and her eyes, though hardly lustreless, had lost just a little of their sparkle. Indeed, she wore the darkened clothes of one who mourns. But the fact that her son, and stepdaughters, and the stepson in Templar clothing who accompanied them wore no such accoutrement, suggested that her loss was an old one, and that she wore the clothes more out of habit than immediate need.

She allowed the bishop, who was waiting for her at the portal, to come forward and replace her son at her side.

'Princess, we are honoured indeed to have the daughter of the great Frederick Barbarossa at the inauguration of our cathedral. The king himself has asked that I conduct you to the memorial to your husband, Johannes von Hartelius,

Baron Sanct Quirinus, that has been built, exactly to your requirements, to the right hand of the altar, neighbouring the chancel.' The bishop halted momentarily, as if he were out of breath, causing the princess to halt with him. 'Of course, it was not without some difficulty that we secured the permission of the Holy Father to allow the image of a Muslim man – and therefore, dare one mention it, a heathen – to accompany that of your husband on the memorial and to be allowed inside the precincts of the cathedral. But in the circumstances that accompanied the restitution and the translation of the Copper Scroll half a century ago, together with the vast sum that followed on from that translation, and which was instrumental in allowing the cathedral to be both built and dedicated according to the Holy Father's wishes, all objections were graciously lifted.'

'The objections of the Jews, you mean, given that Solomon's new temple was to be built here in Chartres and not in Jerusalem as Solomon so clearly intended?'

The bishop shrugged. 'The Jews. Ah. So very unfortunate. Such an ill-omened race. It was felt that they should not be encouraged towards unrealistic expectations. Chartres is so much better, don't you think? The true soul of Christendom transposed from the Holy Land to here. This was surely what Solomon would really have wanted if given the choice.' He indicated that the princess should walk ahead of him up the main aisle. 'He was, after all, renowned for being one of the world's great pragmatists, was he not?'

The princess managed a half smile. Old battles, fought long

ago. She started up the aisle, followed by her son, Johannes von Hartelius, Baron Sanct Quirinus, and her stepson, Grimwald von Hartelius, who had abrogated his droitural rights as eldest son to become a simple Templar Knight, just as his father had been before him. They were followed in their turn by Paulina, Agathe and Ingrid von Hartelius, Grimwald's sisters, daughters of Adelaïde von Kronach, first wife of the dedicatee, and dead now these fifty-two years past.

The seven stopped before the memorial, the echo of their footsteps diminishing behind them as if snatched away by an invisible hand. The princess looked down at the stone image of her husband in full armour, a dog at his feet, his face placid in rest, his features stamped upon both his son's faces as if with a die. Then she looked to his left at the stone image of the Amir, his head partially turned towards his friend, his Saracen armour and chainmail an incongruous presence in a church dedicated to the cult of the Virgin and to the glory of her own son, the King of the Jews. The Amir, unlike the Christian knights and paladins who surrounded him within the precincts of the church, rested his feet on the back of a falcon.

'Your husband, the baron, was killed six years ago in the service of the Holy Roman Emperor, was he not? During the siege of Jerusalem?'

The princess turned away. 'Six years ago, yes.'

'And this man?' The bishop pointed to the Amir.

'His friend. Yes. He died during the sixth Crusade. Betrayed by the Sultan Al-Kamil.'

'Ah. The Crusade that ended in March 1229 with the restitution of an unfortified Jerusalem? And the coronation of your nephew as king? How they all seem to blur in the memory.'

The princess closed her eyes. More old battles, no longer significant. She knew that the bishop wished to ingratiate himself with her by his comments, and by his familiarity, but all she could feel was alienation and irreparable loss.

'They tell me that your husband was a friend, also, of Saint Francis of Assisi?'

'The Amir, too,' said the princess. 'They were Sufi. All three of them. Bound together by love.'

'I am sorry?'

'Saint Francis, the Amir and my husband. Each believed in the love of God above all else.'

The bishop watched the princess in flabbergasted horror.

'They wrote the *Song of the Sun* together. They believed the search for salvation to be a simple expression of vanity.'

The bishop swiftly crossed himself and looked around to see if anyone else was listening.

The princess pointed to the third plinth, which was empty. It was situated at the same height, and to the right, as that of her husband. 'That is for me?'

'Yes, yes,' said the bishop, mopping his brow. 'That is for you.'

The princess smiled, her entire face lighting up. '*Laudato si mi Signore, per sora nostra Morte corporale, da la quale nullu homo uiuente pò skappare.*'

'I speak no Italian, Princess.'

'It is from the "Song of Saint Francis". The one that I mentioned to you before. It means "Be praised, my Lord, through your sister, the death of the body, from whose embrace no living being can escape."'

'And do you seek death, my child?'

The princess looked up at the cathedral vaulting. Then across at her children. Then down at the effigies of her husband and the Amir. She smiled at the bishop, amused at his obvious discomfort in the face of her placidity.

'I am in no hurry. A great man once said that even though you tie a hundred knots in it, the string remains one.'

# Acknowledgements

Thank you to the Yazidis of Lalish for their welcome and their gentleness. I visited their holiest shrine in 2013, and had written them into this book well before the horrors perpetrated on their innocent community by the savages calling themselves ISIS. Thank you, too, to my agent, Oli Munson at A.M. Heath, who has championed my writing so steadfastly over the years. Also to Steve Benbow for all his insights into emergency medical aid, trauma injuries, the best cars to use for car bombings, and other assorted marginalia not normally available to the public. To Michèle O'Connell, who reads my books as they are written and encourages me to surpass myself. To my infant granddaughter, Éloise Alexandrina, who has taught me patience, the value of being able to work under any conditions and not to take myself too seriously. And finally my wife, Claudia, who tolerates all my wayward journeys with the Zog Society, which so often form the backbone of my works – you are my priceless Mexican pearl.

Read on for the thrilling opening chapters of John Hart's next adventure. . .

# ONE

# Katohija, Kosovo

2 SEPTEMBER 1998

The first Lumnije Dardan heard of the event that would shape the rest of her life was the sound of her mother's raised voice.

But Jeta Dardan never raised her voice. She was a placid woman, content with her lot, happily married to Burim Dardan, Associate Professor of Politics at Pristina University, and just now taking a well-earned rest at their country cottage in the village of Katohija, a few kilometres north of Pejë, with her husband and her two children, Azem, just turned eighteen, and Lumnije, sixteen and a half.

The next thing Lumnije heard was the crackle of heavy tyres.

'It is the Serb police,' she said to herself. 'They are returning.'

The Serb police had visited them three times already that summer. They had behaved themselves, for the most part, limiting their aggression to shouting and ordering people to register – Serbs on one side, Albanian Muslims on the other – together with a little minor theft. Chickens, mainly, and the occasional lamb. Always from the Albanians and never from their fellow Serbs.

Lumnije and her family were Albanian Muslims. The last time the police had come they had ordered any Serbians to paint a large S onto the door of their houses. There had been an active discussion amongst the villagers as to whether everybody ought to paint the S onto their doors as a form of protest at this infringement of their liberties by the authorities. It was finally decided, however, that no harm could come from obeying the new law, so the situation had been allowed to lapse into abeyance. The S on every other house was hardly noticed any more.

Lumnije could hear her mother shouting louder now. She began to run. This was the first time the Serb police had come when the men, too, were resident in the village – her brother Azem on leave from his university studies, and her father, given the political situation, on an enforced sabbatical from his professorial duties. Maybe the Serbs were threatening him? Or angry about something one of the villagers had done? Or Azem was mouthing off to the police in the way young men with pent-up political opinions occasionally do?

Lumnije burst into the village square, her hair flowing behind her, her dress flattening against the front of her thighs. It was to be the last time in her life that she was ever able to view anything as remotely normal.

The big trucks she had heard earlier were just pulling up, but paramilitaries on foot, and heavily armed, had infiltrated the village first. Paramilitaries, not policemen.

The soldiers were splitting the men from the women and herding them into two groups. Lumnije was just in time to see her brother and her father being dragged away from her mother, who was shrieking and screaming, her face afire, her cheeks awash with tears.

Lumnije stopped in her tracks. No one – and certainly no man – had ever dared to treat her mother with disrespect.

Now Lumnije added her voice to the screaming and wailing of the women. She ran to her mother's side. A soldier hurried her on her way with a glancing blow from his boot. Lumnije sprawled on the ground, her dress hoicked up, her underwear showing. The soldiers jeered. Lumnije began to retch.

The officer in charge of the soldiers ordered all ethnic Serbs to return to their houses. This they did, hurrying away, without backward glances. Abandoning their neighbours. Terrified too, it seemed, if not for their lives, then at least for what they might be about to witness.

Lumnije looked for her father and her brother amongst the men. The captain of the soldiers called out her father's name. Her father stepped forward. As the most notable individual amongst the Albanian population of the village, it was natural that he should be called first. He began to protest on behalf of the villagers. Lumnije knew the tone he was using well. It was her father's public voice. His professional voice. The voice he used beyond the confines of the home.

The captain of the soldiers raised his pistol. At just this moment, their family dog, Peta, ran in from the periphery of the group, where he had been circling and barking, and leapt into her father's arms. It was his party trick. The thing he knew would always gain him attention, and, if he was lucky, a treat.

The captain's shot took Peta behind the head. He and her father both fell to the ground. Peta was dead, her father still alive. One of the Serb soldiers ran over and slit her father's throat with his knife. Then four more soldiers took his body up, dragged it to a nearby Albanian house, threw it inside, and followed its passage in with two grenades.

'Three times,' said the captain to the howling women. 'We have killed this filth three times.'

It was then that the machine guns opened up. Lumnije sat, cradled in her mother's arms, and watched as the men fell to the ground like scythed corn. Her brother tried to run towards them, shouting for his mother, but he was killed before he took two paces. Any woman who tried to move towards the men was struck down with a rifle butt, or, if she was young and pretty, slapped to the ground by a soldier's hand.

Later as the women watched, still wailing and weeping, a bulldozer was brought into the village and the bodies of the men were raised up on the hoist and dumped into an empty truck bed.

It was at this point, watching the bulldozer manhandling the bodies of her husband and son, that Lumnije's mother broke. She ran at the captain, screaming her husband's name. The captain shot her. It was done so swiftly, and with such contemptuous dispatch, that, for a moment, Lumnije did not realize that her mother, too, was dead.

One of the soldiers dragged Lumnije to her feet and pushed her towards a small group of young women that was being gathered together at the edge of the village. Lumnije knew them all. Each girl was weeping and shrieking, just like her. Some had covered their heads with kerchiefs and scarves in a bid to make themselves less noticeable to the soldiers. Others were too deeply lost in shock even for that. Some of the girls were unable to stay on their feet. When they were raised up they fell down again, like rag dolls. Finally their friends held them, fearing that the soldiers would lose patience and kill them.

When the clearing of the men was complete, the women were loaded onto two empty trucks. There were only young women left. The older women and the children had been herded towards the edge of the village and told to leave for Albania. If any turned back they were warned once and then shot. The bodies of those who disobeyed were loaded onto the same truck that was carrying the dead men.

Two kilometres out of the village, at an abandoned quarry, there was a snarl up. The truck containing the young women stopped. Lumnije, her hands shaking, lifted the tarpaulin to see where they were being taken. She saw the truck containing the dead men tipping its contents into a shallow trench. She thought she saw her father and her brother tumbling with the others. She could not see her mother, although she knew she was with them. As she watched, the Serbs threw cornhusks onto the piled-up bodies and lit them. Soon, great plumes of smoke rose into the air. The heat from the fire was so intense that the rubberized tarpaulin of the truck she was sitting in began to smoke.

The truck lurched forwards. Lumnije hugged the girl beside her. The girl hugged her back. The two young women remained that way, clasped in each other's arms, for the remainder of the two-hour journey.

# TWO

It was the captain himself who came for her. For some time now Lumnije had been hearing the screams of her friends and other women she did not know as the soldiers raped them. She had retreated far inside herself to a place nobody could touch. A dark place, of shadows and mist and the shortages of winter. A place which bore no resemblance to the substance of her normal dreams.

'You. Come with me.'

Lumnije followed the captain. It was the first time she had been outside the room in thirty-six hours. She had been having her period, and this had saved her from the initial free-for-all that had occurred a few minutes after they arrived at the Rape House. Now she knew that it was her turn.

As she walked through the main rooms of the house she saw naked girls walking around in a daze – some with blood down their legs, over their breasts, on the inside of their thighs. Some were being made to clean with mops and brooms and besoms. Some were lying on the floor as if dead. There were Serb soldiers sprawled everywhere, drinking rakia and beer and smoking Domacica. As she walked behind the captain the soldiers called out to her, and made foul movements with their hands. Lumnije thought the captain would hand her over to them, but he continued walking and she followed him. What else could she do?

He took her to a private room in the back of the house and told her to undress and lie on the bed.

'I am a virgin,' she said.

'You are all virgins,' he said. 'That is the point of this.'

'I do not understand,' she said.

'You do not need to understand. You are not a human being. You are Albanian. You were born a whore. I am merely here to remind you of this. Has your period ended?'

Lumnije nodded.

'Then you stay here sixteen days. I've decided to make you mine. I don't like sharing. So you remain in this room. I come in. I use you. If you fight, I give you to my soldiers. If you cry, I give you to my soldiers. If you try to talk to me when I don't wish to be spoken to, I give you to my soldiers. Do you understand me?'

Lumnije nodded.

Later, when the first rape was over, she sat on the bed in the corner of the room and thought about her father and her brother and her mother. This became her pattern. Outside, she could hear the screams of the other women as they were taken by whoever felt the urge.

'You are lucky,' said the captain one day.

'I am lucky?' said Lumnije.

'Yes,' said the captain. 'You could be with those other women. Instead you are safely in here with me.'

Lumnije curled up on the bed and hid her head inside her hands. She could feel the captain watching her. Could feel his eyes travelling over her body.

Lumnije hated her body. Hated her femaleness. Hated the way her hair fell across her face. She wished she might obliterate all that made her desirable to men, but she knew that was an impossible dream.

So the captain came back. Sometimes he was drunk. At these times he used soft words when he was raping her. But the soft words did not help. They only made it worse. She wanted her father's soft words. Her brother's kisses. Not this man's. She wanted her mother's arms round her – to smell the starch in her apron – the dough on her hands from the bread she was baking. Not this man's hands, which were rough, and intrusive, and cold as grave ice.

'Why sixteen days?' she asked him once.

'So you get pregnant,' he said. 'Have a Serb baby.'

'Why?' she said.

'Why?' he said. 'I do not know why. Why is there always a why? Think yourself lucky. Have I mistreated you?'

Lumnije stayed silent.

'You fucking Albanians have no idea,' the captain said. He sat down on the edge of the bed. 'You know how many I have killed these last six months?'

Lumnije shook her head.

He held out his hand. He pointed to the palm with his other hand. 'Imagine that is full of rice. That is how many I have killed. And still there are more of you. Like locusts. Like ants.' He raised his hand as if to hit her.

Lumnije turned towards the wall. She waited a long time. Eventually she heard him get up and walk to the door. He stood there, too, a long time.

She did not turn round.

Finally, without a word, he left.

# THREE

On the fourteenth day of her incarceration Lumnije tried to commit suicide. She tore up the bed sheets and knotted them into ropes. Then she tied the ropes together and attached them to the light. She made a rough noose and placed it round her neck. Then she stood on the bed and jumped off.

Her weight brought the light bracket down. She lay on the floor and looked upwards at the hole left in the ceiling.

One of the soldiers came in. He looked at her lying there, and then at the trailing light. He dragged her to her feet by the rope, and for one moment Lumnije thought that he would take her out into the main room and give her to his brothers. But he contented himself with beating her about the arms and shoulders. She was the captain's woman. More would have been inappropriate.

He unknotted the rope and left her lying on the bed. Five minutes later the captain came in and beat her some more.

'Will you try this again? If so I give you to my men now. Take your clothes off.'

Lumnije shook her head. 'I will not try it again.'

'You swear to this on Allah's head?'

Lumnije nodded.

The captain threw something on the bed. 'Look. I brought you a shawl.'

'I do not want a shawl.'

The captain looked at her for a long time. Then he left.

Lumnije picked up the shawl and threw it into a corner of the room.

That night, with no sheets left, she was forced to retrieve the shawl and use it to keep warm. The captain came in around midnight, drunk, and raped her again. As usual, he spoke soft words to her. As usual she closed her ears and her heart to anything he said.

'Are you pregnant yet?'

'How can I know,' Lumnije said. 'Don't you understand women? How we work? How can I possibly know?'

She would never have spoken to him like this when he was sober.

He looked at her and made a sign of disgust with his hand. 'You are not a woman. What am I thinking? You are Albanian. I kill Albanians.'

'Then kill me. Kill me like you killed my mother and my father and my brother.'

The captain looked at her in horror. 'I have a son,' he said. 'And a wife.'

'Then I hope somebody kills them.'

They looked at each other across the bed. Lumnije was beyond hatred. Beyond fear. Now she simply existed. Two more days, she told herself. In two more days he will let me go.

'I like you,' he said, on the eve of the sixteenth day. The day of her release. 'You suit me. That's why I have given you special privileges. I take no pleasure in breaking in new women. I take no pleasure in rape. So I have decided to keep you.'